BC

SAM BASS

Other books by Bryan Woolley:

Some Sweet Day
We Be Here When the Morning Comes
Time and Place
November 22nd

·A·N·O·V·E·L·

SAM BASS

BY BRYAN WOOLLEY

CORONA PUBLISHING CO.

·1983·

Library of Congress Catalog Card No. 83-70812
ISBN 0-931722-25-X

Cover design by Paul Hudgins
Book design and layout by Patricia Broersma

Printed and bound in the United States of America

Table of Contents

For my sons
Bryan and Patrick
in memory
of the summer of '78

Sam first came out to Texas, a cowboy for to be;
A kinder-hearted fellow you seldom ever see.

—*The Ballad of Sam Bass*
1878

Great God! what a fearful calling was theirs. How the angel mother of Sam Bass, from the battlements of Heaven, must have wept as she looked down upon him in his degradation and infamy . . .

Charles L. Martin
A Sketch of Sam Bass, The Bandit
1880

. . . this ubiquitous wraith, this knight of the road, this generous and open-handed highwayman . . .

Walter Prescott Webb,
The Texas Rangers
1935

Dad Egan

He had seen the dream many times before. It was night, and a horse of some dark color was galloping along the ridge of a long, flat mountain. The mountaintop was strewn with small boulders. Bushes and small trees grew everywhere. The horse's iron shoes struck fire from the rocks sometimes, but it never stumbled.

He was the rider, but he also was standing on the mountain and watching the horse's run, in that way that dreams have of letting you be in two places at once, both doing the thing being dreamed and seeing it done at the same time. As the rider, he felt his hair blown back by the wind of the horse's passage. He felt the wind against his cheeks, too, and in his eyes. He rode bareback and felt the movement of the animal under his legs and the coarseness of its mane between his fingers. The rhythm of the horse was very smooth, and the rocks and the brush seemed to offer no impediment at all to its progress along the ridge. The iron shoes striking fire from the rocks made no sound. As the watcher, he saw the rocks and trees and fire and the horse running. The animal had one spot of white on it, a stocking leg, the left hind one. It glowed in the moonlight as it moved across the ground like a small ghost. He saw his own face, too. It was as pale as the horse's leg and was smiling a smile of such abandon as to suggest madness.

Suddenly the horse would approach a cliff, and instead of stopping or turning aside it would plunge into the void. Not downward, as if falling, but straight out into the darkness, like an arrow, until the horse and rider were swallowed by the gloom.

The dream came to him years ago, when he was a boy on his

uncle's farm in Indiana. It had appeared to him many times since then. It never varied in any detail.

It was always followed by another dream, or a second part of the same dream, that also was always the same.

It was still night in the same hilly country. But now the horse was standing in a corral. It was standing quietly, making no sound at all. Its stocking leg still glowed in the moonlight, and its chest and withers and flanks were flecked with foam. The rider was outside the fence now, gazing at the horse. He was tired. Then he noticed the dark shape of a small house next to the corral. A light was glowing behind a curtained window. The rider thought he had never been in that place before, but he walked to the house and opened the door without knocking, as if he knew he was expected there. He entered a narrow hall, longer than such a small house could have contained. The hall was dark, except for a light at the far end. Standing in front of the light was a woman. He couldn't see her face. Only the black silhouette of a woman wearing a long, straight skirt. "There's a horse for you in the corral," he said. And she said, "Thank you."

That was all. It wasn't particularly unusual, as dreams go. I've dreamed stranger dreams myself. During the war, I dreamed terrible dreams that made me sweat and wake up screaming. Sam's dream wasn't at all frightening. The first part, the running of the horse, made him feel light and free, he said. And the second part made him feel calm.

Sam told me about the dream not long after he arrived in Denton, before he went to work for me and came to live in my house. I was the first person in Denton to meet him, I guess. It was dusk, in the early fall of 1870, and I was sitting on the steps of the courthouse, taking the air. The courthouse was closed at that time of day, of course, but I liked to put the town to bed before I went home. I would inquire politely about the business of any strangers I found and make an early round of the saloons. Not to drink, you understand. Drink is the most dangerous thing an officer of the law can do. Liquor impairs a man's wit and strength when he needs them most, and in a place like Denton, where the forces of decency and the forces of perdition are so delicately balanced, a whiff of whiskey on the breath can destroy a sheriff at the polls as well. The law is the heaviest weight on decency's side of the scale, and the odor of sour mash on the breath of the law inspires a fear in decent people that the scale is tipping against them. In that dark time, only five years after the death of the Confederate States of America, when we were still trying to free ourselves from a carpetbag governor in Austin and a thuggish state police that poured salt into our wounds at every opportunity, it was especially important that the local law be decent and upstanding.

Beyond these professional and political considerations, I abstain from alcohol because I'm a family man, a man of property and a Christian and try to be a friend and worthy example in my own home and in the town and county. And I'm proud that although I was only thirty-six years old at the time, even older men chose to call me "Dad," in place of my Christian name, William. That may be why Sam was so drawn to me. He hadn't called any man "Dad" in such a long time.

Anyway, I was rising from the courthouse steps, about to commence my round of the saloons, when a wagon entered the square. I knew the driver. He was Bob Mayes, who used to run a livery stable in Denton. He had given it up in a fit of homesickness two years before and had gone back to Mississippi. Now he had returned. His wife was on the wagon box beside him. Their sons, Little Bob and Scott, had shot up like saplings since they left. They had the appearance of men now, slouching in their saddles. I didn't know the third rider, a young man about Little Bob's age, eighteen or nineteen. I stepped up to the wagon and shook Bob's hand and welcomed him back to Denton. While Bob climbed down and I helped Mrs. Mayes, the boys dismounted and tied their horses to the courthouse hitching rail. Bob said, "Dad, meet Sam Bass. He's come from Indiana to be a cowboy, and he kept an eye out for Indians all the way across Arkansas." He winked at me.

The lad grinned sheepishly as he shook my hand. He was slightly built, five-foot-eight or so, and stood with a stoop that made him look even smaller. He was wiry, though, and although he didn't grip my hand hard, I knew he was strong and used to hard work. His high cheekbones and black hair and eyes made me think that if he wanted to see an Indian, he should look in a mirror. I welcomed him and told him he had come to the right place to be a cowboy, for Denton is a sort of border between the farming country to the east and the cow country to the west. And if he wanted to see Indians, I said, he could ride on west and find plenty.

The boy didn't reply, and I turned back to Bob and his family and the kind of chat that old acquaintances get into when they haven't seen each other for a long time, inquiring after the health and prosperity of each other's families, comparing carpetbag governments and nigger problems in Texas and Mississippi, and things like that. I remember saying that so few men in Denton County had taken the oath of allegiance to the government in Washington that it was hard sometimes to find twelve white men for a jury. And he said the same was true in Mississippi.

Sam Bass stood listening for fifteen or twenty minutes, shifting from one foot to the other and looking at the ground. Finally he said, "Sheriff Egan, where can I go to get a job on a ranch?"

"Just stay in town and talk to the ranchers when they come in," I said.

"I ain't got the money to hang around," he said, "or the time."

"Well, ride that way in the morning, then," I said, pointing to the road westward out of the square, "and stop at every house you come to. They're far between, but you'll find somebody who can use you."

"Thank you," he said. "I'll start now."

"You won't get far before dark," I said. "You'd better stay the night here and leave in the morning."

"No, I'll go now and get a jump on the day," he said. He shook hands all around, thanked Bob for letting him ride along with him, and promised to look up Little Bob and Scott the next time he came to town. Then he mounted his little buckskin horse and rode out.

"That boy," said Bob, watching him. "He's going to amount to something real fast, or he's going to bust a gut trying."

Sam was hired by Bob Carruth, fourteen miles west of Denton, and I must have seen him sometime during that fall or winter, but if I did, I don't remember it. Maybe I didn't. Some of the cowboys stay on the ranches for months at a time without coming into town, especially those who want to keep their pay for a while. I wish they all would. The town needs their money, of course, and I guess we'd be pretty bad off if they just stayed out on the range or went elsewhere for their good-timing. But I dread seeing them, especially when they arrive in bunches. They get drunk, and then start playing cards. Men who gamble are fools, and men who gamble while drunk are bigger fools. They forget the value of their money while they're losing it, but when it's gone they remember how hard they worked for it and resent the ease with which it's taken from them. They get mad and fight. Sometimes they kill, and then head into the cross-timbers or light out to the west, where, likely as not, their scalps wind up in the belts of the Comanche or the Kiowa. There's no telling how many men in Denton have been wasted on whiskey and cards, some slowly, over a number of years under their awful influence, and others extinguished suddenly in the violence inspired by them. "Wine is a mocker," saith the Lord. And whiskey is worse.

Sam had been drinking when I saw him next, and he had won a few dollars at the card table. He didn't look happy, though, when he sat down beside me on the courthouse steps. "Well," I asked, "how do you like being a cowboy?"

He was rolling a cigarette, and he licked the paper and stuck it down and twisted the ends before he answered, "I don't."

"What's the matter?"

"The hands at my uncle's sawmill in Indiana told stories about Texas," he said. "So did the river men in St. Louis and the boys at the sawmill in Mississippi. They all made it sound like heaven, and said they was coming here someday. But Texas ain't nothing but a barren place where everything bites, and cowboying ain't no more fun than standing in a fire."

I was amused at the bitterness of his complaint, which he spoke in a high, nasal twang that made him sound even younger than he was. "Most people come here expecting more than there is," I said, "especially since the war. But they get used to it. Most even like it after a while."

"Oh, I don't mind the *place* so much," he said. "But I'm a sorry cowhand."

"Who says?"

"Carruth's told me I ain't going on the drive to Kansas. He says I got to learn the tricks before I can be any use on the trail."

"Well, he's right," I said. "If you don't know what you're doing, you'll get yourself killed on the trail. Or get somebody else killed. Be patient, son. You haven't been here long, and you've got all the time in the world to get whatever you want."

Sam squinted through the smoke of his cigarette. "No, I ain't," he said. "What if I spend a year or two learning to rope a cow? What am I then? Just a cowboy. Nothing. Them longhorns ain't nothing but misery, and I ain't going to wear myself out on them."

His face was flushed, perhaps by the alcohol, and I thought he was going to cry. I felt sorry for him, so young and alone. "Why don't you do something else?" I said.

"I'm going west to hunt buffalo," he said. "Hides is bringing up to two dollars apiece, and a lot of boys is going out to get them."

"Are you good with a rifle?" I asked.

"Not very good," he said quietly.

"Have you ever skinned a buffalo? It's the hardest, filthiest work there is. Worse than working cows. And if you're not good with a rifle, you won't get many hides."

Sam stared at the dust at the foot of the steps for some time, then pulled off his hat and swiped his brow with his sleeve. "Well, Dad," he said, "is there nothing here for me?"

"Sure there is, son. Maybe something in town. Maybe you could get work in one of the stores."

He shook his head. "I can't read or write or do numbers."

"Well, what *can* you do?" I asked. "What do you like in this imperfect world?"

"Horses," he said. Then he told me about the dream.

The Widow Lacy hired him. She ran the Lacy House, the biggest and best hotel in Denton, a two-story, white frame structure on the square. She had a fine well, too, and could water as much stock as you brought, which was one reason her place was so popular. That and her cooking. But she had had a hard time of it since her husband died, and she looked worn down by the worry of it. Business was too good. The inside work kept her hopping, and she was having trouble keeping a man around to do the lifting and carrying and taking care of her customers' animals. The pay was low and her tongue was sharp, particularly when she was tired, which was most of the time, and no male helper of hers stayed more than a few months, despite her food. I saw her one evening, drawing and carrying the water for the stock herself. Her hair was coming unpinned, and the hem of her skirt was spotted with manure. I hurried to help her, and while I carried the water buckets I told her about Sam. "Lordy, Dad, if he's got two arms and a back, I'll take him," she said. "I won't even ask for legs."

They hit it off well. Sam worked hard and didn't have to be told what to do. He didn't complain about the work or the wages. The hotel's customers liked him. Some said their horses and mules looked better after a day or two in Sam's care than they'd ever seen them before. That was high praise, because animals are important around Denton, and most men consider themselves better than most at handling them and taking care of them. But Sam had such a special way with them that people could compliment him without taking anything away from themselves.

It's a strange thing. Most people don't think of cleverness with animals as a gift of God, because everyone has to deal with them in one way or another. But some are so much better at it than others that you have to consider it a special gift. And Sam had the gift. That made him popular with the Lacy House customers, and valuable to the Widow. She knew it, and treated him nicer than she had his predecessors. She would save a piece of pie from supper and give it to him right before bedtime. She would buy him a new shirt or a new pair of pantaloons occasionally, and would fuss when he didn't wear them. He did look scruffy much of the time, letting his black hair grow almost to his collar, wearing old patched clothes and going for a week without being shaved. "I ain't no preacher," he would say when the Widow suggested improvements, and she would shrug and let him go, since his appearance didn't harm his good standing with her customers.

He was popular in the town, too. Although he rarely spoke and wore a sad, vaguely troubled expression on his face much of the time, people who saw him around the square learned that he wasn't unfriendly, and after he had a drink or two, he could be congenial. He drank moderately and gambled moderately, and when he lost, he didn't rail against his own bad luck or curse the good luck of others or mumble of cheating as some did. He accepted his losses with grace, and when he won, he always bought a drink or two for the other players, thus taking some of the sting out of their ill fortune or bad sense. Because of that simple courtesy, cowboys and townspeople sought him out for their games.

And he made three special friends. Frank Jackson, who was about five years younger than Sam, seemed to worship him. To this day I don't know why. Frank was a tinner, and worked in the shop of his brother-in-law, Ben Key. He was a blond, gentle boy who read every book he could find and said he wanted to be a doctor. In appearance, manner and mind he was Sam's opposite. Yet he hung on Sam's every word as if it came from an oracle, and sometimes he even aped the peculiar stoop that made Sam appear to be carrying some invisible burden. I've watched them pitch hay and carry water to the Lacy House stock together, Frank babbling of what he had been reading in some book or newspaper, and Sam working silently, maybe listening to Frank's words, maybe not. Frank was only fifteen or sixteen then and didn't have many willing listeners to his book learning, I guess. Maybe Sam's silence was what Frank treasured in him.

The reasons for Sam's friendship with the others were more obvious. Henry Underwood was from Indiana, like Sam, and had worn the Yankee blue in the war, like Sam's older brother, who was killed in Kentucky. Maybe he had known Sam's brother or served under the same commander. I don't know. Anyway, they had Indiana in common, and strangers in a place are always glad to happen onto someone who shares something of the past with them. Henry was married and made his living hauling firewood and driving freight between Denton and Dallas, but I considered him a shiftless sort. He spent too much time in town, drinking and gaming at the Parlor Saloon, and his wife's life was a hard one.

The Parlor was run by Henderson Murphy, and it was there that Sam met Henderson's son, Jim. Although I consider saloon-keeping a questionable way to win a livelihood, no town could ask for a better citizen than Henderson Murphy. He served several terms as alderman, and outside the town he owned even more land than I did. He sired the first white child born in Denton, and several others afterwards. That was lucky for him, for he suffered terribly from consumption and needed all the help he could get to tend his property. And no man could ask for a more helpful son than Jim was, particularly around the saloon. He was blessed with that cheerfulness and gift of talk that makes Irishmen such perfect hosts and a skill with his fists that enabled him to keep order without calling for the law. If the other saloonkeepers in Denton had been as well equipped for their calling as young Jim was, my lot would have been a happier one.

Sam and his friends were an odd bunch. Frank Jackson wasn't far beyond childhood, hardly old enough to need a razor. Henry Underwood was at least a dozen years older than he, and a family man besides. And Jim Murphy, despite his jolly manner, was a man who took his responsibilities seriously, especially his duty to his father, while the others didn't seem to have a care in the world. I think if Sam hadn't been around, they wouldn't have paid any attention at all to one another. They weren't really friends of each other. But each, for his own reasons, was Sam's friend, and whenever he was around, they moved to him like horseshoe nails to a magnet. So the four were often in each other's company, and the town got used to seeing them together. Sam had a charm of some kind, I guess, but I can't say what it was, and he lived with me for three years.

He came to work for me very like the way he had gone to the Widow Lacy. Out of pure restlessness. I was sitting on the courthouse steps one evening as usual, and he sat down beside me, just as he had when he was working for Bob Carruth. He breathed a sigh and slumped forward. "Lord," he said, "that hotel is getting the best of me."

"The Widow's getting her money's worth, is she?" I said.

"She is. I don't know whether I'm coming or going. And the worse thing is, I'm staying in the same place."

The remark didn't make sense to me, and I asked him what he meant.

"I mean I ain't *going* nowhere," he said in that high-pitched twang that he employed when complaining. "I've been around that damn hotel all day and most of the night for nearly two years now, and every time I get out of sight of it, that widow woman hollers so loud you can hear her all over the square. She might as well tie me up like a dog."

"She likes you," I said.

"But I'm too old for that kind of work now. Hotel work is boy's work. And women's. A man's got to move around. In all the time I've been in Texas I ain't been no farther from this spot than Carruth's place." He lapsed into a kind of reverie, just staring into the evening for some time. Then he said, "I shouldn't never have listened to you. I should have went buffalo hunting."

"Well, you'd probably be dead now."

"Dead is better than what I am."

"Pshaw, Sam!"

"Well, I believe it," he said. Then he fell back into his silence.

It was full dark when he spoke again, and the saloon lamps were casting an inviting glow onto the sidewalks around the square. "Come have a drink with me," he said.

"You know I don't drink, son."

"Never?"

"Never."

"Let me drive for you, then."

At that time, besides being sheriff, I had started a small freighting business. Just two wagons that I ran between Denton and Dallas and Sherman to fetch goods from the railroad depots whenever there was call to. Although I had competitors in Henry Underwood and others, my business was growing, and I employed two teamsters. But I didn't need another one.

I did need help, though. In addition to the family ranch west of town, where my brothers did more than their share of the labor, and my twelve-acre town place west of Bolivar Street, where my dear wife was too heavily burdened with the care of our large garden and the domestic animals, I recently had bought a hundred-and-sixty-acre place to the northwest that was in need of improvement. As I said, I'm a man of property. But the growth of the town and the troublesome times were demanding more of me than I had expected when I was persuaded to run for the sheriff's office, and I was proving a neglectful steward of what the Lord had given me. So I said, "I've got no place for another teamster now, but I do need some help." And I told him about the new place and all that needed to be done there, and offered to let him live with Mrs. Egan and me at our town place. I also promised that if one of my teamsters quit, he could have the job.

He accepted my offer with enthusiasm, and wanted to move his belongings into my house that very night, but I refused. "It would be unfair to the Widow," I said. "Tell her what you're going to do and give her a few days to find somebody to take your place."

"She ain't going to like this, Dad," he said.

"No, she won't."

"Will you tell her? She'll kill me."

The prospect of telling the Widow Lacy that she was losing her right hand didn't thrill me, either, but I agreed to do it. Sam wanted me to go to her right then, but I decided to wait until morning, when the woman wouldn't be so tired.

The Widow gave me unshirted hell. She even wept, and

accused me of stealing the boy away from her. But I told her Sam was so restless that she was bound to lose him soon, anyway. And she had begun to suspect that, and finally told me that if she had to lose him, she was glad he was coming to me. She implored me to treat him right, and I promised that I would. She took my hand and pressed it and wiped her eyes, and that was that.

A few days later, Sam moved his gear into the little room off my back porch. I rode out to the new place with him and my younger brother Armstrong, who is called "Army," and showed Sam the work he would have to do, with Army's help. The prospect would have disheartened almost anybody. Nobody had lived on the place in years, and the cabin was in ruins. I didn't care about that, since I didn't plan to live there anyway, but the land was on the verge of ruin, too. The fields were overgrown with weeds, and the brush was making a vigorous comeback in the pasture, and the fences would have to be rebuilt. The improvements I wanted were minimal, since I intended to use the land for grazing and for the firewood I could get out of the bottom on the back side of the place. But Sam and Army would have to spend days in the pasture with grubbing hoes and axes, hacking at the brush and snaking timbers out of the woods and splitting them to rebuild the fences, and chopping and hauling the firewood. Just looking at it made my back ache, but Sam and Army regarded it as nothing. Youth is wonderful.

Within a month they had the fences up, and I bought a few head of stock and moved them there. The boys cut enough firewood to last the whole winter and hauled it to town. Then Army went back to the ranch and left Sam alone with his grubbing hoe and ax and the brush. Every morning Mrs. Egan fixed him bacon and biscuits to take with him, and he would saddle the little buckskin and ride out just after daylight. He would stay out there all day by himself, working like a nigger, and ride back in time to milk our cow, gather the eggs and do anything else he could to help my wife. He would dandle my daughter Minnie on his knee, and let little John ride him piggyback. He called John "Little Pard." He made a lot of progress on the pasture, too, and I guess he would have grubbed brush all winter if Billy Chick hadn't quit.

Billy was one of my teamsters. When the weather started getting cold, he looked for an inside job and found one. I wasn't sorry. He was lazy, and I probably would have let him go anyhow.

I was looking for a way to reward Sam, since he hadn't uttered a word of complaint and I knew he wouldn't be happy hacking brush forever. So when Billy quit, I offered his job to Sam.

I'll never forget the day of his first trip to Dallas. The wagon was piled high with buffalo hides, and they stank to high heaven. But Sam had a brand new haircut and a shave and was wearing new black pantaloons and a checkered shirt that the Widow Lacy had given him. I don't guess he had worn them more than twice before.

"Lord, son," I said, "you look like you're going to church."

"Better than that," he said. "I been tending these goddamn horses all my life, and now they're going to *take* me somewhere."

He came back a few days later full of tales about the city. His eyes flashed as he described the iron toll bridge across the Trinity River, the street with the outdoor gas lights that made night almost as plain as day, the huffing of the steam locomotives, the mule-drawn cars for the public to ride on Main Street. You would have thought he was Marco Polo home from Cathay. His taste of the wider world had given him such a thrill that he was a pleasure to see.

He hinted of sampling the city's darker pleasures, too, offhandedly mentioning the elaborate gambling setups in some of the saloons there, the piano music and the women with uncovered shoulders and plumes in their hair who knew how to separate a man from his money. I suspected they had separated Sam from some, but if they did, it was his own money and not mine. He returned with every penny he was supposed to, so I didn't ask how he took his ease in Dallas. I had sent Sam to the city to do a job for me, and he had done it. I was satisfied.

And I was more satisfied as time passed. Sam was the most willing, capable hand I ever had. He became the man I relied on for any duty requiring intelligence and a sense of responsibility. It was he who hauled the first load of ice from Sherman to Denton, a day of note in the history of the town. The ice had come all the way from the Great Lakes by riverboat and train, but so much of it could have been lost on the hot fifty miles from Sherman that the enterprise wouldn't have been worth the effort in the hands of a careless man. Sam packed the big blocks in the wagon with a care befitting glass, surrounding and covering them with straw before he lashed the canvas over them. When he arrived, he and Frank Jackson chipped off two big chunks and danced a jig in the street, holding the ice over their heads, shouting its coming to the town. The butchers and saloonkeepers bought it quickly at a premium price, and the ice run to Sherman became one of Sam's regular duties. I wouldn't have trusted it to anybody else.

Sam lived in my house and ate at my table and had my leave to treat most of my goods and belongings as his own. My children worshipped him. My wife pitied him and tried to teach him to read and write. He wasn't much of a pupil, but he did learn to write his name. When my wife concluded that he was enduring her instruction only to please her and not out of a desire for learning, she gave up. He received two or three letters from his family in Indiana, and Mrs. Egan would read them to him and write out his replies for him. In one, I remember, a couple of his brothers were inquiring about Texas and expressing an interest in joining him here. And he told Mrs. Egan to tell them they were better off in Indiana.

Sam had several brothers, I gathered from his rare mentions of his family. One was named Denton, the same as our town, I recall, but if I ever heard the names of the others, I've forgotten them. He had some sisters, too, I think. They were orphaned when Sam was just a boy. Their farm and everything on it were sold at auction, and Sam and the others went to live with an uncle, who had a large family of his own.

From Sam's vague references to that time I deduced that he was a runaway. He mentioned a quarrel with his uncle, about wages, I think. "I walked away without nothing but the shirt on my back," he said. He went to St. Louis and hung around the waterfront for a while, then drifted downriver to Mississippi and got a job at a sawmill. It was the same work he had done for his uncle, but they paid him for it in Mississippi. He saved enough money to buy a horse and a gun, somehow hooked up with Bob Mayes and his family, and wound up in Denton because that was where Bob Mayes was going, and one destination was as good as another to Sam, just so it was Texas.

There was nothing interesting in his story, and nothing unusual. The world is full of runaways, and many of the best citizens of Denton admit to scrawling "GTT" on their doors back home, a message to friends or the law or creditors that they had gone to Texas. There's no shame in being a runaway or even an outlaw here, so long as the wrong was done somewhere else. Since the war, many decent people have fled carpetbag debt and carpetbag law, and there's no disgrace in that, just as there's no disgrace in being a poor freedman, now that the Yankees have cut the niggers loose from the secure places they used to know. What matters here is what people make of themselves after they get here, not what they were where they came from.

Nobody tried harder to make something of himself than Sam did. As I've already said, he was a hard worker, and at that time there wasn't a cheating bone in his body. He returned from every freighting trip with all the goods and money he was supposed to bring back, and sometimes more. Once he returned so much of the expense money I had given him that I asked if he had fed the horses during the trip. He just said, "Don't worry till you see their ribs."

I didn't worry. I would have trusted him with anything, especially my horses. People around town took to calling him "Honest Eph." I don't know why, unless they just thought "Honest Eph" sounded better than "Honest Sam." Anyway, he earned the name. And I couldn't have felt closer to him if he had been my brother or son. I even invited him to sit with me and Mrs. Egan at night when we read the Bible to each other. "Are you reading the Old Testament or the New Testament?" he would ask. When we were reading the Old Testament, he would join us sometimes, but he wouldn't when we were reading the New. He didn't care about Jesus and Paul, but he loved some of the stories in the Old Testament, especially those about Samson and those about David before he became king, when he was a bandit.

One night I read the story about Pharaoh's dream and Joseph's interpretation of it as a sign that Egypt would have seven years of plenty and seven years of famine. "And Pharaoh took off his ring from his hand," I read, "and put it upon Joseph's hand, and arrayed him in vestures of fine linen, and put a gold chain about his neck."

"Did what Joseph said come true?" Sam asked.

"Yes," I said, and I went on to read about the famine that hit Egypt, and how Joseph's preparations had saved the people and brought his brothers out of the land of the Hebrews to buy corn from him.

Sam was astonished. "Is there really people that tell you what dreams mean?"

"Things happened in Bible days that don't happen now," I said. "It was a special time, and God was closer to people than He is now."

"I was thinking of my horse dream," he said. "I ain't no Pharaoh, but I'd give a penny to know what it means."

"I don't think dreams mean anything," I said. "Not anymore."

"Why does it come to me all the time if it don't mean nothing?"

"You've just got horses on the brain," I said.

No one could doubt that he *did* have horses on the brain. His whole life was horses. My freight animals were entirely under his supervision, and he had begun spending more and more of his idle time at the racetrack at the edge of town. Army was responsible for that, I regret to say. Army shared Sam's love of horseflesh. They also shared a love of gambling. Army loved the races and had known most of the sporting men around Denton for years. He introduced them to Sam, and after a while the races became a regular part of their Sunday afternoons. Sometimes Frank Jackson or Henry Underwood would go with them.

By the standards of my native Kentucky, the Denton races were pitiful. The track was just a quarter-mile stretch of harrowed prairie with a row of primitive chutes at one end and a finish line at the other. The performers were usually just cowboys and cow ponies racing for a new hat or a new suit of clothes or a bottle of whiskey. A few townspeople who owned good horses but didn't know how to ride them would hire the young darkies who hung around the track to climb into the saddle in their stead. A few of the niggers were excellent riders and fulfilled all their worldly needs in that way, never turning a hand at honest labor.

Those races were taken very seriously by many, though, especially those who bet habitually and heavily. And since those chosen to judge them often were incompetent and all the spectators and many of the riders were drinking, there were many cries of foul and many accusations, threats and fights resulting from them. It was as unholy a way to observe the sabbath as the devil has devised, and I had as little to do with it as possible. Any attempt of mine to break up a fight out there likely would have led to another fight, so I left the sportsmen to settle their own disputes. I rarely even went to the track except when a stranger would ride into town leading a thoroughbred behind him. I knew that he was a professional, and that he was going to taunt the locals into laying outlandish bets on some hometown favorite, and I knew he was going to win the race. On those occasions I would go to the track and do what I could to see that the race was run fairly, that the professional got his money, and that he got out of town quickly and safely.

The track was a thorn in my side, and I'm sorry that my brother was so devoted to it. But nobody can be his brother's keeper in all things. Nor could anyone foresee what terrible consequences would result when Sam caught the contagion in earnest.

That happened the day he returned from a freighting trip to Sherman and walked into my office at the courthouse and stood trembling before me. "Dad!" he said. "The horse in my dream is tied outside!"

The beast that had galloped through Sam's sleep was a little sorrel mare, about two years old and fifteen hands high. She had only one marking, a white stocking leg, the left hind one. She was a fine animal, but I saw nothing about her that should inspire such ecstasy in a man. I've never seen an expression on another face to compare with what I saw on Sam's. Moses must have looked like that when he beheld the burning bush, and the Emmaus pilgrims when the risen Christ revealed himself to them. It's blasphemous, I suppose, to compare the effect of a mere horse on a man to revelations of God, but no other comparison will do. Sam trembled as he stood there staring at that animal, and his face shone with a light that I can only call holy. Finally he stepped to the mare as if in a trance and extended his hand, and the mare nuzzled his palm.

"How do you know it's the one in your dream?" I asked.

"I just know."

"That mare belongs to Mose Taylor. I've seen her many times."

"I never seen her but in my dream," he said. "I know she's the one. I must have her."

"I doubt Mose will sell."

"He'll sell. God wants me to have her."

That's the only time I ever heard Sam speak the Lord's name outside our evening Bible readings, except in curses. His admission that God lives and works in our lives surprised me, and I was moved by it. "Come on," I said. "I'll help you find him."

Mose Taylor was a farmer. He lived in the eastern part of the county, off the McKinney road, and didn't come to Denton often. But I knew him and, as I said, I had seen the mare before. Mose was standing at the bar in the Wheeler Saloon when I introduced him to Sam.

Sam said, "I want to buy your mare."

Mose laughed. "So do a lot of people."

"I don't want to haggle. How much will you take for her?"

Mose regarded Sam with some surprise. "Six hundred dollars," he said. His eyes roved over Sam, over his shaggy black hair, his unshaven face, his patched pantaloons and scuffed boots. "Not a penny less."

He might as well have demanded a million. I knew that, and I knew that Mose knew that. It was a ridiculous price for any horse in Denton County. But Sam didn't bat an eye. "Give me time to raise the money, and you've got a deal," he said. "Will you shake on that?"

Mose didn't want to sell the mare. He glanced at me, but I just gave a slight shrug. Then Mose extended his hand. "The shake is good for a week," he said. "After that there's no deal. Dad is our witness."

Sam shook his hand and walked out without another word. I followed him. "You don't have anywhere near six hundred dollars," I said.

"No."

"How much *do* you have?"

"About two hundred."

"You're crazy. Where are you going to raise four hundred dollars in a week?"

Sam gave me a tight little smile. "Don't worry, Dad. I'll get it."

He did, too. He got it from Army. The next Sunday, they rode out of town together in the morning and returned near sundown, Sam astride the mare and leading his buckskin. He was grinning bigger than I'd ever seen him. "Dad, meet Jenny," he said. "The fastest horse in Texas."

Army was grinning, too. He said, "There's many a dollar in Jenny."

Then I knew what their intention was, and I was troubled.

Army owned two-thirds of Jenny, but she really belonged to Sam. I gave permission to stable her in my barn, and every day when he finished his work Sam went straight there and put a hackamore over her head and leapt upon her bareback and rode out to the racetrack. There he galloped her up and down the harrowed stretch until darkness brought him home. Sometimes he wouldn't arrive until after supper, and Mrs. Egan complained of that, but Sam always refused to let her warm it for him. She complained of his no longer milking the cow or gathering the eggs, too, but I reminded her that those were no part of the duties for which I was paying him. Nor was he obligated to carry the children piggyback or attend the Bible readings, which he no longer did. He tended the animals and drove my wagons with the same care and profit as before, and that was all I had a right to ask of him.

We were hurt by his withdrawal from our family circle, though. Even I, who as a horseman understood his enthusiasm for his new possession, couldn't help being offended by the indifference he displayed toward us, since we had gone the extra mile to befriend him.

I won't say I was angry. I was disappointed. Yes. And my disappointment wasn't eased by his constant company with the least worthy of his companions, the derelict husband and freighter, Henry Underwood. That ne'er-do-well now walked in Sam's shadow like a cur, and he rode out to the track every day, too. I mentioned to Sam one night that I didn't like the company he was keeping.

"What's wrong with Henry, Dad?" he asked.

"He's no good."

"Aw, there ain't nothing wrong with Henry. He's just helping me train Jenny."

"Yes, when he should be at home with his wife."

"His wife's a bitch, Dad. There ain't nothing wrong with Henry."

I had never heard Sam refer to a woman in that way, and I bit my tongue to hold back the reply I wanted to make. It would serve no purpose, and I might wind up losing my most valuable hand. So I said nothing. But I didn't like Sam's new cockiness, and I didn't like his mare for inspiring it, and I didn't like Army's involvement with either of them. That part of it came to a head on the day the mare won her first race.

I heard Sam and Army long before they reached the house. They were shouting and singing in the night, and I knew they were drunk. I stood at the gate, watching for them to come up the lane. They were on foot, weaving hither and yon, leading their three horses. I sent Mrs. Egan and the children into the house and told them to shut the door. I stood waiting, and when they reached the house Army handed his reins to Sam and staggered up to me. He grinned in a silly way and took off his hat and handed it to me. "Hold it with both hands, brother," he said. Then he stuck his hands into his pockets and dropped several silver dollars into the hat. He rummaged in other pockets and found more and dropped them in, too. "Wooo!" he hollered.

"Quiet!" I said. "The children will hear you."

He grinned in the same stupid way and tipped his absent hat and took the reins from Sam, who stepped up and dropped more money into the hat. He said, "Old Army told you there were lots of dollars in that Jenny. That's how many she throwed up for us today."

But it wasn't Jenny who had "throwed up." Army's shirt and vest were covered with vomit, and his sour odor filled the air between us. Sam noticed my disgust. "Old Army taken sick and fell off his horse," he said. "That's why we was walking."

I gave the hat and its heavy contents to Sam and gathered the reins from Army's hand. "I'll help Army with the horses," I said.

"Army, he's too drunk . . ."

"I want to talk to my brother in private," I said. "Don't go inside until you're sober." I put my arm around Army's shoulders and half led, half carried him toward the barn, pulling the horses behind. Army mumbled, and leaned heavily against me, and it was hard to keep my balance in the darkness. But I made it to the barn and managed to prop Army against the wall. I unlatched the door and lit the lantern and led the horses inside and unsaddled them. While I was currying Jenny I called out, "How much will you take for your part of this mare, brother?"

"Ten thousand dollars," he called back. Then he giggled to himself, and I didn't speak to him again until I had put the animals up and fed and watered them.

When I closed the door Army was sitting against the barn. His chin lay on his chest. He appeared to be asleep, but he raised his head when I nudged him with my toe, and I said, "I'll give you four hundred dollars in the morning, brother. Take it or be damned."

He frowned, trying to focus on me, but said nothing. "Our dead mother demands it," I said. "She would weep to see you now."

Army wept. He tried to get to his feet, but couldn't. "Sleep in the barn," I said. "I don't want you in my house." Then I left him.

Sam was slouched on the porch still, but seemed fairly sober. Either he hadn't drunk as much as Army or he held it better. Army's hat was in his lap, and he was counting the silver into two neat stacks. "So you won," I said.

"Yeah. Where's Army?"

"Asleep."

"I couldn't stop him, Dad."

I shrugged. "He's a grown man. He's responsible for himself. But I'm buying his part of the mare."

Sam smiled and offered his hand. "Good," he said. "Shake, pard."

"No, I won't be your partner. The four hundred is a loan. The mare is all yours."

Sam gazed thoughtfully at the stacks of dollars. "It'll take a while to pay back four hundred of those."

"Take as long as you need. I should have loaned you the money in the first place. It's not good for me or my family to be mixed up in horse racing."

"I'm sorry about Army, Dad."

"It's not your fault. Sam, do you have to race her?"

"Yeah. If I do it right, she'll be my ticket to big things."

"What things, Sam?"

He waved at the stacks of dollars. "Money's what makes us men, ain't it, Dad? Without it, nobody can be much more than a nigger. You've treated me good, and now I'm your head nigger. But I'm still a nigger. I've been a nigger all my life. But I come to Texas to stop being a nigger, and Jenny's going to help me do that."

I laid my hand on his knee. "You're looking for a short cut where there isn't any," I said, "but that's none of my business. Let's go inside."

"No, I'll stay with Army," he said.

That happened in the fall of '74, and I'm proud to say that Army never went to the track again. But the races became the most important thing in Sam's life. He associated himself with a skinny nigger called Dick, who became his jockey, and a remarkable one. He rode Jenny without saddle or bridle. He used only a hackamore, and slathered the mare's back and sides with molasses before each race. He stuck to her like a fly, and seemed to communicate with her in a mysterious way that no one, except maybe Sam, understood. It wasn't long before Dick and Jenny had beaten every fast horse in Denton County and several challengers from other parts.

By the spring of '75 Jenny had become known far and wide as The Denton Mare, and Dick's unorthodox way of riding her gave rise to tall tales about the animal's speed and the human fly who urged her to her victories. As the mare's owner, Sam was regarded as something of a gentleman, and became one of the better-known men in Denton County. Sometimes his winnings were considerable, and even though he presented generous shares of them to the darky and Henry Underwood, who now bragged of being Jenny's manager, Sam always made at least a small payment on the loan.

The rest he squandered, like the Prodigal Son in the far country. When the sporting crowd rode into town from the track on Sunday evenings, he made the rounds of all the saloons, usually with Dick and Henry in his train, and bought drinks for all present. When he left one saloon to move to another, many of the drinkers would follow, in hope of picking up another free drink at the next stop. Sam never turned them down, so he became a popular man. But he was popular with trash. Henry Underwood and the darky were pet dog and monkey to him, and most of his crowd were worse. Hard drinkers, gamblers, thieves and such, men who lived by guile and wit. The boy Frank Jackson and Jim Murphy were the only decent people in his company.

Inevitably there came the day when the owners of other horses and those who bet on the losers ceased to wonder at the speed and consistency of The Denton Mare and began to suspect that she was helped along by some clandestine means. The quarrels began with a mound of dirt in The Denton Mare's starting chute. Since our racetrack has no turns, a horse's place in the chutes gives it no advantage or handicap, you see, as it would on an oval track. But some horsemen held a superstitious affection for one chute or another, and out of courtesy their competitors usually didn't object to their always using their favorites. Sam was one who always used the same chute, and he somehow got the idea that a downhill start would give his mare an advantage over the other horses. So he and Dick built a mound of dirt, about three feet high, in her chute, so Jenny's first stride or two would be downhill.

I don't know whether the mound gave the mare an advantage or not, but the judges allowed it, and the owners of rival horses found it a convenient excuse for their losses. Cries of foul became a part of the regular Sunday doings at the track, and the quarrels and bickerings that started there continued into the carousing in town and became more bitter and dangerous with every glass of whiskey consumed.

I told Sam that his dirt mound was playing hob with my Sunday nights, and he gave his rivals a headstart of a length or two thereafter. But no pride is larger or more easily injured than that of the owner of a fast horse, and as The Denton Mare continued undefeated the alibis of the losers' backers became more and more farfetched until one finally accused Sam of outright crime.

The beaten horse was from out of town, and his owner didn't know how well Sam was liked in Denton. Otherwise, he probably wouldn't have made such a foolish accusation, especially in the Parlor Saloon. Maybe the man knew Sam was in the place at the time, maybe he didn't. Anyway, the stranger was standing at the bar, and the man next to him, a staunch Bass supporter, started needling him about the drubbing his horse had taken from The Denton Mare. And he replied: "Well, he would have done better if he hadn't been poisoned before the race."

Sam was sitting at a table nearby and heard him. He got up and confronted the man. "Who do you think poisoned your horse?" he asked.

The fool persisted. "Somebody who was afraid of a fair race," he said.

Sam struck him hard in the face. The man reeled back against the bar, then reached under his coat and came up with a gun. But Jim Murphy, who was standing behind the bar, grabbed him by the hair and jerked his head back very hard. The man screamed and dropped the gun, and somebody kicked it out of reach. If Jim hadn't been where he was, Sam might have been killed, for he wasn't armed, and the man had the drop on him anyway. As I said, Jim Murphy was a handy man around a saloon.

The man could have filed a complaint against Sam for striking the first blow, I guess, but no Denton County jury would have convicted him. Maybe he figured as much. He left town that night and never raced in Denton again.

That incident was the end for Sam and me, though. I had worried all along that Sam's involvement with racing and the racing crowd held a potential for my political disgrace. That's why I forced Army to end his association with Sam and The Denton Mare. No decent man can consort with thieves and gamblers indefinitely without sharing their taint, and Army's drunkenness after that first race showed me he didn't have the will to resist even the grossest temptations. Indeed, his stupor convinced me that his slide to hell was greased, and his upright behavior since that drunken night proves I did right in invoking our dead mother's name and asserting my authority as elder brother.

Of course I didn't hold that kind of sway over Sam. He was in my hire and lived in my house, and The Denton Mare was stabled in my barn, but I knew those facts didn't give me the right to dictate to a man who was free, white and over twenty-one and wasn't my kin.

However, the incident in the Parlor convinced me that Sam was in for trouble, so long as The Denton Mare beat all comers. I knew it was only a matter of time until Sam would be a party to some violence or other, and whether he was the victor or the vanquished, my impartiality as an officer would be put in jeopardy. From any point of view racing and its attendant vices are bad, and my association with them, even in so remote a way as through my hired hand, could ruin what good I might do for peace in Denton County, not to mention any political aspirations I might have now that the carpetbaggers were losing their power in Austin. So I called Sam into my office and told him he would have to give up either his mare or his job.

I might as well have clubbed him between the eyes. He groped to a chair and sat down. Those Indian eyes stared so long at me that I became nervous, which isn't characteristic of me, and began shifting in my chair.

"Do you really mean that, Dad?" he asked.

"Yes," I said, and I began explaining my reasons, but he interrupted me.

"You know I can't give up Jenny," he said. "Remember my dream?"

"That dream means nothing," I said. "Jenny's a fine animal, but she's not *that* special."

"Then why ain't nobody beat her?"

"There seem to be several opinions about that," I said. Sam glared and started to rise, but I waved him down. "I'm not accusing you of anything. I'm not even dropping any hints. I just can't afford the sort of thing that happened last night. I can't have it associated with me in any way. Don't you understand that?"

"Well, I can't give up Jenny."

"Stop racing her then."

Sam smiled. "What's the good of owning a race horse if you don't race her?"

"I'm sorry, but that's your choice. Stop racing or stop working for me."

He was silent for some time, just sitting there twisting the brim of his hat in his hands, never taking his eyes from mine. Then he expelled his breath in a kind of hopeless sigh and said, "It ain't much of a choice, Dad. I'll be out of your house by tonight."

"I'm sorry you see it that way. You can pick up your wages tomorrow."

"I still owe you better than two hundred dollars."

"Pay me when you can. I trust you."

He put on his hat and started toward the door, then said, "I ain't had that dream no more since I got Jenny."

I still wonder sometimes if things would have turned out differently if I hadn't made him leave me. But it's foolish to speculate on what might have been. If Adam hadn't bitten the apple, we would still be in the Garden, wouldn't we? Or maybe Cain or Enoch or Methuselah would have bitten it later. The snake would have kept trying, that's for sure.

Frank Jackson

I'm free to say I don't regret riding with Sam Bass. And if some miracle happened and Sam tracked me into New Mexico and found this village, and if he could divine that the strange name on the shingle over my office door designates his old friend, Frank Jackson, and if he asked me to live it all again, I would do it.

Sam and I were brothers as surely as if we had been pulled from the same womb. Fate had made us orphans. Fate had decreed that we find one another. Only other orphans on equally harsh frontiers might understand the loneliness in which we lived before we met. The Widow Lacy and Dad Egan were kind to him. They even tried in various ways to make him a part of their own households. But that kind of kindness only salts the pain of an orphan's loneliness, making it intolerable. An orphan knows that anything that's given out of no obligation can also be withdrawn, and he's afraid to accept the gift, for fear that he would love it and then have it taken from him. The wisdom of that wariness was proved for Sam when Dad Egan made him choose between keeping his mare or his job. Sam had never permitted himself to think that he was *really* a part of Dad's family, so he could defy Dad with a clear conscience, knowing he had earned everything he received from his benefactor and had accepted nothing free.

My situation was a little different. Ben Key, in whose shop I worked, was married to my sister, so I was, at least in the formal sense, a member of his family. But my sister was a brood mare. It was a rare year that didn't witness the arrival of another tiny Key in their tiny house. And when Dr. Ross, after his delivery of one of them, turned to me and said, "Pack your gear, son, and come live with me," Ben and my sister exchanged a glance of such amazement and hope that I didn't even hesitate. But the ease with which people parted with Sam and me inspired an anger in both of us, I think.

Dr. Ross was lonely, too, and old, and angry and a drunkard. He was a graduate of Transylvania University in Kentucky, and even in his drunkenness he possessed an aristocratic dignity that made people respect him, even as he staggered from saloon to saloon. He even staggered with a certain high-born deliberateness. He was a noble-looking man, tall and broad-shouldered, with long white hair and beard that contrasted vividly with his black, professional coat. His eyes were icy blue and gazed steadily, hardly ever seeming to blink. They had sadness in them, and anger. Behind them, constantly in his mind, must have been the memory of something terrible or tragic, the reason for his being in Texas and a drunkard. But he never told me what it was, and he wasn't the kind of person you could ask. The most unusual thing about him was his feet and hands, which were tiny, like a woman's. Those hands, slender, smooth and white, holding the whiskey glass delicately between thumb and forefinger, were what set him really apart in a country full of big, rough, knobby hands.

His house set him apart, too. It was a small white frame structure not far from the square, very ordinary looking from the outside. Inside, though, it was a clutter of books and journals and shiny medical instruments of brass and steel and bottles full of mysterious powders and liquids. In a corner of one room was his bed, always rumpled, and in the corner of another was my own, always rumpled, too. The rest of the house was given over to the clutter.

He never suggested that I read any of the books, and never objected when I did. When I asked questions about them, he would answer them, but he never elaborated. He wouldn't lecture. It was the same with the instruments and bottles. I would pick up some tool or bottle and ask its medical use, and he would tell me. He even allowed me to be present when he treated patients. I assisted him any way I could, fetching things for him, holding patients still while he poked and probed at them, and he answered any questions I asked.

I was free to take or use anything he possessed, but he never *offered* anything. I was a colt wandering in a pasture of learning, free to nibble what I pleased. All Dr. Ross expected of me was to keep his horse groomed and fed, his hack in good repair and his liquor supply ample. In return I received food and shelter and access to the clutter.

I discovered a copy of Alexander Pope's translation of *The Iliad* among Dr. Ross's clutter and tried to read it. It was damn difficult until Dr. Ross showed me it was poetry, which I had never seen before, and read a passage aloud, showing me the cadence of Pope's lines. Then I began to love it. I memorized snatches of it and recited them to Sam while he fed the animals at the Lacy House. The verses bored him. He liked Homer's stories, though, and when I told them in my own words he would listen. The same with Shakespeare. He loved the blood and guts of *Othello* and *Julius Caesar* and *Macbeth*. Later he would see his mare, Jenny, as the fulfillment of a dream he had about a horse, and would become a believer in omens and portents. I think *Macbeth* and *Caesar* were responsible for that.

When Mrs. Egan gave up trying to teach Sam to read, I offered to tutor him. "What for?" he asked. "I got you, and you tell tales better than them old bastards in the books." But I think the real reason he rejected even rudimentary book learning was the slowness of it. Sam would give himself completely to any enterprise that interested him, no matter what labor or danger it involved. But he was impatient. Progress toward the goal in his mind had to be quick, in giant strides. If he had ever seen an hour glass he would have considered it a hideously boring means of measuring life. Grains of sand, falling silently from one small chamber to another, over and over again. It's a fitting symbol of most lives, I guess, but Sam's should be measured by boulders thrown into a pond. Each would splash and make ripples, and when the pond was full of rocks, well, that would be that. No turning the glass over and over again.

Well, I'm no poet, but you get my drift. He was as angry at life as I, and wild, and I loved him. The day he rode off to Indian Territory with Henry Underwood and the nigger Dick, I wept. I thought I would never see him again, and I was angry at myself for loving him so, for thinking him different from the others. He, too, had parted from me without much regret. One morning he rode up to Dr. Ross's house and hollered for me to come out. He was on his little buckskin, grinning. The nigger was mounted on a mule and leading another with a pack on it. Henry was on a big chestnut. The Denton Mare's lead rope was tied to his saddle horn. "Leaving?" I asked.

"Yeah," Sam said. "Jenny and me is running out of suckers around here."

"Where you headed?"

"Up to Montague County to find somebody that ain't heard of Jenny yet. Then up to Injun Territory. I hear them Injuns up there is mighty proud of their horseflesh."

"That's dangerous," I said. "Indians don't like to lose. And when they lose they don't like to pay."

Sam smiled. "We'll find a way." He leaned down and shook my hand, then wheeled the buckskin and headed northwest at a fast trot. After all we had been to each other, that was it.

Stories soon began drifting back to Denton. Jenny had won in Montague County and in Indian Territory as well. As I had predicted, the Indians hadn't taken kindly to her victories, and Sam and his bunch had fled back south of the Red River. The following spring I heard he was in San Antonio, that Dick had been killed in a knife fight, that Underwood had split with Sam and joined a cattle drive to Kansas.

Then I heard that Sam had gone into partnership with a saloonkeeper named Joel Collins. They were pretending that Collins owned The Denton Mare, and she was racing at South Texas tracks under his name. Meanwhile Sam was pretending to be a trainer and judge of racing stock and was roaming the southern part of the state checking other people's horses. Whenever he found one that he knew Jenny could beat, he advised the owner to match it against the Collins mare and bet heavily. Of course, Jenny always won. If rumor can be trusted, Sam and Collins played that trick from San Antonio to the Rio Grande, and even in Mexico. Then I heard that Sam and Collins had bought a herd and headed north.

But in the fall of '77 the horrible story came down the trails. A gang headed by Joel Collins had robbed a Union Pacific train in Nebraska. Collins was dead, the cowboys said, and Sam Bass was on the run.

One night not long after that, I was in Ben's shop, mending a coffee pot for a traveling preacher, and Sam stepped in and closed the door. I glanced up, but his side of the room was dark, and he had grown a mustache. I didn't recognize him. "I'm closed," I said. "Soon as I finish this job, I'll be going home."

"Still lazy, ain't you, Frank?"

"Sam!" I fairly sprang to him and embraced him, and he laughed. We made the nonsense noises that friends or brothers make when they meet after a long time and slapped backs and patted arms. I poked him in the belly with my thumb and touched something hard. He unbuttoned his shirt and whipped out a money belt and held it out like a fat, heavy snake.

"Me and Joel got lucky," he said. He laid his hat on my work bench beside the lamp. He opened the belt and tilted it into the hat, as if pouring grain into a trough. Coins glittered in the lamp light, clinked into the hat until it was full. "That's what's in them Black Hills."

"Your partner's dead," I said.

"I heard." His black eyes flickered in the dim light. "What the hell, Frank. We all go sometime."

"Not Collins's way. They shot him down like a dog."

Sam scooped up a handful of the coins and dropped them into the hat one by one. "I've got five hundred of these," he said. "Ten thousand dollars."

"You oughtn't have come here, Sam. Everybody in Denton knows you."

"How many coffeepots would you have to fix to get ten thousand dollars, Frank?"

"Every one in the world, I guess. You better ride out of here."

He shook his head. "I got plans. Lay down them tools and come with us."

"Who's 'us'?"

"Me and Underwood. He's with me. I need you, too, Frank."

"Not me, Sam."

He gazed into my eyes for several seconds, and I gazed right back, refusing to look away, thinking of Joel Collins, determined to convince Sam I was staying put. Then without a word he picked up the money belt and began scooping the coins back into it. The last fistful he held out to me. "Take this, pard," he said. "I'm giving it to you."

"Keep it. You're likely to need it."

He held his hand there, extended, the gold so shiny it seemed alive. If the eagles had flapped their wings and ascended from his palm, I wouldn't have been amazed.

"You keep it, Sam."

He shook his head and slowly dropped the money into the belt, then held out his hand again, holding only one coin. "Here. At least drink to my luck."

"No, you keep it," I said. "Who knows you're back?"

"Just you and Henry."

"I'll bet the law's connected you with Collins already."

"Maybe. But I've got some time."

"You shouldn't have done it, Honest Eph."

He smiled. "It was easy. Blow out the lamp." He opened the door and slipped into the darkness.

I went home. Dr. Ross was standing in front of the fireplace, still wearing his black coat, his hands clasped behind his back. He had built a fire. His glass of whiskey was on the mantel. "It'll be an early winter," he said.

"Yes, I reckon so."

"Your friend Bass is in Denton."

"How do you know?"

His blue eyes narrowed. "The Denton Mare was tied behind your shop."

"Yes, he's here."

"Hmm," he said.

Every time I would doze I saw Sam's hand full of gold. Until that night I had never thought much about money. I knew little about it, having had so little. The wages Ben paid me were small. Dr. Ross paid me none. But lying in my bed with the vision of Sam's gold in my head, I began to make connections between money and things I wanted. The house in which I was lying. Hadn't it cost money? How much? I had no idea. And the things that mattered more, Dr. Ross's books, his instruments and bottles. It had never occurred to me that he hadn't been born with them. He had acquired them with money. How much money? I had no idea. Not to mention his education. How much did it cost to go to Transylvania University and become a doctor and learn about poetry? I had no idea.

I reached to the small table beside my bed and picked up a book I had found among the clutter almost five years before, not long after I moved to the doctor's house. It was written by an English doctor named John Aiken and was called *Essays on Song-Writing*. I mentioned to Dr. Ross when I found it that song-writing was a strange subject for a doctor, and he looked surprised and took the volume from my hand. "My God," he said, "I haven't seen this in years." He leafed through it, smiling now and then. "An old professor of mine gave it to me, to teach me that physicians needn't think *constantly* of disease and death." He handed it back to me. "Keep it," he said. "I learned its lesson long ago, and then forgot it."

I loved the book. Not only because it was the only one I owned, but because Dr. Aiken had included with his essays a "Collection of Such English Songs as are Most Eminent for

Poetical Merit." They were short and most of them merry and easy to remember, and just the thing for reading at bedtime. The book was over a hundred years old, and I've never heard any of the songs sung, but I still keep them beside my bed. Reading them keeps the memory of Dr. Ross fresh in my mind.

But Dr. Aiken's songs couldn't compete with Sam's gold that night. So I finally closed the book, blew out the lamp and stared at the dark ceiling, thinking about money and what it could do for me, if I had any.

I got up before Dr. Ross did, which was rare, and fried the bacon and made the biscuits and gravy and coffee. I was eating, reading Dr. John Eberle's *Notes of Lectures on the Theory and Practice of Medicine*, when Dr. Ross came in half dressed, his suspenders flapping about his legs, and poured his coffee. He grabbed four biscuits and opened them and poured the hot gravy over them and sat down across the table from me. He craned his neck to see my book. "Eberle," he said. "My God, you're a serious young man."

"Weren't you?" I asked.

"Ah, yes. I was. It's a curse that afflicts some people. There's nothing to be done about it."

"Am I smart enough to be a doctor?"

"Of course you are. Intelligence has little to do with it, anyway. It's the being serious that's important. You'll know nothing about most things that ail people, but if you're serious, they feel better, and Mother Nature takes care of the rest, one way or the other. You must grow a beard, though, so you can tug on it at the right moments."

"You're not serious now."

He laughed. "You'll find out. Your reputation will depend on the fullness of your beard and your use of it." He sucked at his coffee, making a noise like a horse at water. "What did young Bass want?"

"He wants me to go with him."

"Where to?"

"I don't know."

"Are you going?"

"No."

"But you want to."

I said nothing.

"You tossed all night. Come, Frank, am I not your doctor?

Didn't I cure your croup? Doctors are sacred, like priests. We don't have to testify to anything."

"Testify?"

"Bass is a bandit, isn't he? He helped that Collins fellow rob a train, didn't he? Amazing! He probably has some similar adventure in mind."

"I don't know."

"Well, he'll have an exciting life. It's a good thing he didn't ask me. I would go."

"Now you're *not* serious."

Dr. Ross arched his eyebrows. "Oh, I wouldn't have gone with him when I was *young*. I was *much* too serious. I thought an exciting life couldn't be a responsible one, and I chose responsibility. Now look at it." He waved toward the clutter. "That's all there is."

"It's not so bad," I said.

"But this is all there has *ever* been, Frank. And it was my choice."

"Do you regret it?"

"Yes. It isn't so bad for an ending, but the beginning was the same. That's what I regret. A young man should gather memories that he'll enjoy living with when he's old. All my memories are of denying foolish impulses and being responsible."

We had never talked like that. I didn't know what to think of it. "I don't want trouble," I said.

"And I'm not saying you should go," he replied. "You're a good tinner."

"But I'm going to be a doctor."

"As long as you stay here, you'll be a tinner. That's the nature of things, my boy." He pushed his chair back and got up and pulled his suspenders over his shoulders and buttoned them.

Well, that conversation and the memory of Sam's hand full of gold wove themselves in and out of my mind all day while I worked in Ben's shop. I had never paid much attention to the shop before, never looked at it closely. But I did now, and the battered work benches, the worn tools, the bits of metal littering the floor seemed squalid and hopeless. I tried to imagine myself ten years older, Ben's age, standing in the same spot, holding the same pair of shears. The ease with which I imagined it frightened me, angered me. All I had to do to make it happen was nothing more than what I was doing now. Just keep on living as I was living now, and it would happen. Wasn't that what everyone was doing? A man could ride into Denton, write a list of all the people he saw and a description of what they were doing, then leave and come back ten years later and do the same, and the lists would be almost identical. Oh, some would have died or moved on, but their places would be filled by others, and nothing would have really changed. And it was the sameness that people valued. A man who did the same thing over and over again for years, and nothing else, was a *good* man, like Ben. A man who refused to submit to sameness or got tired of it and got drunk too often or tumbled the wrong woman or got money in other than the prescribed commercial ways was soon dead, or was driven farther westward to places that were still uncivilized.

I wasn't really surprised to find Sam in Dr. Ross's barn when I went to tend the horses that evening. He had already fed them, including Jenny, who was in the stall next to my bay, still saddled. "Look at that gal eat," he said. "She ain't had grain in a while."

He was armed with two pistols and a Bowie knife, all tucked into a belt that bristled with bullets. The bulge above them told me he still wore the money belt under his shirt. Large spurs graced his heels. His gray hat was pushed back from his forehead. He looked nothing like a teamster now, sitting there on a grain sack, smoking and grinning.

"Hello," I said.

"I got here before the doc."

"He knows, then."

"Yeah. Look, I come to make you an offer. I'll guarantee you a hundred dollars a month. There's little danger. I've never had no trouble yet . . ." He hesitated, studying my face, trying to determine what last card would play best. "I'll even let you ride Jenny sometimes."

"All right, Sam," I said.

He looked surprised, and answered so quietly I barely heard him. "Good," he said. "Good."

We walked to the house. Dr. Ross had built a roaring fire, and the room was stifling. He stood with his back to the fireplace, as usual, still wearing his coat, stroking his beard. He wasn't drinking, though. "You've made your decision?" he asked.

"Yes. I'm going."

He nodded. "God help me. You could be killed."

"Sam says it's safe."

"Well." He frowned and rubbed the side of his nose with his forefinger. "Let an old man advise you. Don't hurt the people. They'll be your friends if you don't hurt them. It's the nature of this place. And Frank, when you get enough money, go to Lexington, Kentucky, and write to me. I'll see that you have a chance to become a doctor. I swear." He stooped and picked up a set of saddlebags. I hadn't noticed them there at his feet. He handed them to me. "This is all you really need, anyway," he said. "This and a beard."

Sam, whose presence Dr. Ross hadn't acknowledged, was shifting from foot to foot, impatient. "Pack your gear," he said. "It's dark. It's time we went."

I started to unbuckle one of the saddlebags, but Dr. Ross said, "He's right. It's time."

I carried the saddlebags to my room and laid them on my chair while I stripped the two blankets from my bed, wadded my spare shirt and pantaloons and rolled them into the blankets. Then I saw Dr. Aiken's book of songs on the table, unrolled the blankets and nestled the little volume among my clothes. I stuck my pistol in my belt, laid the saddlebags across my shoulder, picked up my old Spencer rifle and the bedroll and was ready. I looked around the small room that had been my home for five years and was grieved. But I blew out the lamp and closed the door.

Dr. Ross and Sam were standing just within the back door, talking quietly. "Say your goodbyes," Sam told me. "I'll go saddle your horse." He opened the door just wide enough to slide through, and Dr. Ross closed it and turned to me. I could barely see his face in the darkness.

"I'm sorry I encouraged this," he said.

"Don't be sorry," I said. "You were right. I'll be fine."

"Stay alive."

"Yes."

"And don't kill, Frank. For God's sake, don't kill."

"I won't. Really. I'll be all right."

I felt his beard against my face. He kissed me. He opened the door again, and I slipped through. I looked back and gave a small wave, and he closed the door.

Sam was cinching my saddle when I got to the barn. "Tie on your gear, and let's ride," he said.

The moon was high and almost bright enough to cast shadows. We avoided the square and stuck to the alleys and the streets where only a few lamps burned inside the houses until we were beyond Denton, riding at a trot toward the northwest. The horses were rested and moved effortlessly through the cool night. The moon flashed dimly off the withers and haunches of Sam's mare and the silver conchos of his saddle. It was a fine night for a ride, and although there was an emptiness in my gut at leaving the home and life I had known, I felt good. I knew I was not only leaving something but moving *toward* something, too, toward the fulfillment of some dream, the keeping of some right, unclear promise, something unknown and inevitable but not at all bad. Destiny, I suppose you could call it. And I had no wish to avoid it. Sam and I didn't speak until we were beyond the town and well into the prairie, which rolled before us in the moonlight like a sea. I asked where we were going.

"Cove Hollow. Do you know it?"

"No."

"It's on Henderson Murphy's ranch, about forty miles from here. It's perfect for the likes of us. Prairie to run in and woods to hide in." He flashed a grin in the moonlight. "It's good to have you, Frank. We can't lose now."

"Joel Collins lost," I said.

"He wasn't among friends, and we are."

He spurred Jenny into an easy gallop, and I followed. We said nothing then for what seemed hours. We galloped until the horses began to tire, then we trotted, then walked awhile until they were rested, then galloped again. Both horses were strong, and I knew we were covering the ground fast. Just as I was beginning to tire, Sam reined to the left, toward a line of trees that grew along a watercourse. He pointed. "We'll stop there. We'll have an easy trip tomorrow."

We entered the woods, ducking to avoid the branches of the scrubby, close-growing trees. Sam picked his way carefully through the brush, and I followed. Most of the leaves were gone, but the thickness of the branches above and around us almost shut out the moonlight, and I was suddenly blind, depending on my horse to follow Jenny's lead. "Hickory Creek," Sam said. "I know a good spot by the water." And soon we were in a tiny, grassy clearing beside the creek. Sam dismounted and started unsaddling. "We can have a fire," he said. "I'll take care of your horse if you'll gather the wood."

The night was cool enough to make the fire's warmth inviting, and when the blaze was well established we spread our saddle blankets on the ground and sat cross-legged on them. Sam pulled a bottle of whiskey from his saddlebags, uncorked it and passed it to me. "Warm yourself, pard. The first drink of a prosperous life together. One to remember when we're rich."

I drank and passed the bottle back. He raised it in salute. "Here's to Joel," he said. "May them that killed him fry in hell." He drank, but didn't pass the bottle back to me. He held it a moment, then drank again. I knew then that he was more troubled by Joel's death than he admitted, and that if I wanted another drink I would have to ask for it. I did ask, and he stared at me without offering the bottle. "Let's see what the doc give you," he said. While I was unbuckling the saddlebags he took another drink.

In the first saddlebag were three books and a leather case with a green velvet lining containing forceps, three scalpels, several probes and a pair of scissors. The books were Eberle's small volume of *Notes*, Dr. Henry H. Smith's *Minor Surgery* and Dr. Thompson McGown's *A Practical Treatise on the Most Common Diseases of the South*. The other bag was full of vials of various sizes, all filled and labeled with their contents: quinine, opium, sulphur, calomel, mercury, camphor, digitalis and just about every other medicine I had seen Dr. Ross dispense during my years with him. There was also a large packet of bandages, tied up in a piece of canvas. I passed the case of instruments to Sam, and he examined them with mild interest. I was returning the books to the saddlebag when I noticed a white envelope protruding from Eberle's *Notes*. It was a letter, sealed, with my name written in Dr. Ross's beautiful hand. I broke the seal and read it:

Dear Frank,

You can't imagine the remorse I am feeling at this moment, having advised you to take a course that may well be the road to ruin. I was stupid to tell you that you were doomed to the tin shop forever. Of course that isn't true! You're a fine, intelligent boy, capable of a good life and many fine deeds. Instead, you're in the wilderness, embarking on a life of crime, and at my urging! I was foolish, made so by drink. If you can forgive, and if you can endure the company of a lonely old man a while longer, please return to my house at once.

But if your decision is truly made, accept this poor gift and go with my blessing. I used these saddlebags when I was young and made my rounds on horseback, but the chemicals are fresh and the instruments are in good condition. The books will teach you how to use them. I particularly recommend McGown, who was a classmate of mine at Transylvania. He's a fine, practical physician.

I've given you all you need to be a physician in this wild land. All except a cool, comforting hand (which you may have already) and a beard. And, O yes, a black coat, which I urge you to purchase as soon as possible. The rest will come with experience, and no one will ask to see a diploma.

Goodbye, my son. Be kind to the people. Do not kill.

Yr. frnd.,
Ross

"What is it?" Sam asked.

"A letter from Dr. Ross."

"Read it to me."

"It's nothing. Just about the medicines he gave me." I folded the paper and stuck it in Eberle's book and buckled the bag.

"I hope you don't get a chance to use none of that on me," Sam said. "Or nobody, for that matter." He gave me the whiskey bottle. He rolled and lit a cigarette and leaned back against his saddle and gazed upward into the dark trees. "This here's what you call freedom, Frank. It's worth taking chances for. No Dad Egan, no Ben Key, no doc telling us when to jump and how high. Just you and me and Henry. Horses, whiskey, cards, women and money. You'll like it, Frank."

"I'm here, Sam."

He smiled. He watched the horses grazing quietly just beyond the small circle of firelight. He waved his cigarette toward them. "That Jenny. She's to thank for it. Without her I'd still be freighting for old Dad. That ain't no life for us, Frank. It's no better than being a nigger. That ain't no life at all for the likes of us. The world belongs to them that grabs onto it and pulls, and that's what we're going to do, ain't it, Frank?"

"Yeah, Sam, that's what we'll do."

"Lord, Frank, you sure are quiet tonight. You ain't saying nothing."

"I just feel quiet. You know."

"Hey, old Henry's going to be glad to see you."

"I'll be glad to see him, too. It's been a long time."

"Remember when we used to go to the track together? That

was good times, wasn't it? We'll do that again one of these days, to watch old Jenny make us rich."

"Yeah. But what are we going to do now?"

"Well, we're going to see Henry."

"And after that?"

"Well, we'll sit down and decide what to do next. Maybe find us a couple more good men."

"And then?"

"Well, a stagecoach, probably. I've did them before. They're easy. Give you a chance to learn the business." He held out the bottle against the firelight. The whiskey was nearly gone. He handed it to me. "Finish her, and let's turn in."

I killed the bottle and threw it into the fire. We unrolled our blankets, arranged our saddles for pillows and threw two logs onto the flame. When we were bedded down Sam said, "Dream of gold, Frank."

Lying there, I began to miss Dr. Ross and my room back home, and even the tin shop. I couldn't sleep, despite the whiskey, and Sam couldn't either. I heard him get up very late, when the fire was low. He pulled on his boots and walked out beyond the firelight to where the horses were. He spoke quietly to Jenny, and she snorted. He talked and talked. He was still talking when I fell asleep.

The morning was chilly. Sam poked at the embers, and soon a small flame flared. I fed it dry grass and twigs until it was strong enough to take a few small logs and make enough heat to drive the night cold from our bodies. As we hunkered there, I saw we were in a jungle. Most of the trees and bushes were bare, but grew so thickly they almost blocked out the early sun. I had seen such thickets, but had never ventured into one for fear of tearing myself and my horse on the sharp branches and the almost certain presence of snakes. It wasn't a large wood, not more than a hundred yards across, with Hickory Creek running down its center. But I supposed it stretched as far as the creek did, a vein of marsh and jungle winding across the dry, brown prairie where nothing grew but grass, a testimony to the difference water makes on the face of the land.

"Learn this place," Sam said. "You'll be seeing a lot of it. Only a fool would come in here after an armed man." He took a hunk of jerky from his saddlebags and sliced off several slivers with his knife and passed them to me. "It's all I got."

"No coffee?"

"No, but old Henry's got the pot on the fire."

"Let's move, then," I said. "Morning's a grim time without coffee."

We bridled the horses and led them to the water. We lay on our bellies on the bank, sucking at the water with the horses, trying to moisten the dry, hard meat in our mouths. Then we led the animals back to the fire and saddled them in its warmth, scattered our embers and kicked dirt over them and mounted. We picked our way through the brush more quickly than we had in the darkness, and soon we were on the prairie, and the sun was full on us and warm.

We rode in silence in the pattern we had established the night before. Trot, gallop, trot, walk, trot, gallop, trot, walk. The rhythm of it took over my body, and as we traveled across the empty prairie I began to think of myself as a small boat, drifting on an ocean. If I had been in Denton at that hour, I would be fixing breakfast for Dr. Ross and myself, and the changeless pattern of my days would be beginning again. After breakfast I would wash the dishes and harness the doctor's horse, then walk to the tin shop and do again what I had always done. But here I was, drifting on an empty ocean of grass. Not drifting, really, but moving toward the young man's adventure that Dr. Ross wished he had had, a memory to store up and bring out again before the fireplace of Dr. Frank Jackson, an old man.

It was freedom I was feeling. A young man's freedom, which is the absence of responsibility and the prospect of unlimited possibility. And danger! I was riding with a man who owned ten thousand dollars, taken at gunpoint from a Union Pacific train. A man who had tended animals at a hotel and grubbed brush, but who now was considered dangerous because he dared take what others wanted to keep. I liked that. I didn't think of that as a crime, nor did many others. I had read in a newspaper that the Texas government had compiled descriptions of more than forty-five hundred men in the state who were wanted by the law somewhere, and almost a quarter of the counties hadn't even filed reports. Oh, many people railed against the "lawless element," I guess. But I venture to say that those who railed were rich, or had arrived in Texas with prospects of getting rich. Yankees, most of them, who hadn't suffered the war and its humiliation or the carpetbaggers. Some had even profited from our misery. And many of those on the state's list had got there for trying to keep what was theirs or regain what was taken from them. There were many others, weaker or more timid than they, who had suffered their losses silently, but cheered on and protected those willing to "grab onto the world and pull," as Sam had put it. A man who had nothing to pull but a gun and who took only from those who had plenty was considered a criminal only by those who had plenty and feared for it. Believe me, there weren't many of those in Texas in those days. Not in the countryside. So as Sam and I rode across the prairie in silence, dreaming our dreams, I felt like an outlaw but not like a criminal, and the beauty of the day and its freedom filled me.

When the sun was almost straight overhead we entered a thicket very like the one we had left in the morning. It, too, was bisected by a creek, which we began following upstream. This one was even more overgrown than the other, full of walnuts, oaks and acacias and thick tangles of vines and brush. High walls rose on both sides, not far from the banks of the stream. Large outcroppings of limestone gleamed white near the tops of the walls, shading caves and crevices whose depths I couldn't determine. "Cove Hollow," Sam said. "It runs about six miles up yonder, but we don't have to ride that far." We dismounted and led the horses to the creek and dropped the reins. The horses, their necks extended, their noses close to the ground, sniffing the water, stepped gingerly down the bank, found firm footing and dipped their muzzles into the stream. Sam and I flopped on the grass. He took off his hat and rubbed his sleeve across the sweat and dirt of his brow. "Welcome home, Frank," he said.

When we were refreshed we remounted and picked our way up the creek. I could see that Cove Hollow was ideal for our purpose, but it struck me as an unpleasant, unhealthy place. The ground was spongy under our horses' hooves. Clear Creek, as it was called, was dark and sluggish, and our course along its bank stank of rotting vegetation that had collected in numerous stagnant pools. Miasma and fever and snakes displaced freedom and adventure in my thoughts.

We had ridden about two miles into the hollow when a high, rasping voice screeched: "Throw up your props!" Sam halted his mare and raised his hands above his head. I looked around me, confused. I could see no one. The voice came again: "Throw up your props, Frank!" I did, and the voice laughed. "Can you see me?" it asked.

"No," Sam said. "Come on out."

Henry Underwood rode out of the shadow of the limestone outcropping above us, disappeared into the trees, then emerged on the creek bank only a few feet ahead of us. He carried a new Winchester rifle across his lap. "I've had you in my sights for fifteen minutes," he said. "Hello, Frank."

I had lied when I told Sam I would be glad to see Henry. I didn't like the man and didn't trust him and didn't understand Sam's affection for him. His eyes were the meanest I've ever seen, little round dots of blue ice that squinted from under heavy red lids. If snakes had blue eyes, they would be like Henry's. If snakes had eyelids, they would be like Henry's. His skin was florid and scaly, his hair long and rusty and matted, and so was his beard, which was streaked below the corners of his mouth with the tobacco juice he drooled when he spoke. He drooled now as he squinted from under the droopy brim of his dirty black hat. He wore no shirt. Dirty suspenders crossed the shoulders of his dirty red underwear, and a pistol butt protruded from the unbelted waistband of his dirty brown pantaloons. His squint, amused and curious, was directed at me, and I knew why. He had returned to Denton months before Sam had, but I had avoided his company, for his company meant trouble. He had made part of his living as a bill collector among the nigger part of Denton's population. Merchants who had trouble collecting from nigger customers would set Henry on them. They never inquired about his methods, and he always collected. He was a brutal, treacherous man, feared by many, and I could never abide his company outside of Sam's presence.

Sam said, "Let's go." Henry turned his horse and headed up the creek, with Sam and me following single-file. About a mile farther up the stream he turned into the woods, and we began climbing toward the limestone outcropping near the ridge. It was a tough climb, and the horses lunged, grabbing for footholds, kicking small stones down the slope behind us. Soon we came to a small level place, a sort of stone porch jutting from the base of the limestone, and in this place someone long ago had built a tiny log cabin. It leaned a bit, and most of the chinking was gone from between the logs. There were holes in its rough shingle roof. A small fire burned outside the low door, and as Sam had predicted, the coffeepot sat on a bed of coals near the blaze. Beside the cabin was a limestone cave, shallow, but large enough to shelter the horses. A crude corral had been built across its mouth. The rails, held in place by piles of stones, were newly cut, and their ends glistened yellow in the sun.

"Jim Murphy brought us to this place," Sam said. "It's on his daddy's land."

"Why doesn't Jim come with us?" I asked.

"He's worried about what his daddy would think. But he's promised to help us on the sly. I guess old Jim has something of a yellow streak."

Henry laughed harshly and spat a stream of tobacco juice into the fire. I resented their belittlement of our old friend, who had shown no sign of a yellow streak during my acquaintance with him. I would have preferred his company to Henry's any day, but I said nothing.

We dismounted and unsaddled the horses and turned them into the corral. Sam handed me a tin cup, and I poured myself some coffee and hunkered by the fire, settling myself into the bandit life.

We played cards on a blanket spread by the fire in the daytime and moved the blanket into the cabin at dark. The nights were getting cool, and I guess we were lucky to have that cabin, but I hated it. The chimney, or what was left of it, didn't draw well, and the place stank of smoke even when no fire was in the fireplace. When there *was* a fire we almost choked. But at night the fire and the walls offered some semblance of a real dwelling place, and the soft yellow light of the lantern on the edge of the blanket where we played created a certain intimacy among us that I needed and welcomed.

Sam and Henry talked endlessly. Sam described his Nebraska robbery in detail. How he and Joel and the others attacked the train. How he had discovered the forty thousand dollars in newly minted gold by accident, by kicking a wooden crate in the express car. How he and Joel and the others divided the gold, then split into pairs to make their getaway. How he and a man named Jack Davis bought a hack and stashed their gold under its seat, and how that sedate means of transportation had fooled the posses that pursued them. How he and Davis, posing as cattlemen, had driven part of the way to Texas in the company of a troop of soldiers who were searching for them. How he and Davis had split in Fort Worth, with Sam returning to Denton and Davis making his way toward New Orleans. Frankly, I found some of it hard to believe, but Sam told it with such detail and conviction that I didn't challenge him.

Henry's tales were less exciting and not as well told. They were about petty cattle thefts, scrapes with vigilantes, his escape from a doctor's office where he had been taken after he was wounded by a posse that proved too merciful. If he had headed up the posse, he said, he would have strung up the thief, meaning himself, on the spot, wounded or not. I silently agreed with him. Why anyone would be merciful to Henry was beyond me. Just the odor of him day and night for weeks on end was enough to plant thoughts of murder in my mind. But among his wretched tales of barroom knife fights and nights in jail, drunk and puking, there were also warm references to his long-suffering wife and his two children, a boy and a girl whom he loved deeply. I couldn't imagine Henry as a husband and father. How a woman or child could bear to embrace that filthy body or kiss that brown, juicy mouth was beyond me. But they did, and I envied Henry for that.

I had nothing to contribute to all the boasting, and one night I got bored and pulled Dr. Aiken's book of songs out of my saddlebag and stretched out on the blanket by the lantern.

"What the hell you doing?" Henry asked.

"Reading."

"What is it?" Sam asked.

"Songs. Poems, really. There isn't any music with them."

"Read out loud," Sam said.

"Why?" Henry said.

"Quiet," Sam said. "Read, Frank."

I opened the book at random and began reading.

When all was wrapt in dark midnight
And all were fast asleep,
In glided Margaret's grimly ghost
And stood at William's feet.

Her face was like an April morn
Clad in a wintry cloud,
And clay-cold was her lily hand
That held her sable shroud.

"What the hell's going on?" Henry asked.

"Hush," Sam said. "Read, Frank."

Well, it was a long poem, about the ghost of a woman who comes back to haunt her lover, who has been unfaithful to her. Most of the verses are her cussing him out, and he, of course, is scared almost to death. When morning comes and the ghost leaves, William jumps out of bed raving mad, runs to Margaret's grave, throws himself on it, and promptly dies.

And thrice he call'd on Marg'ret's name,
And thrice he wept full sore;
Then laid his cheek to the cold earth,
And word spake nevermore.

Well, I guess he dies. Either that or he's struck dumb. Either way, it's a good poem, and Sam liked it. "A ghost," he said. "Just like them stories you used to tell me. Do you believe in ghosts, Henry?"

"Hell, no," Henry said.

My reading became a part of our daily entertainment, and from time to time Sam would ask me to read about Margaret and William. Whenever I did, Henry would get up and walk out of the cabin. He believed in ghosts, all right. So did Sam.

From time to time we would ride down the creek to a little frame house that Jim Murphy had not far from the mouth of Cove Hollow. Jim would meet us there and bring us groceries and whiskey from town, and we would sit around all evening and drink. I liked Jim, and I enjoyed those times. Jim's house was more comfortable than our cabin, and his conversation, full of gossip from town, was a nice relief from the tedium of our camp.

Some bandits we were! I had been with Sam for almost a month, and we had done nothing but sit on our behinds. "Sam," I said one day, "you promised me a hundred dollars a month, and so far I haven't seen a nickel."

He pulled out several double-eagles and tried to give them to me, but I refused them. "I don't work for wages anymore," I said. "I just want to *do* something."

"All right," he said. "We'll go to Fort Worth and have a party."

That wasn't what I had in mind, but I was ready for anything that would get us out of Cove Hollow. So we rode to Fort Worth.

I hadn't been there in years, and the town had changed a lot. The railroad had reached it, and it had boomed as Dallas had a few years before. Sam got us rooms at the El Paso Hotel, which was new then and had gas lights and carpets. Sam and I spent three days bathing, getting shaved, drinking, playing cards and dancing with the ladies in the saloons. Sam's gold was welcome everywhere. He also bought me a new rifle like Henry's and a new suit of clothes, including a long black coat like Dr. Ross's. He would have done the same for Henry, but that savage had different fun in mind. As soon as we hit Fort Worth, he ducked into a dance hall, grabbed himself a whore, took her with us to the hotel and disappeared into his room with her. Neither emerged until the morning of the fourth day, when Sam banged on his door and told him we were leaving.

"I'm ready for that!" the woman replied.

While we were at the livery stable saddling up, I said to Sam, "Before we go home, I think we ought to do some business."

He stopped his work and glanced across at Henry in the next stall. "What do *you* think?" he asked.

"I think Frank's right."

As we led our horses out of the stable, Sam asked the hostler, "What time is the Fort Concho stage due?"

We rode toward Granbury, the last stop of the Fort Concho stage on the road to the city. The sky was gray and the sun so dim that we cast no shadows, but we were in a jolly mood. Sam talked and talked as we rode along. We were in no hurry. The stage wasn't due in Fort Worth until evening, and we had nearly all day to find a place to lie in wait for it. Even Henry wore what may have been a smile, and from time to time he let loose a screechy "Hee, hee!" and spat and wiped his mouth with his sleeve. His laugh seemed to have nothing to do with what Sam was saying. Maybe he just felt as I did, light-bodied and light-headed at the prospect of ending our long idleness and *acting*. Yes. The long, dreary month was ending, and my new life about to begin in truth. Somewhere along this road I would start to make my fortune. On this very day! It was a fine feeling, and not dampened at all by the likelihood that we were about to get rained on. The sky in the west was getting darker and darker, and the wind was rising, but we didn't care.

Nine or ten miles out of Fort Worth the road curved around a low hill with a small grove of live oaks at its foot. Sam decided this was the place to do the deed, that we would wait in the grove and step into the road when we heard the stage coming. The driver wouldn't see us until he rounded the hill, so we would have a good drop on him.

We tied our horses in the grove. A large flat rock lay under one of the oaks, and Henry flopped there with the whiskey bottle and a deck of cards. We drank and played penny-ante poker for I don't know how long, for the clouds hid the sun, and we couldn't judge the time. As the thunderheads kept building and building in the west, I took off my new black coat and rolled it into my blankets. At what would have been sundown, maybe, if there had been a sun, a bolt of lightning lit the landscape. Thunder cracked and rolled, and raindrops hit us like stones. The horses nickered in panic, and I dashed into the grove. Sure enough, we had almost lost them. Sam's mare had freed her reins from the tree and was backing away, about to sprint for the open country. I grabbed her reins and untied the other horses, which were kicking and rearing, too. I led them out of the grove, and Sam ran to help me with them while Henry chased his cards, trying to save them from the wind and water. "Mount up, Henry, or you're going to lose this horse!" Sam hollered.

Henry looked at him, open-mouthed and frowning, then recognized the situation and hurried to claim his horse from me. We mounted and quieted the animals, then just sat looking at each other in the flickering lightning. The rain had plastered our clothes to our bodies and was pouring off our hatbrims.

"Them cards is ruint," Henry said, and for some reason, maybe the whiskey, that seemed funny. We laughed until tears mingled with the rain in our faces. If the stage had come at that moment, the driver would have thought us lunatics and whipped his horses past us so fast that we wouldn't have known he had come and already gone. Then Henry remembered why we were sitting in the storm, and he said, "Hey! Where's that damn coach?"

"Maybe it's held up by high water," Sam said.

"Well, hell, it might not even come tonight!"

And suddenly we were miserable. The idea of sitting on the prairie, wet to the bone and waiting for the lightning to strike us while those we had hoped to rob were warming themselves in Granbury didn't appeal to us at all.

But the wind finally blew the storm on by, and our spirits improved. The moon, high and silver, encouraged us to believe the coach would be along, after all. We secured the horses again, and Sam handed us each a large white handkerchief. We folded them corner-wise and tied them around our necks. And as we sat talking and smoking through what must have been the early morning hours, Sam suddenly raised his hand. The jingle of trace chains was on the wind.

Silently we raised the masks over our faces, drew our pistols and stepped into the road. My breath came fast and heavy through the handkerchief. I wasn't scared. It was a delicious excitement that I would feel many times after that night, but never as wildly and acutely as I did then.

The coach rounded the bend. It was only a two-horse hack, moving slowly through the mud. When the driver saw us and pulled on the lines, in that instant when he had to decide whether to stop or whip his tired team past us, Sam presented his pistols and shouted, "Throw up your props!"

The driver held onto the lines but raised his hands above his head, and Henry grabbed the nose band of the closest horse and aimed his pistol at the man's head. "You got a gun?" he asked.

"Yes."

"Pull it out easy and throw it down."

The man did as Henry told him, and Sam and I dashed to the coach and raised the side-curtains. Two men, both well dressed and middle-aged, sat inside. One looked scared, the other disgusted. "This is outrageous!" the disgusted one said.

"Shut up," Sam said.

My man, the frightened one, was unarmed and carried only six dollars in greenbacks. "This bastard's almost broke," I said to Sam. "How about yours?"

"Five dollars," he replied. "God amighty, they're letting white trash ride the stage now. You fellows was heading to buy Fort Worth, lock, stock and barrel, wasn't you? You oughtn't travel with your whole fortune, though. No telling who you might meet on some dark road."

"And who *have* we met?" asked his man, the disgusted one.

"Why, General Robert E. Lee," Sam said. "And this here's President Jefferson Davis."

"Those gentlemen didn't hide behind masks," the man said.

"Well, I apologize," Sam said, "but me and Jeff's trying to keep our whiskers out of the rain. Please be our guests for breakfast." He handed each man a silver dollar. "We recommend the El Paso Hotel. Please climb aboard our carriage, and our man will take you there."

The men returned to their seats, and I lowered the side-curtains. "All right, drive!" Henry said. The driver slapped his lines on the horses' backs, and the wheels of the hack spattered mud on our boots and pantaloons as they turned down the road much faster than they had arrived. We stood watching until our victims disappeared into the darkness, and watched the spot where they had disappeared until we no longer heard the wheels and the harness and the cries of the driver. Henry lowered his mask. "All this for just three dollars each," he said.

"Don't fret," Sam said. "This was just something to do. Just a start. The big one's coming."

We divided the money and mounted and headed northeast at an easy gallop. The wind dried our clothes quickly, and the prairie smelled clean and alive, and the soft, wet sound of the horses' hooves in the long grass was soothing to the spirit. We skirted Fort Worth close enough to see its lamps, and by daybreak we were well on the way to Denton. "Hey, you know what today is?" Henry asked.

"What day?" Sam replied.

"Christmas Eve. Tomorrow's Christmas."

Sam said nothing, and neither did I. Henry's words had turned us lonely, I guess, and we rode for some distance in the private company of our thoughts. Then Henry said, "I'd like to spend it with my younguns, Sam."

"Then do. Just be careful."

"Just Christmas Day," Henry said. "Then I'll come back." He reined his horse toward Denton and spurred it into a run. He waved goodbye without looking back.

Sam said, "You got any place you want to be, Frank?"

"No."

"Good," he said.

Christmas never meant much to me. In Ben Key's house we had a noon meal on that day that was more than we had on other days, but that was the sum of our celebration. Dr. Ross observed it by drinking a toast to the Christ Child early in the morning and then forgetting it. I don't know what the day meant to Sam, but it couldn't have been much, and our edginess that day wasn't because of Christmas. It was because a face that we were accustomed to having around was missing, and Sam and I had only one face each to look at and nothing else to do but look at it. It was bitterly cold. The wind howled around the corners of the cabin and whistled through the holes like a pack of wild, insane animals. We kept the fire burning in the fireplace, and its smoke almost choked us at times, and we had to wear our coats all day. We finally gave up our attempt to play cards because our hands were so stiff we couldn't shuffle well. So we quit and kept our hands in our pockets and sat and stared into the fire. From time to time one of us would get up and grab a stick and poke at the fire and then sit down. We fried bacon and made biscuits and coffee, and that was our Christmas meal, then I grabbed the water bucket and worked my way down the slope to the creek, just to get away for a while. The creek wasn't frozen, but its water seemed to flow even more sluggishly than usual, and the wind whipped the bare branches of the trees in a dance as wild and insane as the animal sound at the cabin. I stood staring into the water until I couldn't stand the cold anymore and dipped the bucket into the stream and climbed back up the slope with it. When I stepped through the door Sam said, "I guess I'll check the horses," and *he* left. That's how the day went.

So we were glad when in the late afternoon we heard a voice drifting on the wind from below, shouting, "Sam! Sam Bass!" It was Jim Murphy, and Sam and I ran out of the cabin, waving our arms and calling back to him. Jim worked his horse up the slope and dismounted and took a quart of whiskey from his saddlebags. He handed it to me and said, "In honor of the day, from the Murphy family and the Parlor Saloon." His face, what I could see of it between his hatbrim and his turned-up collar, was red and not at all cheerful. He led his horse to the corral and turned it in and walked back to us, rubbing his hands together. "The law's got Henry," he said.

"What for?" Sam exclaimed.

Jim waved us toward the cabin, and we followed him inside. He stood in front of the fire, his back to us, warming his hands. "It's colder than a witch's tit out there," he said. "Let's have a drink."

"Damn it, Jim, what happened?" Sam said.

Jim drew the cork and took a long pull on the bottle. He coughed quietly. "It was Pinkertons," he said. "They kept saying Henry's name was Nixon and that he was with Joel Collins in Nebraska. Them and Dad Egan surrounded his house last night and kept hollering for him to give hisself up. And Henry kept hollering back that he ain't been out of Denton since summer. Hell, Dad knowed that."

"Tom Nixon's in Canada," Sam said. "Henry wasn't nowhere near us."

"I know that!" Jim yelled angrily. "You think I don't know that? Now let me tell it! Old Henry wouldn't give hisself up. He just kept telling them he was innocent. But this morning they said they was going to storm the house if Henry didn't give hisself up, so he did. He was afraid his wife and younguns would get hurt. So he just walked out and give hisself up on this fine Christmas morning." Jim waved the bottle toward the door, where the wind was howling. "And his wife and kids come to me crying, and his wife says, 'Do something, Jim. You know this ain't right.' "

"It *ain't* right, by God! Tom Nixon's in Canada!"

"Go tell that to Dad Egan and them Yankee detectives. I went to Dad's house and said, 'Look, Dad, Henry was working for me all during September. That's when that robbery was, ain't it?' And old Dad just picked at his fingernails with his knife, and he said, 'The Pinkertons said he was their man, and who am I to doubt it? I ain't sorry to see Henry Underwood out of Denton County. I hope he goes to the gallows.' "

"That righteous bastard!" Sam yelled. "We'll get Henry back, by God!"

"They done taken him straight to Sherman and put him on a train," Jim said. "And there was about four Pinkertons with him. Even if you was to catch up with them, they'd just kill Henry and say you done it. There's a reward for him. For Nixon, anyway."

"How much?" Sam asked.

"Five hundred dollars."

"How much for me?"

"The same, I guess, if they know you was in it. They figure Collins for the leader, and they done got him."

We fell into silence. Jim, standing with his back to the fire, looked at me and then at Sam and then back again, and Sam and I were looking at him. The wind seemed to be dying a little. The logs were popping and cracking in the fire. I couldn't think of a thing to say, but I knew somebody ought to say something. Then Jim said quietly, "How's things, Frank?"

"Fine."

"We miss you in town. When you coming back?"

"Leave Frank alone," Sam said. "He's staying with me."

I kept thinking about Henry's wife and children and how confused they must be by it all, and what a rotten Christmas it had been for everybody, and what a tiny bandit band we were now. Sam must have been thinking the same thing, for he said, "Join us, Jim. We need a good man."

"It would kill Daddy," Jim said. "Look what it's doing to Henry's family."

"Henry's been in trouble all his life. You know that. And your Daddy wouldn't never know."

"I can't, Sam."

"Later, maybe?"

"Maybe."

"Do you know a man or two who want some easy money? We need help."

"I'll check around," Jim said.

"Make sure they're good ones," Sam said. "We won't have time to teach them much."

"All right." Jim rose and stretched like a cat. "I got to go. It's Christmas, and I'm expected."

We walked him out to the corral and watched him swing into the saddle. As he was about to start down the hill Sam said, "Wait." He took five double-eagles out of his pocket and handed them to Jim. "Send them to Henry when you know where he's at."

Jim looked at the coins and smiled. "I'll send him greenbacks. These wouldn't help his case if the law got hold of them."

The wind definitely was dying, and the cold, fresh air felt good after the smokey confinement of the cabin. When Jim had gone, we led our horses to the water and watched them drink. They were quiet and rested, and the cold hair of their hides and the strong animal warmth underneath was pleasant to the touch. "I'm sick of this place," Sam said. "Let's get out of here."

"And go where?"

"To steal something."

So we saddled up and rode out of Cove Hollow. I was glad to go.

When the driver sighted us my rifle was aimed straight at him. Alarm spread over his face. He pulled frantically on his lines, shouting, "Whoa! Whoa!" The man on the box beside him, whom I guessed to be a passenger from his fancy dress, grabbed at the side of the seat to avoid being toppled overboard.

"One move, and you die!" Sam shouted.

"No trouble!" the driver replied. "You won't get no trouble out of me!"

Sam ran to the coach and opened the door. I shifted the rifle from the driver to the man beside him. "Get down," I said. "Go for a gun, and your brains will be all over this road."

The man climbed down and joined the four men Sam rousted from the inside. He lined them in a row and began searching them. I kept my rifle pointed at the driver's chest. He was a small, skinny man with a droopy mustache and squinty brown eyes that stared at me without blinking. He wore a pistol in a holster, but it was well back from his hands, which still held the lines. "Stay away from that gun, and you won't die," I said.

"I will. I can't hit the side of a barn, nohow."

I smiled behind my mask. "You ever been robbed before?"

"Once. The other side of Weatherford."

His horses seemed to welcome the stop. They cocked their hind legs and dropped their heads as if sleeping. One snorted and shook his head. The harness jingled. "Whoa!" the driver said.

"How long you been driving these nags?" I asked.

"Nigh onto three years. It was four men that robbed me last time. Mighty chancey doing it with just two, ain't it?"

"No. It's easy."

"I told them they ought to give me a shotgun guard. Cheap company!"

Sam was herding the passengers back into the coach. The man who had sat beside the driver got inside with the others. Sam slammed the door, and I said, "You can go now."

"All right, son. Take it easy, hear?"

The driver slapped the lines. The horses bolted like one animal and left us standing in their dust. A passenger poked his head out the window, then pulled it quickly back inside. The driver never looked back. Sam jerked his mask down and grinned. "Better class customers this time, pard. Four hundred dollars." He sauntered to me, holding his hands behind his back. "And I got a Christmas present for you. Pick a hand."

I tapped his left shoulder, and he said, "You got the pretty one." He held up two gold watches swinging like pendulums on gold chains and handed me the one I had picked. It was one of those with a lid. The letters G.W.C. were engraved on the lid, and when I pushed the stem it opened and played a little music box tune and revealed the picture of a woman inside the lid, a young woman with long black hair and brown eyes, wearing a blue dress.

"Hoo!" Sam said. "No wonder he didn't want to give it up!"

Sam divided the money, and we rode toward Denton. And I felt wonderful. I had never owned two hundred dollars, and my possession of the musical watch seemed to lift me into a different class of humanity altogether. I pulled it out now and then and popped the lid and listened to the music, and Sam and I would laugh to see the horses' ears whipping back and forward, trying to figure out what they were hearing. "Hey," Sam said. "Why don't we ride up north and tap another stage. It's a shame to quit while we're on a winning streak."

"Fine. But I've got to eat first. My backbone's rubbing a hole in my gut."

In the early afternoon we came upon a tiny cabin standing alone on the prairie, unprotected from the wind by trees or hills. The stalks of last year's corn stood rotting in a small field beside the place. Smoke curled from the mud chimney, and I persuaded Sam to stop and ask for food. We rode to the door, and he yelled, "Hello! Anybody home?" We heard movement inside, but no one replied. Sam yelled, "Open! We're friends!" The latch moved, and the door opened a crack, "We're traveling through," Sam said. "We need food. We're willing to pay."

The door opened wider, and a voice said, "Pay?"

"Yes. We've got money. Do you have food?"

The door swung open then and revealed the muzzle of a shotgun and a woman holding it. She was a gaunt creature in a ragged gray dress. Her brown hair was matted and hung almost to her waist, and her close-set black eyes glared with a heat that verged on madness. I knew she wouldn't hesitate to blast us if she took the notion. "We mean no harm, ma'am," I said. "We're just hungry."

"You've got money?" Her voice had a strange, faraway quality, as if it came out of darkness.

"Yes, ma'am," Sam said. "We're willing to pay."

She grabbed the door, still holding the shotgun on us with her free hand. It was a heavy gun, but she held it steadily. She backed into the cabin and pulled the door shut. I heard voices and the clatter of pans inside. Then she swung the door open so hard that it banged against the wall. Two filthy, almost naked children that seemed to be girls clung to her skirt. She and they moved slowly toward us, she holding the shotgun in the crook of her elbow, her finger still on the trigger. She offered me something wrapped in a towel. "Cornbread," she said. "It's all I got."

"That's fine, ma'am," I said. "Is your man about?"

She swung the gun to my chest again. "Mind your business. Where's the money?"

Sam leaned down and handed her a double-eagle. She stared at it, frenzy in her eyes. "What is it? Is that gold?"

"Yes, ma'am," Sam said.

"How much? I ain't never seen none."

"Twenty dollars, ma'am."

It was so quiet I could hear one of the children sucking her thumb. "It's only cornbread," the woman said. "I ain't got nothing else."

"It's all right," Sam said. "The money's yours."

"You ain't Yankees, are you, having gold?"

"No, ma'am. Not Yankees."

"Then bless you, son. God bless you." Her voice was on the verge of tears. "What's your name?"

"Sam Bass, ma'am."

"I'll remember you. I'll pray for you."

"Thank you, ma'am."

She swung the gun toward him. "Go now." She backed through the door, pulling her children after her.

As we rode away I threw the towel on the ground and broke the pone in half and handed Sam a piece. The cornbread was old and cold, but my empty gut didn't care. Sam and I didn't speak until the pone was gone, washed down with water from Sam's canteen. Then he said, "Poor woman. I wonder if she's *got* a man."

"If she does, I pity him, too," I said. And we rode in silence for some distance, the woman much on my mind.

It was full dark when we arrived at Cove Hollow and bedded down. I felt as if I had just fallen asleep when Sam rousted me. It wasn't yet daybreak. We had our coffee and made a sackful of bacon-and-biscuit sandwiches, then saddled up and struck out toward Sherman. About midafternoon we sighted the town but avoided it and turned westward on the road to Gainesville. When we reached the cross-timbers we scouted for a thicket where we could conceal ourselves and still have a good view of the road. Sam's mood was cloudy that day. Whenever I tried to start a conversation, he answered shortly and let it die. So I amused myself with my new watch, popping the lid, checking the time, listening to the music, studying the face of the beautiful black-haired woman. But Sam said, "Stop that. It makes me nervous."

At last we heard the sounds of the coach, and I jumped up and pulled my mask over my face. But Sam grabbed my arm and said, "No, let's skip it."

"*What?*"

"It's a feeling I got. I think this stage is unlucky."

"Christ, Sam!" But anger clouded his eyes now, and I knew that if I pushed him we would fight. So I jerked my mask down and watched helplessly as the stage passed our hiding place. Nothing about it looked unlucky to me. But we climbed back into our saddles and had a long, quiet ride back to Cove Hollow. Our horses were exhausted when we arrived, and so was I. I rolled myself into my blankets and laid my watch beside my head, next to my pistol. The initials G.W.C. winked at me in the firelight. Those are the initials of the name on my shingle now, and my children hear many stories I make up about the lady in blue.

For weeks Sam was jumpy, and every effort of mine to find out what was troubling him met with angry looks and sharp words. He spent days sitting before the fire, smoking cigarette after cigarette and staring into the flames while I read my medical books and did whatever else I could find to keep my mind and hands occupied. I began to suspect that my friend had lost his nerve. I considered leaving him and striking out on my own, lest my career wither like the brittle leaves that still clung to some of the trees around us. But one night in the middle of February we were awakened by a horse nickering below us. We rolled out of our blankets, pistols in hand, and went to the door. The horses were scrambling up the slope now. "Who goes?" Sam shouted.

"Are you Sam Bass?" a voice replied.

"Who wants to know?"

"Friends. From Jim Murphy."

"How many friends?"

"Two."

"Keep your hands in sight."

Two horsemen rode onto our limestone ledge. One, a short, stocky man, rode a small black, and the other, a lanky fellow with long, light hair and beard, sat a gray pacing pony. "Jim told us you was looking for help," he said.

Sam stuck his pistols in his belt, and I stirred up the fire to put on the coffee. "Who are you?" Sam asked.

The stocky one, whose eyes and hair were almost as dark as Sam's, said his name was Seaborn Barnes. He worked in a pottery five miles south of Denton, he said, and was tired of the confinement of a potter's life. He was no older than I, but he had spent a year in the Fort Worth jail for killing a man. When he finally went to trial, the jury had pronounced him innocent. People, he said, called him "Seab," which was what he liked to be called. His face was somber. He spoke so softly I had trouble catching his words.

His lanky companion spoke loudly in a high, sing-song voice and laughed a lot, showing a mouth with few teeth. His cheeks were sunken. Long blond whiskers covered his narrow jaw. His pale blue eyes were grotesque. The left one twinkled and shifted from Sam to me and back while he talked. But the right one, which was larger than the other, had no light in it and gazed always straight ahead. I must have stared at it, for he said, "It's glass," and tapped it with his finger. The click of his fingernail against his eye sent a shiver up my spine.

"Can you shoot with that eye?" Sam asked.

"Not with that one. But I can with the other one." He laughed loudly at his joke.

His name was Tom Spotswood, and he had left a wife and a small son on a ranch somewhere northeast of Denton. Although his shiny yellow hair, which hung almost to his shoulders, made him appear young, he said he fled to Texas from Missouri just after the war, so he must have been between thirty-five and forty.

"What for?" Sam asked.

Spotswood stopped talking and glared at Sam with his good eye.

"I like to know who I'm working with," Sam said.

"Killed a man. Two, in fact. The circus come to Sedalia. I had taken a fancy to a young lady that worked for it. Bareback rider. I got drunked up and was in an argument with a carpenter about which one was going to carry her home. I shot him. A store clerk caught one of my bullets, too. I climbed on my horse and lit out of there. The clerk died, too, I heared later. I reckon nobody carried that young lady home."

"Had any trouble in Texas?" Sam asked.

"Not much. Tried to nail me for cattle-stealing in Wise County. Killed two niggers in Collin County. Got off both times."

The coffee boiled over, and Barnes got up and lifted the pot off the fire. I handed him the cups. "Speaking of women," he said, "I was in Dallas the other day. Met one that knows you, Sam."

"I don't know no women in Dallas," Sam said.

Barnes handed us the cups of steaming coffee. "Well, she said she knowed you. I told her I was from Denton County, and she asked about you. Name's Maude."

"Maude? I knowed a Maude, but that was way up north."

Barnes nodded. "She's the one."

"Son of a bitch! Joel's girl!"

"She's working in Norene's house on Main Street," Barnes said.

Sam laughed for the first time in a long time. He slapped my shoulder. "We're ready, pard!" he said. "You find Jim and stock this place with all the grub and oats and ammunition he can rustle. When I get back, we're going to work on the railroad!"

"Back from where?" I asked.

"Dallas!" he said.

While Sam was whoring, I found Jim at his Cove Hollow house. He left immediately for Denton and returned two days later on a wagon laden with sides of bacon, flour, coffee, tobacco, whiskey, beans, dried fruit, rifle and pistol ammunition and oats for the horses. We transferred it all to two pack horses Jim kept at his place and moved it up to our cabin. It took us several trips. Spotswood and Barnes and I slept at Jim's house that night, and the next morning he headed back to Denton, and we rode up Clear Creek to the cabin. Sam showed up about sundown, grinning. "Well, we're ready to move," he said.

"What's it to be?" I asked.

Sam was full of excitement. "The Houston and Texas Central's Number 4 train. The Nebraska train was Number 4, so this one ought to be lucky, too."

He had done some long and careful thinking while he was with Joel's woman. The Houston and Texas Central passed through Collin County just east of the Denton County line. It was the nearest railroad to Cove Hollow, and we could have the cover of the cross-timbers and creek bottoms almost all the way to its tracks. Sam had learned that the Houston and Texas Central connected with the Katy for St. Louis, and it stood to reason that it might carry a bit of Yankee money. He had decided to strike the train at Allen, a tiny prairie station twenty-four miles north of Dallas. "The southbound is due there about eight o'clock in the evening," he said, "so we'll have the darkness working for us. We can hit it and be back in the bottoms before anybody knows what happened. Frank and Seab will rush the locomotive and put the engineer and the fireman under their guns. Me and Tom will tap the express car."

"What about the passenger cars?" Barnes asked.

"Forget them. It would take too long to search everybody, and some fool might try to make a fight of it."

We fed the horses well and let them rest that night and all the next day and the following night. Shortly after noon on the next day we packed a few supplies and rode down Clear Creek single file. We rode in silence over the rough Cove Hollow terrain, but when we cleared the hollow and passed Jim's house we left the woods and rode abreast, following the course of the creek. Just northeast of Denton, where Clear Creek and Little Elm Creek flow into the Elm Fork of the Trinity River, we moved into the river bottom and turned southward, riding single file again. A couple of miles south of Hilltown Sam called a halt, and we pitched camp in the bottom. "The rest is open prairie," he said. "We can make it fast when the time comes."

The next day, George Washington's Birthday, 1878, Sam told Spotswood to ride into Allen and check out the situation. I thought Tom was a poor choice, because his gray horse and his yellow hair and glass eye made him the most conspicuous member of our band, but I said nothing. "Take your time," Sam told him. "Don't waste your horse. Find out if there's anybody there that might give us trouble, and ask what time the train's due, just to make sure I'm right."

Tom gave Sam a mock salute and spurred his gray up the river bank. Fog lay in the Trinity bottom that morning, and we quickly lost sight of him.

The fog lifted later in the morning, but the day remained gray and misty. We spent a great deal of time straining our eyes toward the east, looking for Spotswood's return long before he could have ridden to Allen and back. He emerged out of the mist about midafternoon. "Easy as pie," he said. "Not a lawman in the place, and the train's still due at eight o'clock."

We cooked the last of our food and ate every morsel, since it likely would be our last meal until we returned to Cove Hollow. In late afternoon we headed toward Allen. Not long after dark we arrived at the edge of town and dismounted. Tom pointed to a lighted building and said, "That's the station." He swung his arm northward. "And the train will come from there. If it was daylight you could see the tracks. We've got a good view here."

I looked at my watch. It was fifteen minutes until eight. Sam touched my wrist. "Don't pull that out again till we're out of here," he said. "We don't want nobody remembering the music." We sat down under a tree and Sam took out his own watch and laid it on the ground in front of him. We could hear its ticking, and although we couldn't read its hands in the darkness, we kept staring at it as if mesmerized. I felt tension building in us. Barnes, sitting beside me, drew a long breath and expelled it in a great rush. Spotswood fooled with the rowel of one of his spurs. Sam picked up his watch and held it close to his face. "It's eight o'clock," he said. "The train's late."

I strained my eyes toward the station, half entertaining the foolish notion that the train had pulled in without our seeing or hearing it. But the station and the village around it were quiet. The tension grew even faster now, for we had no idea how long our wait would be. My hands were sweating and beginning to tremble. I grasped one with the other, trying to hold them still. Every few minutes, Sam would announce the time. "Eight-thirty." "Twenty till nine." "Fifteen till nine." I didn't see the point of it, since we had no way of knowing when the train would arrive, and his announcements were adding to my nervousness.

Then suddenly it was there. The headlight cut through the misty darkness, and the whistle shrilled. Without a word we jumped to our feet, lifted our masks and sprang into our saddles. We dashed pell-mell across the stretch of prairie separating us from the station, reined in sharply at the platform and swung down with guns already drawn. Two men standing together on the platform stared at us, surprise and terror in their faces. "Oh, my Lord!" one of them said.

"Move and you're dead!" Sam cried.

Amidst plumes of smoke and steam the locomotive moved slowly alongside the platform, its bell clanging. Its headlight was bright in my eyes, but I could see its big wheel, and when it stopped turning I screamed, "*Now!*" In a flash Seab and I were up the engine steps and had our gun muzzles under the chins of the engineer and the fireman. The firebox door was open, and the dancing lights and shadows created by the flames made hellish imps of the men, who raised their hands above their heads. Four terrified, white eyes stared out of their sooty faces, and little streams of sweat coursed down the hard muscles of the fireman's bare chest. "Don't move!" I said and poked my gun closer to the engineer's face. My gun hand was steady now. With my left hand I drew my knife and cut the bell rope. I heard Sam's voice: "Throw up your hands and give us your money!" Then came a shot, and then another.

"God!" said the engineer.

"Shut up!" I said.

I heard three more shots, then one, then three more, then Sam's voice, but I couldn't understand his words. Seab's eyes, shiny in the firelight, shifted quickly to me, then back to the fireman.

"Pard! Back it up!" Sam shouted. "We're going to uncouple!"

I waved the engineer to the controls with my gun. "You heard him. Do it."

The engine chuffed, and the shock of the cars slamming against each other almost knocked me down. Barnes waved the fireman toward the steps. "Go uncouple it behind the express car," he said. "Don't do nothing funny. I'm right behind you." A few seconds later his masked face appeared at the bottom of the steps. "She's uncoupled," he said. "Take her up."

"You heard him," I told the engineer. He moved the locomotive forward. When we had moved sixty or seventy feet I said, "Stop. Shut her down."

I heard more shouts from the express car, then silence. The engineer and I gazed at each other, both of us listening, trying to figure out what was happening behind us. Then spurred feet were running, and Sam said from the bottom of the steps, "We've got it, pard. Bring him down."

I herded the engineer into the small cluster of men standing on the platform under the guns of my companions. Sam and Tom clutched large parcels to their chests with their left hands. Seab was searching the men. Shouts and screams issued from the passenger cars farther down the track. "They're clean," Seab said.

"All right," Sam said to our prisoners. "Stand where you are till we're out of sight. Otherwise, you'll die."

We mounted and rode out fast. When we were beyond sight of the train and the station and Allen we halted, and Sam said to Tom, "Did he get a good look at you?"

"I don't think so. I got it back up pretty fast."

"What happened?" I asked.

"Tom's mask fell down when he jumped into the express car," Sam said.

"Damn!" I said.

"Well, we'll hope for the best," Sam said. "We made a good haul, I think."

"What is it?" Seab asked.

"Silver, mostly. Some greenbacks. Quite a bit, I think."

"What was the ruckus?" I asked.

"The bastard in the express car cut loose on us. He hid behind the boxes, and we had to shoot back to keep him down. I finally told him if he didn't give up we'd set fire to his car, so he come out."

We camped in the Trinity bottom again. Sam brought the parcels to the fire, opened them and counted the silver and the greenbacks into four equal stacks.

"Are you just taking an equal share?" Spotswood asked him.

"Yes. We all did equal work."

We got three hundred and twenty dollars apiece.

The morning was cold, and since we hadn't waited to eat or even make coffee, we were a groggy, cranky crowd, not fit company for each other. Spotswood's mood was the worst. He complained in his sing-song way of aches in his joints from sleeping on the damp ground, of hunger, of the long ride, of anything that came into his mind. The rest of us made no replies, but each was miserable in his own way, and I, at least, had no desire to have Tom's unhappinesses heaped upon mine. I wasn't sorry when he pulled his pacer to a halt and announced he would go no farther. "I've had enough cold camp," he said. "I want my woman and a good dinner, and I'm going to go get them."

"All right." Sam's voice had a little anger in it.

Spotswood's departure called to my mind Henry Underwood's Christmas visit to Denton, and I said, "Family men. They aren't very reliable, are they?"

"Tom's all right," Sam replied. "He just ain't cut out for being rich."

"It was his mask that fell down," Barnes said. "He might be trouble. Maybe I should go get him."

"And do what?"

"Make sure he don't talk."

What he was suggesting was murder. Sam studied Seab's face. "No," he said. I was relieved.

We arrived at our cabin late the next afternoon. After we took care of the horses we flopped on the bare stone in front of the fireplace and slept for hours before we mustered energy enough to eat. Seab, as it turned out, was a decent cook, and he fixed a meal of beans and bacon and stewed apricots and biscuits and coffee. Then we unrolled our blankets and slept like babies until well after daylight.

I got up before the others and went down to the creek and plunged my face into the cold water. While lying on the bank, I heard a woodpecker working. I looked around until I spotted him not high up on the trunk of an old acacia. I eased my hand down and unbuckled my spurs and then grabbed my hat. I tiptoed to the tree as quietly as I could, careful to keep out of the bird's line of sight, and slapped the hat down on top of him. Barnes was stumbling down the slope, yawning and rubbing his eyes, and I said, "Seab! Guess what I've got under this hat."

"A buffalo," he said.

"A woodpecker. I caught him."

"What the hell for?"

"Come help me get him."

He made a face and stumbled on down the slope, and I said, "Stick your hand under there and grab him."

"He'll peck the hell out of me," he said.

"No, he won't."

"I'll hold the hat, and *you* stick *your* hand under there."

The bird did peck me pretty hard, but I held him. The pecker was a big one. His yellow-and-black eyes glared at me. He raised a terrible fuss and kept trying to get at me with his beak.

"Now what?" Seab asked.

"Get something to tie him with."

Seab went to the cabin and returned with an empty coffee sack and a piece of twine, and I dropped the bird in and tied it shut.

Seab grinned. "You ain't nothing but a kid."

"Well, how many people you know have caught a woodpecker?"

"Don't know none that wanted to," he said. "I caught me a jay once. He flew in the house, and I slammed the door and chased him around till I stunned him with Mama's broom."

"What did you do with him?"

"Made me a cage out of sumac sticks. Kept him for some time, too, before he died."

"Let's do that!"

He laughed.

"It'll give us something to do."

"It's your woodpecker."

"Will you help me?"

He raised his hands in an expression of helplessness. "All right."

Sam thought we both were crazy, and Seab tried to lay off all the craziness onto me. "If I don't help him, he might get dangerous," he said. But I knew he was enjoying my childish idea as much as I was, and we set about constructing the cage with enthusiasm and care. Seab and I went back to the creek and hacked down far more young, flexible sumac whips than we needed and shaved the bark off. I rubbed the strips of bark into several strands of crude string, while Seab gouged holes around the edge of a shingle that had blown off the cabin, to serve as the floor of the cage. We poked the ends of the sumac whips into the holes and tied them together at the top to form a sort of dome. Then Seab wove thinner branches in and out among them and lashed them with my string, leaving no opening big enough to allow the woodpecker to escape. He even made a small door and lashed it on. Sam sat ridiculing us while we worked, but I enjoyed it. It was the first careful work I had done with my hands since leaving Ben's shop, and it felt good. Maybe the potter in Seab felt the same way, for he stopped saying "he" and started saying "we" when responding to Sam's rawhiding. He even winked at me a couple of times, and a bond grew between us that never really broke. From then on, in any arguments or discussions, Seab was always on my side, except for one matter farther down the road.

We worked on the cage all day, and it was with a great deal of pride that we released the woodpecker into it and hung it from a rafter with the twine that had held it in the sack. The bird raised a ruckus, flapping about the cage, blinking at us with those yellow-and-black eyes. I don't know whether dumb animals feel hatred or not, but those eyes looked like they were full of it.

After all the work was done, Sam became interested in the bird, too, and would stick his finger between the bars and withdraw it when the woodpecker attacked it. "Does he have a name?" he asked.

"Yeah," I said. "Honest Eph."

Sam laughed, and Seab asked, "What does that mean?"

"We used to call our chief that when he grubbed brush for Dad Egan."

"That ain't no good," Sam said. "Honest Eph won't never be behind bars."

The name stuck, anyway. And during the long days of nothing that followed, that bird was a godsend. "What do woodpeckers eat?" I asked, and Seab said, "Bugs, I guess. That's probably what they're looking for when they hammer the trees." So he and I spent hours crawling along the banks of the creek, looking for the few bugs to be had at that time of year. Maybe we *were* crazy. I don't know. I even tried to teach the bird to talk once, and realized how foolish I was when I saw my friends looking at me as if I were a freak.

When we had been in the hollow about a week, Jim Murphy rode up with the Dallas newspapers of several days before. We had created a sensation. The papers said several posses had gone to Allen but failed to pick up our trail. The Texas Rangers were investigating, and everybody was offering money for our scalps. The governor had posted a reward of five hundred dollars per man, which was matched by both the railroad and the Texas Express Company. "Fifteen hundred apiece. That almost makes it worth my while," Jim said. "Two thousand for you, Sam, counting Nebraska."

"I reckon nobody wants it," Sam said. "I ain't seen nobody coming to get it."

"They ain't identified you," Jim said. "But life's getting livelier. They picked up Spotswood yesterday, and the express messenger identified him. They just walked up to his wagon and arrested him. His little boy was with him, too."

We were too stunned to speak. We glanced nervously at each other and at the ground until Jim said, "I wish I hadn't sent him up here. I didn't do nobody no favor."

"Did he have the money on him?" Seab asked.

"Just twelve dollars."

"Well, they'll never convict him on just the messenger's say-so," Seab said. "It was dark."

"Maybe. You never can tell about juries."

After Jim left, the three of us sat around the cabin, saying nothing. We were scared, I guess, and I was empty inside, without hope and angry. In a fit of rage I grabbed a stick and jumped up and jabbed it between the bars of the woodpecker's cage, trying to hit the bird with it. "Hey, Honest Eph! You damn train robber!" I yelled. "Stand around there, boy! Stand around there, son! This is what Dad Egan's going to do when he catches you!"

Sam leapt up and jerked the stick from my hand and whipped it across my belly. The stick broke, and a piece of it flew across the room and almost hit Barnes. Sam's hand was trembling. He flung the other half of the stick out the door and made a fist in my face, his eyes black with fury. "Don't never say that!" he screamed. "You'll be in *hell* before they put Sam Bass behind bars!" Then he grabbed the cage and tried to yank it down. The twine held, but a couple of the bars broke, and the woodpecker was out and gone in a flash of red and blue.

Sam's eyes and mine were locked on each other, unable to move. We didn't move a muscle, and neither did Barnes. It was deathly quiet. And suddenly I felt sad and thought that if something didn't move I would cry. Then Sam's eyes softened. He breathed out a big breath and laid his hand on my shoulder. "I'm sorry, pard," he said. "There wasn't no call for that."

"I shouldn't have done what I did, either," I said. "I was just nervous."

"We're all nervous." Then he threw up his hands and laughed. "Hey! Tomorrow we'll find us another train!"

Seab was in front of the fireplace wearing his coat and hat, hugging himself. The fire was huge, roaring up the chimney. "I'm freezing," he said. "Something's wrong with me."

I stepped over Sam, who was still rolled in his blankets, and Seab turned and looked at me. His face was drawn and pale, his eyes very bright. His teeth were chattering. "Something *is* wrong with you," I said.

"I ache all over. My head hurts."

His lips and fingernails were blue. I pushed his hat back and laid my hand on his forehead.

"What's wrong with me?" he asked. "I ain't never felt so."

"Some kind of fever, probably. We'll know soon. If it's fever, you'll get hot."

"I wish I was getting hot now. I'm freezing."

Sam stirred, then sat up. "Seab's sick," I said.

"Bad?"

"Don't know. I just got up."

Sam stretched and got up himself. He looked at Barnes and said, "Jesus, you look like hell."

"Your bedside manner isn't the best, Dr. Bass," I said.

"Well, you're the great healer. Do something."

I arched my eyebrows at him. "I will, Dr. Bass."

"It ain't funny," Seab mumbled.

I opened the saddlebags that Dr. Ross had given me and pulled out McGown and Eberle and flipped the pages to the sections on fevers. "You're cold, ache all over, and your head hurts, right?"

"Yes."

"Anything else?"

"Like what?"

"Well, let's see. He's pale and shivering. Do you agree, Dr. Bass?"

"I do, Dr. Jackson."

"His lips and fingernails are blue. Do you agree, Dr. Bass?"

"Yes, indeed, Dr. Jackson. Very blue."

"It ain't funny, damn it," Seab said.

"Are you thirsty, Mr. Barnes?"

"Yes."

"Is your mind confused?"

"His mind's always confused, Dr. Jackson," Sam said.

"Have you pissed this morning, Mr. Barnes?"

"Yes."

"What color was it?"

"What color was it? Yellow."

"Pale yellow or bright yellow?"

"Are you funning me, Frank?"

"No. I'm trying to find out what's wrong with you."

"Well, I don't know what kind of yellow it was."

"You probably have an intermitting fever. We'll know for sure if you get hot. Dr. McGown says hardly anybody dies of intermitting fever. You're lucky, Mr. Barnes."

"Can you fix him?" Sam asked.

I had seen Seab's symptoms many times on my rounds with Dr. Ross, and I thought I knew what would happen to him. "Yes, I can." The words gave me a feeling of immense power. I opened the medicine side of my saddlebags and got the quinine and laudanum. "Give me a cup, then go get some water." Sam jumped to obey, and I poured what I guessed to be about fifty drops of laudanum into the cup. McGown didn't say whether the laudanum and quinine should be given separately or together, so I assumed it didn't matter and dropped what I guessed to be about ten grains of quinine into the laudanum and stirred it with a stick and gave it to Seab. "Drink this."

He obeyed and made a face. "Sam's getting some water," I said. "Sulphuric ether would make you better faster, but I don't have any. This will do it, though."

"Do you know what you're doing?" Seab asked.

"Yes," I said, not really sure.

Sam brought a bucket of water. I dipped Seab's cup into it, and he drank gratefully. "Now roll up in your blankets and lie down," I said. "You're going to get hot and then go to sleep and then start sweating, but don't worry. You'll be all right."

Without a word he did as I told him, and a few minutes later he was asleep. Sam and I sat watching him. "Well, no trains will run today," Sam said.

"Not for several days," I said. "It takes a little time."

"Could he die?" Sam's eyes were full of respect.

"No. He'll be all right."

Suddenly I understood all that Dr. Ross had told me. My real knowledge of Seab's illness was scarcely deeper than his own or Sam's. But because I could read and because I possessed and had administered the medicines and was answering Sam's questions with an air of confidence, I was a doctor. I found myself wishing I had a beard, and pretending I was chilly, I put on the black coat that Sam had bought me in Fort Worth. I *was* a physician, for I had a patient and a concerned friend, a relative of the patient almost, who needed comforting and believed whatever I said.

My professional reputation grew when Barnes became feverish and then broke into a sweat, as I had predicted. I bathed his head and neck in cold water, gave him draughts from the cup, and followed the nursing procedures dictated by McGown and Eberle with a great deal of ceremony, barking orders to Sam to fetch whatever I needed. By nightfall Seab was feeling better, and he smiled weakly at me and said, "You ain't so dumb." I gave him more quinine and laudanum and a little calomel and said, "You're not through it yet, but you're going to be all right."

Sure enough, the chill-fever-sweat cycle recurred during the night, but with less intensity and shorter duration. I reckoned that my diagnosis must have been right and followed the instructions of McGown and Eberle to the letter, wishing that Dr. Ross were present to judge my performance. I remained at Seab's side until he lapsed into his sweat. Then I went to sleep, since there was nothing to be done at that stage, and I knew it would be followed by remission.

In the morning Seab asked, "What made me sick, Frank?"

"It could be any number of things," I replied casually. "My guess would be miasma."

"What the hell's that?"

"Bad air from swamps or marshes. You've been sleeping in too many creek bottoms lately."

"It's the best place for them that's in our trade," Sam said.

"He'll be all right," I said.

In four days Seab was up and around, though still weak and shaky. Sam asked if it would be safe to leave him alone and ride out to scout our next job, and I said it would.

We left that morning and spent the next three days scouting the Houston and Texas Central through Collin and Dallas counties. We struck the railroad just south of Allen and rode southward in a leisurely manner, sticking to the roads most of the time and stopping and talking to people whenever and wherever we liked. We posed as ranchers looking for land to buy, bought drinks and shared tobacco with men lounging at crossroads stores and talked about cattle, weather and, of course, trains. Sam could be a good talker when he wanted to, and his generosity with his money made many whiskey-jug friends who were eager to tell him everything he wanted to know about anything under the sun.

We chose the village of Hutchins, about eight miles south of Dallas, as the site of our next adventure. The layout there was almost identical to Allen, and the southbound train arrived about ten o'clock at night, which would give us the advantage of the darkness again.

Our decision made, we headed north. When we neared Dallas Sam said, "I'm going to town and visit Maude. Want to come?"

"No, I'd better go on and check on Seab."

"There's lots of pretty girls there. You ain't had a woman in a long time, Frank, and Maude has lots of friends."

"Next time."

Sam touched his hatbrim and rode away toward Dallas. It was the first time I had been alone in four months, and I was glad to have the chance. It had been a good winter for rain, and the countryside was bright in the new green of spring. The sky was cloudless and the sun warm, and everyone, it seemed, had found work to do outdoors. Women were washing clothes and yelling at children. Men were mending or building fence, and a few had already begun their spring plowing, trudging the rows behind their patient mules. It was still cool, and a great day for that kind of work. I envied them. I stopped at midday at a farm just south of Lewisville and was given fried chicken for dinner and held a little girl, the youngest child of seven, on my knee while I had my final cup of coffee and speculated with her father about when the first herds would pass through on their drive north. I could feel the sap running in me, and regretted that I had declined Sam's invitation.

But I was getting close to Denton now, so I left the road and struck out across the open prairie, aiming in a general way toward Cove Hollow. I was in no hurry, but my horse felt the juice of spring, too, and I let him have his head. He moved at a long-striding, lazy gallop for a while, then, receiving no restraining signal from me, broke into a run. The cool breeze roared in my ears, and I could feel my blood pumping through me. The bright grass passed under my horse's hooves in a blur. God, it all felt good after the long winter in the creek bottoms. When we reached Hickory Creek we stopped and drank and rested, then continued at a slower but still brisk pace. If horses could sing, I believe mine would have that day.

Seab was enjoying the spring, too. He was stretched on a blanket on the limestone ledge in front of our cabin, soaking in the sun. He sat up when I started my horse up the slope. "Where's Sam?" he asked.

"He got the itch. He went whoring."

He watched us plunge up the slope, then asked, "What's the plan?"

He looked fit as a fiddle, which made me very proud.

On the night of March 18 Sam and Seab and I rode into Hutchins and tied up at the station platform. We had passed the train on our way into town, so we already were masked, and our guns were drawn. Only the agent and a nigger porter were in the station, and they threw up their hands when we entered. "All right, keep them up and move out to the platform," Sam ordered.

As soon as the train stopped, I leapt to the engine. The engineer and the fireman raised their hands, too, and I recognized them. "Is this Number 4?" I asked. The engineer nodded, and I said, "You probably remember me, then."

"I sure do, son," he said.

I herded them down the steps, and as my foot touched the platform a face appeared around the front of the engine. I swung my gun to it and said, "Join us." Two men crept slowly around the engine and climbed the platform steps.

"Riding free on the cowcatcher," Sam said. "The railroad don't like that, boys."

The men, shabbily dressed, grinned weakly and took off their caps and held them against their chests, as they no doubt did when asking for handouts. We moved them and our other hostages down the platform until they were opposite the express car door, which was open and lighted. A man holding a bag appeared at the mail car door, just behind the express car, and shouted, "What's the matter?"

"We want money, and there's no use kicking!" Sam called back.

The man stepped back and slammed the door and yelled, "Robbers on the platform!" The light went out in the express car, and its door slammed, too. Sam cursed and ran into the station and returned with two axes. He handed one to Seab, and they attacked the door. Soon its splintered parts fell away, and Sam and Barnes were facing the muzzle of a pistol. The express agent was backed against the far wall, taking aim. The station agent yelled, "Don't shoot! You'll kill us!" The man lowered his gun, and Seab and Sam jumped into the car while I held our prisoners under my gun. In less than a minute they came out carrying two cloth sacks and ran to the mail car. Sam banged on the door with his pistol butt. "We've got you! Come out or it'll go hard for you!" The mail clerk made up his mind quickly and opened the door.

While my companions were ransacking the mail, a burst of gunfire issued from the rear of the train. One of the tramps groaned and fell. I fired two blind shots into the darkness, then a shotgun boomed, and the station agent grabbed his face. Sam and Seab backed out of the mail car, and we retreated slowly toward our horses, laying down heavy fire toward the muzzle flashes. We mounted and lit out toward the west. A few miles out of Hutchins we swung north toward the Hickory bottoms. It wasn't until then that we slowed and Sam asked, "Any casualties?"

"Not on our side," I said.

Our haul was disappointing. Three hundred and eighty-four dollars from the express car and a hundred and thirteen from the mail. One sixty-five apiece. "It's a good thing old Spotswood ain't along," Barnes said.

Barnes ran into the cabin, grabbed his rifle and said, "Riders!" Sam and I grabbed our rifles, too, and we bellied down behind the rocks on the slope. "They're coming slow and quiet," Barnes said. "Two of them."

At last my eye caught the sun glinting on something, then I saw a black hat and part of a face. "Here they come!" I whispered.

They emerged into the clearing. Sam screamed, "Freeze!"

The riders showed no signs of panic. They turned their horses slowly until they faced us, and one called, "You ain't going to kill me, are you, Sam?"

It was Henry Underwood. I could name fifty people I would rather have seen, but I was relieved that the face was a friendly, although ugly, one. Henry's companion rivalled Henry himself in ugliness. A big, florid, pig-eyed man with a flat nose and pock-marked jowls, he dismounted and watched, his mouth hanging open stupidly, while Sam and I shook hands with Henry and introduced him to Barnes. "This here's Arkansas Johnson," Henry said. "Him and me's rode all the way from Nebraska together. And spent a long spell together before that."

I took their horses, and Sam threw his arm around Henry's shoulders and walked him toward the cabin. Barnes glanced at me skeptically, then followed with Johnson. The horses had been ridden hard and looked as if they hadn't eaten in days. Their noses never left the grain while I rubbed them down.

When I entered the cabin Underwood was bragging loudly of his escape from the jail in Nebraska. "Your money done it, Sam," he said. "I give part of it to a man that was getting out, and he proved true to his word. He got me a file and some saw blades, and Arkansas's wife fetched them to us in a bucket of butter."

Seab Barnes showed little interest in Henry's narrative, but the silent Arkansas Johnson made not the slightest move without Seab noticing it. When Henry paused for breath, Seab pointed at the new man and said, "Tell us about yourself."

Johnson turned his pig eyes to Barnes and gazed stolidly at him. "Ain't nothing to tell," he mumbled.

"Where in Arkansas are you from?" Seab asked.

"I ain't. Missouri."

"Ever know a man named Tom Spotswood?"

"No."

"What was you in jail for?"

Again Johnson lapsed into silence, regarding Barnes with a vacant stare, as if he couldn't remember. Then he said, "Stole some lumber. I got to piss." He got up and slouched outside.

"I don't like him," Seab said.

"I don't, either," I said.

"Come on!" Henry whined. "Me and him's rode a long way together."

"I don't like him, either," Sam said. "He's white trash, and this here's a high-class outfit. We ain't got no use for trash, Henry."

"Aw, Sam," Henry pleaded, "I couldn't have made it without him. I promised him."

"Promised what?"

"Why, that he'd get rich!"

Sam smiled. "Well, all right," he said. "I'll try him once. Then we'll see."

So we had two hogs in our sty that night.

Two days later, on a Sunday afternoon, another rider came up the creek. "We don't have to go looking for no trains," Sam said. "This place is a railroad station."

It was Jim Murphy, looking for me. "You got visitors at my place," he said.

"Who?"

"Ben Key. Your sister. Dr. Ross."

"What do they want?"

He shrugged. "They want to see you."

I rode down the creek with Jim. "I'd listen to them if I was you, Frank," he said.

Dr. Ross's hack was standing in front of the house, and my visitors were in the tiny parlor, drinking coffee. They rose when

I went in, and my sister hugged me. Jim went outside. Through the window I saw him walking toward the barn. My sister held a small handkerchief, and she twisted it into a small roll and wove it in and out among her fingers. Ben and Dr. Ross shifted in their chairs. Their feet were noisy on the bare floor. I was glad to see them, but felt embarrassed. Finally Dr. Ross said, "We want you to come back, Frank."

"Yeah," Ben said. "We want you to come home with us."

"I can't," I said.

Tears welled into my sister's eyes. She unrolled her handkerchief and daubed them away.

"Dad Egan's looking for you," Ben said, "but who he really wants is Sam. He's getting hell from the railroads, and he thinks Sam is some kind of traitor. But come home now, and I think he'll leave you alone."

"Did Spotswood say something?"

"No, but he might when he's tried. Everybody knows he was hanging out with you and Sam."

"That doesn't have to mean anything," I said. "We have a right to our friends."

"That's my point," Ben said. "If you come home before the trial, I don't think your name will ever come up. Dad won't try to prove anything on you."

"Did he tell you that?"

"Yes. He likes you, Frank."

"He used to like Sam, too."

"He thinks Sam betrayed him," Ben said.

A breeze blew the curtains into the room, and the sun shining through them made patterns like maps on my sister's gray skirt. Dr. Ross was slouching in his chair, stroking his beard, not fidgeting anymore. "I cured a man," I told him.

His eyes narrowed. "What was wrong with him?"

"Fever."

"What did you do?"

"Gave him laudanum and quinine. A little calomel."

He smiled. "Did you enjoy it?"

"Yes. And I have a black coat now."

Dr. Ross laughed.

"Come with us, Frank," Ben said. His high forehead was furrowed. I had never noticed he was getting bald. "The shop ain't the same without you. Nothing's the same without you.

Ain't that right, doc?"

"I won't go back to the shop," I said.

"Well, do something else, then!" Ben said. "But come back!"

"I'll have to think about it," I said.

"Come with us *now*," my sister said.

"Let him think about it," Dr. Ross said. "I'm sure Frank will do what's best." He slapped his knees and stood up. "I brought you something." He pulled a small book from his coat pocket and gave it to me. It was *The Odyssey*. "It's about a man who traveled to many places and had many adventures, but he finally came home. You'll remember him from another book you read once."

"Thank you." I shook hands with him and Ben. I grasped my sister's hands and pulled them away from her face and lifted her gently from the chair and kissed her on the cheek. "Don't worry," I said.

I was deeply moved by their care for me, and by the time I reached our cabin I had decided to return to Denton.

"What did they want?" Sam asked me.

"I've got to talk to you," I said. "In private."

We walked down the slope and sat down on the grass. "They want me to go home," I said, "and I'm going."

Sam stared in disbelief and hurt.

"We're getting nowhere," I said. "I'm getting no closer to what I really want."

"You'll go to prison," he said.

"I think I could get off if I leave now, even if they tried me."

"No, you'll go to prison."

"It's no good," I said. "We're not making much money, and we're getting in a lot of trouble. I think we should all quit now."

Sam picked at the short green grass with his fingers. "I can't, Frank," he said. "Even if I beat everything here, they'd get me for that Nebraska job. And I need you. I don't even have Joel anymore. I can do without Johnson, and I can do without Underwood. I can even do without Barnes. But I can't do without you, pard. You and me's friends, ain't we? Brothers, almost. We been together too long. Without you and Joel, I'd be too alone to stand it, no matter who else was with me."

I looked at the ground. Why was I embarrassed? I felt awful.

"I know it ain't gone good, Frank. Maybe I just don't have Joel's brain. But all we need is one break, one big haul. Then you can go off to Kentucky and become a doctor. Hell, maybe I'll go with you. They race a lot of horses there."

I said nothing.

"I got plans for a big haul," he said. "We're going to hit the Texas and Pacific at Eagle Ford. It ought to be a rich train. Then we'll go to Kentucky or somewhere. Deal?"

I figured he was making it up as he went. I shook my head. "I'm not going. To Eagle Ford, I mean."

"Frank! We got five men now! It'll be a cinch!"

"My head isn't in it, Sam. I wouldn't be any good to you. I just don't feel like going."

"All right, pard. I'll deal you out of this one. But stay here till we get back, and we'll talk some more. You can do that, can't you, Frank?"

"Yes. I'll do that. Then I'm leaving."

"Well, we'll talk about it." He got up and started up the slope, then turned. "Can Henry and Arkansas use your guns? They ain't got none."

"No, I might need them."

"Well, it don't matter. We'll stop in Dallas and buy some."

Henry didn't go to Eagle Ford, either. Jim rode back up the hollow that night and told him his wife and children were at Henderson Murphy's place, anxious to see him. He rode away with Jim.

"This *is* a goddamn railroad station," Sam said.

Next morning, he and Seab and Arkansas left to meet the train. I stood in the door and watched their horses struggle down the slope. Halfway down, Sam turned and looked at me, his eyes full of questions. I started to wave, but didn't.

I spent the morning on a blanket outside the cabin, reading *The Odyssey.* I had read nothing but Dr. Aiken's songs and my medical books since leaving Dr. Ross, and my mind soon was far away from Cove Hollow, wandering the Aegean Sea. I read slowly and with difficulty, as I still do. But even skipping over the words I didn't know, I didn't miss the majesty of Homer's lines. Or Alexander Pope's lines. I didn't know and still don't know who gave them their grace and beauty. It didn't matter then and doesn't matter now. I was far from Cove Hollow, hearing the waves dash against the open ship that Odysseus and I were sailing in, as unsuspecting as he was that it would take us so long to get to Ithaca and reclaim the faithful Penelope.

I would sit up to rest my eyes and back and arm from time to time and look around at the woods and the creek and the tiny clearing below me. I knew they weren't as beautiful as they looked, that the woods were full of snakes and tangles of vines, and that mosquitos soon would be breeding in the water. But the sun shining through the young leaves clothed the morning in emeralds, and cardinals and jays flashed red and blue among them, and a mockingbird set it all to an intricate, meditative music that made me sigh.

All day I was glad I hadn't gone to Eagle Ford and was alone. That night, though, the cabin was lonely and oppressive to me. I resented its squalor and the necessity of living in the wild like a fox waiting for the dogs to come. I moved my blankets outside and felt better in the company of the night, but concluded that I would go to Denton the next day. Not to stay, for I had promised

Sam I would be in Cove Hollow when he returned, but just to taste the larger human society again.

I rode down after breakfast. Just beyond Jim Murphy's place I saw Henry Underwood moving toward me. I wasn't glad to see him, but I knew he had seen me, so I stopped and waited. "How's the family?" I asked.

"Fine. They're going to stay with Henderson a while. Where you going?"

"To Denton, and have a drink and be seen. If I'm seen in Denton, that'll give Sam something of an alibi."

"Good," he said. "I'll go with you."

I cursed him silently.

Bob Murphy, Jim's brother, was running the Parlor that day, and he wasn't eager to have our business. We had been fools to open the mails, he whispered, because the federals were interested in us now, and the Dallas newspapers were mentioning Sam and Henry and me by name and calling us train robbers. Most people in Denton didn't believe it or didn't care, he said, but if we gave Dad Egan an excuse to lock us up, we shouldn't expect to get out.

We were determined to brave it out, and chose a corner table where we wouldn't be conspicuous, but wouldn't be hidden, either. We drank whiskey and played cards the rest of the day and left town not long after dark without trouble. We had too much whiskey in us to ride far, though, so we stopped and unsaddled our horses and tied them in the timber beside the road not many miles outside of Denton, and made ourselves as comfortable as we could on the bare ground. Henry had armed himself with a pistol and a rifle at Henderson Murphy's, and we laid our arms beside us and went to sleep. We slept a long time, for the sun was well up when Henry poked me in the gut and said, "Horses."

I jumped up and stuck my pistol in my belt and levered a cartridge into the chamber of my rifle. The riders, eight or ten of them, had rounded a bend in the road and spotted our horses among the trees. They had halted, and the man who seemed to be their leader was talking and gesturing. All but two of the riders split from the group and rode off, some to the left and some to the right.

"They're trying to surround us!" I said. I raised my rifle and fired too quickly at the man who seemed to be the leader. He drew his pistol and fired back. His bullet went so far astray that I knew he hadn't seen us, only our horses. The leader and the man remaining with him in the road dismounted. I raised my rifle again, but before I could pull the trigger Henry yelled, "Look out, Frank!" I dropped to the ground, and the bullet, fired by the man with the leader, missed me, but was close enough to tell me I had been seen.

Henry and I took shelter behind two large trees and waited, but no more shots came. The posse had taken shelter, too. The road was empty, and I could hear no one moving in the woods. "They must not have rifles," Henry said. "They can't fight us at long range."

We waited for some time without hearing sound of man or horse, and I began to think they had gone. To find out, I shouted, "Why did you shoot at me?"

From somewhere near the road a voice replied, "Why did *you* shoot at *me*?"

"I didn't!" I said. "I shot at a rabbit!"

The other side was silent for some time, then the voice came again. "Come on out and tell us who you are!"

"No!" I replied. "We don't know you! Go away!"

There was another long silence, then the voice said, "Come on back, boys! I think we've flushed the wrong game!"

Hooves rustled in the timber to the left and right of us, then the men were reassembling in the road. Henry grinned at me. "See anybody you know?"

"No."

"They must be from Dallas County. Hutchins, maybe."

The men were bunched in the road now, but they weren't going away. They sat their horses quietly, looking up toward us. "Cover me," I said. "I'm going to saddle my horse."

Keeping our rifles trained on the posse, we left our shelter and walked into plain view. Henry sat down by the horses and rested his elbows on his knees, keeping the posse in the sights of his rifle. The horsemen didn't move. I picked up my saddle and blanket and lifted them to my bay. When I was finished, I covered the posse while Henry saddled. We mounted and rode casually into the road. The posse was motionless about fifty yards from us. We trotted fifty yards farther on, then I turned in my saddle and waved my hat and shouted, "All right, boys! Come and get us!"

The posse spurred after us, firing crazily into the air, but we had too big a lead. After half a mile or so, our pursuers reined in and watched us sprint away.

When we left the road and started across the open prairie, Henry shouted, "There goes another rabbit!" and pointed his finger at the ground and said, "Bang!" We laughed, and a few minutes later he did it again. "That bunny was wearing a hat," he said and we laughed again. He did that all the way to Cove Hollow, and we laughed every time.

But our jolly mood wasn't shared by the crew that rode in from Eagle Ford that night. They had ridden constantly since the robbery the night before, and men and horses were exhausted. Their job had gone without a hitch. Although the express company had a guard in its car with the messenger, the man had a yellow streak, and our bunch had robbed both the express and mail cars without a shot being fired. But their loot had amounted to only fifty-three dollars, and Sam and Barnes were in a cranky mood. Arkansas Johnson was as silent and oxlike as ever.

Henry's wild account of our "rabbit hunt" cheered them, though, and after a few drinks Sam and Seab were able to laugh at themselves, too, and the labor and danger they had endured to earn their seventeen dollars apiece.

"Bob Murphy says we shouldn't have meddled with the mails," I told Sam. "He says the federals are looking for us now."

"Who gives a damn?" Sam said. "Let the whole world be looking for us. I've got the best damn bunch in the whole damn world." The whiskey was working on him fast because of his fatigue.

Seab was drunk, too. "It's too bad you don't get a cut of this haul, Frank," he said. "Now you can't retire with Sam and Arkansas and me."

That reminded Sam of my decision to return to Denton, I guess. He picked up a bottle and asked me to go outside with him. We walked far enough down the slope to put us out of earshot of the others and sat down on the rocks. He said, "You ain't really leaving me, are you, pard?"

"Yes, I am. Eagle Ford proves my point, Sam. We ought to all give it up."

"Hell, Frank! All we need is one good one! Look at my Union Pacific haul. All we need is one like that, and then we'll quit.

All we've got to do is get lucky."

"We can all die before we get lucky," I said.

Sam leaned back on his elbows and looked at the sky. "How far away do you reckon them stars is?" he asked.

"I don't know."

"What are they, anyway?"

"I don't know, Sam."

"Hell, pard, I thought you knowed everything."

I didn't reply. He just gazed at the stars and drank from the bottle. Then he said, "Well, you're the best man around, even if you don't know everything."

I said nothing to that, either. And he said, "I've got a lot of that Nebraska gold left. I'll give it all to you if you'll stay."

"You can't do that. You're paying the freight for the whole outfit with that. When that goes, all the boys will go."

"Well, I can do without them. But I can't do without *you*. If I got a friend in the world, you're it." He looked at the stars again. "Pretty, ain't they? I don't remember them so pretty. I *have* got a friend, ain't I, Frank?"

I gave up. "All right, Sam," I said. "I'll stay with you for one more job. But if it isn't a good one, I'm leaving. That's fair, isn't it?"

"That's fair," he said. He got up and climbed back to the cabin and the drunken laughter.

We were at Mesquite, twelve miles east of Dallas. Our train was late, but that wasn't our biggest worry. Less than a hundred yards beyond the station, another train stood on a sidetrack. Its cars were lighted, and now and then a man would walk out of the shadows and cross the bright windows. He cradled a rifle or shotgun in his arms. "Convict train," Arkansas said. "Construction gang, most likely."

"How many guards, I wonder," Sam said.

"I've saw just one," Arkansas said, "but there's bound to be more."

"More trouble," I said.

In the darkness beside me Sam was breathing heavily. He shifted in his saddle. The leather squeaked. "They won't bother us," he said. "If their prisoners was to get away, they'd be in a peck of trouble."

"We can't count on that," I said.

We heard the whistle then, and Sam raised his mask. "Let's go."

As we stepped onto the platform, the station agent came out carrying a mail bag. "Hold up your hands!" Sam ordered. Then the train pulled alongside the platform, and he said, "Onto her, boys!"

Seab and I dashed up the engine steps, and the engineer and the fireman raised their hands. I cut the bell rope and said, "Take it easy. All we want is money."

"That ain't no skin off my back," the engineer said.

Then I heard a popping sound, and the guns of our companions roared in reply. "What's that?" I asked.

"The conductor, probably," the engineer said. "Julius carries a derringer."

"Climb down."

Seab and I herded the engine crew to the platform. Arkansas had the station agent and another man under his gun there. The station door opened, framing a woman's head in the lamplight. "Come out here, lady," Arkansas said, but she ducked back inside and slammed the door. He fired a shot into the door.

"Don't do that!" I said.

The engineer tried to break away, and I clubbed him. The man rolled into the space between the platform and the train. I thought he was out cold, but he must have crawled under the train, for suddenly he was running through the darkness toward the convict train. I fired a couple of shots in his direction, but I couldn't tell whether I hit him or not.

Sam and Henry banged on the door of the express car, shouting something. A pistol roared from one of the sleeping cars. It was the conductor again. "The bastard has a six-gun now," Arkansas said. He and Seab and I let fly at him at the same time, and he tumbled down the steps. "Die, you son of a bitch!" Arkansas said. But the man wriggled under the car and fired at us until his gun was empty. In the confusion, the fireman had disappeared.

A shotgun blast and several pistol shots came at Sam and Henry from the express car windows, and they ducked into the space between the platform and the train as the engineer had done. Sam crawled down the space to the engine, jumped to the steps and returned with a can of oil and splashed it on the express car door. "I'll count to fifty!" he yelled. "If you don't come out, I set fire to your car! One! Two! Three! Four!" He was counting fast. At twenty-five the door opened a crack, and Sam stood up. But the man in the car fired a shot and slammed the door again. Sam resumed his count. When he shouted, "Forty!" someone inside the car yelled, "Don't be in such a rush! Give us time to counsel a little!"

"You better talk fast!" Sam said. He counted again. When he reached fifty he said, "Are you going to open up?" There was no reply. Sam struck a match and was moving it toward the splash of oil when the door opened. The express messenger and two guards threw out their guns and stepped to the platform. Sam and Henry and Arkansas jumped into the car, leaving Seab and me to guard the prisoners.

Then the goddamn peanut vendor showed up on the steps of one of the coaches, his peanut box still slung around his neck and a pistol in his hand. I ran to him and stuck my own pistol in the boy's face. "We don't want any peanuts," I said. "Drop it and get back inside." The boy obeyed. I walked back to Seab and said, "We're getting it from every direction, aren't we?"

It was a bad luck comment, I guess, for several shotguns boomed from the convict train, and Seab groaned, "God, they got me."

"Where?"

"The legs."

"Stop it!" one of our prisoners yelled toward the convict train. "We'll be killed!"

"Stop it!" I screamed. "We'll free your goddamn convicts!"

The guards must have thought there were a lot of us, for they stopped firing. I ran to the door of the express car and yelled, "Hurry! We've got a casualty!"

Sam jumped to the platform. He had a cloth sack in his hand, but Henry and Arkansas were empty-handed. Seab was sitting on the platform, still holding his gun on the prisoners. His pantaloons were bloody in several places. "Can you walk?" I asked him.

"Help me up." He raised a hand, and I pulled him to his feet and helped him to his horse.

"Hurt bad?" I asked.

"It's beginning to."

I held his stirrup with one hand and put the other under his butt and pushed him into the saddle. We departed Mesquite at a run.

I don't remember much else about that night. We moved fast, afraid a posse would be coming. And for all we knew, the prairie and woods were full of posses still after us for Allen and Hutchins and Eagle Ford. We left the road and galloped, galloped across the prairie for a long time. We crossed a creek. I remember Henry asking, "Are we going to stop?"

"Not yet," Sam replied.

We moved on and on through the night. We crossed another creek, and Seab's horse stumbled on the rocks. He wailed, "Oh, what shall I do? I can't stand it!"

"We'll stop," Sam said, "and Frank will fix you."

My medical bags were at the cabin, but I took off my shirt and tore it into strips and wrapped them around Seab's wounds, outside the pantaloons. "Buckshot," I said. "I don't think your legs are broken."

"They hurt like hell," he said.

We stayed at the creek long enough to let our horses blow and drink, then started again at a slower pace. The night was so black I could barely see my companions. We said nothing. Seab groaned with every step of his horse.

We didn't reach our cabin until dark the next day. Arkansas and Henry took our horses to the corral, and Sam and I helped Barnes inside and laid him on a blanket near the fireplace. "Give him a bottle," I said, "and build a big fire. I'll need all the light I can get." While we waited for Barnes to get drunk and the blaze to grow, I pulled Dr. Smith's *Minor Surgery* from my saddlebags and looked for gunshot wounds. The closest thing I found was "The Extraction of Foreign Matter from Wounds." I turned to the page and found that the section was only a paragraph:

Requires the use of forceps which are modified according to circumstances, and generally treated of in the works on Gun-shot Injuries. But when the substance is only particles of dirt, or such fine matter as cannot well be seized by the forceps, the free use of a stream of tepid water, either by means of a syringe or from a sponge, will suffice.

I cursed Dr. Smith and returned the book to the saddlebags and got out the case of instruments that Dr. Ross had given me. Henry and Arkansas came in from the corral. Henry grabbed the cloth bag we had taken from the train and poured the contents on the floor. He and Arkansas began counting the money aloud. Sam hunkered beside me, watching me. I opened the case. Seab groaned. The fire gave a glow to the green velvet lining of the case. The instruments glinted like treasure. "Do you want me to do something?" Sam asked.

"Not yet. Let me think." The fire was hot against my face.

"A hundred and fifty dollars," Henry said, and he was through.

I looked at my hands. They seemed as big as hams, and they were trembling. "Give me a drink," I told Sam. "And then come hold him."

Maude

It was after midnight, but men were arming themselves. Groups were riding off in all directions, as if to a war. Men and women, some in nightshirts and gowns, ran past our house toward the depot. As soon as my customer left my room, I got dressed and joined them. La! The train was a mess. The sides of nearly all the cars showed splintered places where bullets had hit them. Oil was splashed on the door and wall of the express car. The conductor's shirt was bloody. Two men were helping him away. The platform was a swirl of people, all babbling at once. "They'll be in the banks next," a man said.

"Four trains in two months, and within twenty-five miles," said another. "Nobody will want to settle in Dallas."

Policemen cleared a path through the crowd for the passengers, who were climbing down from the coaches, women and children in tears, men red in the face. From time to time a hand would reach from the crowd and touch a passenger, then there would be embraces and loud cries.

I went back to the house and went to bed. About noon the next day Norene knocked on my door and handed me a copy of the *Herald*. "Your friend's name is in the paper," she said.

"Which friend?" I closed the door and unfolded the paper. They named him, all right, in the sixth and smallest headline at the top of the article:

> *Unsuccessful Pursuit After the Eagle Ford Gang—*
> *Sam Bass, Underwood and Jackson in Denton County,*
> *Where They Defy the Law and Out-general their pursuers.*

He wasn't named, though, in the account of the robbery at Mesquite. I glanced quickly over the first part of the article, about the train's arrival in Dallas, and began reading in the middle:

Mr. Sam Finley and others of the Texas Express Company, although they had just returned from a trip after the Eagle Ford robbers, started in pursuit of the robbers at about half-past two o'clock this morning.

The number of shots fired could not, of course, be ascertained, for it was almost continual for ten or fifteen minutes, the coaches and express car being riddled with bullets, though fortunately no one was hurt on the train, as far as learned, but the conductor.

Several have offered the opinion that the robbers were cowboys, headed by a man who is nearly six feet high, with beard all over his face. He had a fine, shrill voice; wore a broad-brim light-colored, low-crown hat; and a slouch coat of coarse texture.

Great apprehension was felt by people on the streets when the news spread last night that the robbers might make a dash into this city and attempt to rob the banks. Precautionary measures in the shape of shotguns have been prepared for them, however, and a warm reception will be given them if they come this way. The excitement on the streets was intense.

La! Sam Bass six feet high and with a beard, too! The rest of the story was a heroic tale of a posse crashing about the bushes of Denton County and finding nothing. I dropped the paper to the floor. "Sam Bass," I said aloud. "You silly little clown."

I got up and pulled on my stockings. I wanted to eat before the customers began arriving.

You may think a woman of my calling never loves anyone, but I *did* love Joel Collins. He loved me, too, in his way.

He was a pretty man, over six feet high, slender as a reed and hard as rock. He dressed well, even when he didn't have much money, and his black hair and heavy mustache were so fine and silky that a woman's fingers itched to touch them. His blue eyes had the light of the devil in them. It was that light that got him into trouble, I think.

We met in Deadwood, after he and Sam had driven some cattle there and sold them. They weren't in a hurry to go home. They owed somebody in Texas a lot of money or had stolen the cattle they sold. Something like that. Joel bought a house on the outskirts of Deadwood. He and Sam called it a ranch, but there wasn't much land to it, and no cattle. It was really a sporting house, with a bar and a couple of gaming tables in the front and cribs in the back, where they worked four girls. I was one of them. After I became Joel's woman, I didn't take customers unless Joel told me to. I didn't mind. Sam had eyes for me, too. Sometimes we would close the house and have little parties, and all of us would get drunk and dance and laugh. Sam would make eyes at me, and Joel would notice and wave his hand and tell Sam, "Be my guest." I didn't mind that either, much. I liked Sam. But I loved Joel.

Then he closed the house and told me that he and Sam were going back to Texas. Just like that. It like to broke my heart. I didn't want to go back to work in some Deadwood saloon, or to someone else's cribs. But I kept my feelings to myself and said goodbye. I didn't know he planned to rob a train.

They had been gone just a few days when I decided to go to Dallas myself. And I did. And went to work for Norene. Then the news came down. I had known them all. Berry killed in Missouri. Heffridge and Joel shot down by soldiers in Kansas without a chance of saving themselves. They had twenty thousand dollars in gold tied up in a pair of pantaloons on their pack horse. And they say that one of the papers in Joel's pocket was a beautiful love poem. I wish I had it. The newspapers and the rumors said six men held up that train in Nebraska, and I knew one of them was Sam. Joel was like a big brother to him.

Then Seab Barnes was in my bed. He said he was from Denton. That was where Sam was from, and I asked Seab if he knew him. He said, "No." I said, "Well, he's not there anymore. He was way up north when I knew him."

A couple of weeks later, I was walking down the stairs to greet my next customer, and there was Sam, sitting on Norene's horsehair sofa with his hat on his knee and a glass of whiskey in his hand, just as I remembered him. He stood up and gave me a little bow. Beth was in the parlor, too, entertaining a customer, and I didn't know whether Sam was calling himself by his real name or not, so I said, "Good evening, sir."

We went up to my room, and I locked the door. He kissed me on the cheek. "Joel's gone," I said.

"Yeah." He patted my shoulder. "I hope to run into them that killed him someday."

"It was soldiers. We'll never know."

"Well, men get to bragging sometimes. You never can tell."

I looked up at him. I didn't have to look up far, because he wasn't much higher than me. "Well, let the dead bury the dead," I said.

He seemed shy and awkward. Maybe it was because he was in my room without Joel's permission. I poured two glasses of whiskey from the decanter on the table beside my bed. I handed him his glass and asked, "Do you want me?"

"Well, yeah." He laughed nervously.

I undid my dress and stepped out of it and laid it across the back of the chair. I wore only a chemise under it. I lifted a foot to the chair and said, "Unbutton my boots, will you?"

His face turned red, but he bent to unbutton the boot. His fingers didn't seem able to do what he wanted. He fumbled with the buttons and laughed that nervous laugh again, but he finally got the boot undone and did better with the other one. He stepped back and watched me roll my stockings and garters down. I was about to get into bed, and he said, "Take that off, too." So I pulled the chemise over my head and dropped it to the floor. I lay back on the feather mattress. Sam stood at the foot of the bed and just looked at me. I didn't mind. I like my body, especially in gaslight. I smiled at him. "Aren't you coming?"

He set his drink on the table. His fingers trembled while he unbuttoned his shirt, but he undressed quickly and crawled into bed and took me in his arms and kissed me on the neck, then on my breasts. I'm proud of my breasts. They aren't too large, and they aren't too small, and I rouge the nipples nice and rosy.

"La! You're trembling all over!" I said.

"It's been so long," he said.

"We've plenty of time."

But Sam didn't want to wait. He made love to me then.

You laugh when I say "made love"? Well, that's what he did. I had never before had such a tender time with a man. You may call it what you like, but what Sam did was make love to me. I kept wishing he was Joel.

Later we sat up against the big feather pillows, and Sam poured us each a drink from the decanter. He rolled a cigarette and lit it and breathed out the smoke in a long sigh. "Your bed smells pretty," he said.

"Lavender," I said.

We sipped our whiskey slowly and didn't say anything else. When our drinks were gone, Sam set the glasses on the table and shifted down into the bed and laid his head on my breasts. He made love to me again, and it was longer than before. When he finished he lay quietly inside me for a while. He smelled of old sweat. "You expecting somebody else tonight?" he asked.

"We don't make engagements. We just take what comes."

"I want to stay the night, then."

"All right."

I slapped him on the rump, and he moved away. I slipped on my dress and went downstairs barefoot. Business was slow, and Norene was pleased that Sam was staying. I went back to my room and locked the door and took off my dress again. "Turn off the gas," he said.

I made his breakfast myself and carried it to him. "Scrambled eggs!" he said. "I ain't had them in a coon's age." I sat on the edge of the bed and watched him. He ate like he hadn't had *anything* in a coon's age. He drank the whole pot of coffee himself.

"I told Norene you'd be here all day," I said. "And tonight, too."

He smiled.

"Is that all right?"

"Yeah."

After breakfast I heated the water and poured it in Norene's big brass bathtub for him. He splashed like a child. "If you get water on this carpet, Norene'll kill you," I said.

He held the soap to his nose and sniffed it. "It's been a long time. Soon I'll be rich enough to do this whenever I want to."

I lathered his face and sat down on a stool beside the tub and tried to shave him, but he kept moving, like a child. "Get still, or I'll cut your nose off." He got still, like a little boy minding his mother.

That night, long after I thought he was asleep, he rolled over and touched my shoulder. "Maude?"

"Hmm?"

"I want you to be my woman someday. Like you were Joel's. Would you like that?"

"Yes. When you can afford me."

He was dressing, standing by the door. "How much?"

"Nothing for me. It was for old times. But Norene will want something."

He laid five double-eagles on the bureau. "Give her whatever she wants," he said.

Dallas was like a circus. Every politician was writing letters to the governor, demanding that every resource of the state be slung against poor Sam. They always sent copies to the newspapers, which always published them, along with the governor's replies assuring us that we wouldn't be murdered in our beds and that the precious railroads would prevail in the end. That's not *how* they said it, but it's *what* they said.

Every tin badge in North Texas was in the city. The saloons and sporting houses were full of sheriffs, deputies, constables, city policemen from burgs I never heard of and farm boys toting old cap-and-ball pistols, who styled themselves "bounty hunters" and bragged that they would soon have the scalps of Sam Bass and his gang, and the reward money in their pockets. A couple of girls in our house received proposals of marriage from those idiots, who thought their prospects of future riches sufficient to buy themselves permanent professional bedfellows.

There were reporters, too, from St. Louis and Chicago and Baltimore and New York. They were funny men who took themselves very seriously and imagined themselves on a dangerous adventure on the wild frontier. They wrote long, lurid dispatches about the desperate characters they found and interviewed at the bottom of their bottles. I had one of those, a young man from St. Louis. As soon as he finished his puny work on me, he asked, "Have you ever met Sam Bass?"

"Of course," I said.

He jumped out of bed and rummaged through his clothes, his white rump glistening in the gaslight. He found his pad and pencil and climbed back into bed and asked, "What does he look like."

"He's nine feet tall, and his face is blue. He can't keep his hat on because of the horns on his head."

"Please be serious," he said.

"He's a very large and powerful man. It'll take a lot of bullets to bring him down. If you go with the posses, I hope you'll arm yourself."

"Oh, I *am* armed," he said. He sprang out of bed and rummaged in his clothing again and brought out a shiny little derringer with a mother-of-pearl handle and showed it to me.

"How pretty!" I said.

"My wife gave it to me. She worries about me."

Not all who came were fools, though. The governor sent Major John B. Jones, commander of the Frontier Battalion of the Texas Rangers, to Dallas to calm the people and organize the search. He brought several members of his battalion with him, and I feared for poor Sam when I saw them. La! They were tall, hard men who dressed in dark pantaloons and vests and hats. They bristled with pistols and knives, but they walked erect, unburdened by the weight. The weapons were as natural to them as parts of their bodies, and one unarmed would have been incomplete. They rarely spoke except to each other, and they walked with long strides, but the swing of their arms didn't match their step. Their hands were never far from the sweat-stained wooden butts of their pistols. Their faces were burned darker than even the buffalo hunters', and their pale eyes moved constantly and slowly, scanning their surroundings with a kind of calm deadliness. The Texas Rangers were older than the Republic of Texas itself and had spent more than forty years killing Mexicans and Indians and Yankees. They had begun hunting outlaws only recently, and the arrogance of Major Jones's men told Dallas that they considered the job unworthy of them. They never came to our house.

Some of the Pinkertons came, though. There were about forty, most of them from Chicago, headquartered in the Le Grand Hotel. They worked for the railroads, and had a sleek, big-city Yankee look that made them easy to distinguish from the bumpkins who followed them about, aping their dress and manner. La! One afternoon I saw two hicks in five-dollar suits riding up St. Paul Street. The beard of one of them flew off his face and fluttered to the ground! He jumped off his horse and grabbed it and shook the dust from it and stuffed it in his coat pocket. He heard me laugh and glared at me, then jumped back on his horse and galloped up St. Paul.

The *real* Pinkertons were dangerous though. They didn't have the cool, open deadliness of the Rangers, but they were crafty. When they looked at you, you felt guilty and a little afraid and became more careful in your talk. One, at least, hated all of us. "You don't believe Sam Bass is just a simple robber, do you?" he asked.

He was stretched on my sheets. His soft, pale body was absolutely still, and our brief exertion hadn't disturbed a hair of his oily, center-parted hair. But for his spent sex lolling against his thigh, you would have thought him dressed and relaxing in an office.

I didn't reply. We hadn't been talking about Sam.

"It's a plot," he said. "Against the North. The United States." He smirked, but there was no humor in his eyes. "You Rebs never give up, do you? Bass is out there raising money for another try at us, isn't he? And he's not the only one."

"That's ridiculous!" I laughed, but he didn't.

"The South is full of men like him. Texas is the worst. Nothing but thieves and brigands from Marse Robert's ragtag mob, hating our guts and waiting for another try."

I pictured him in some Chicago saloon, his feet crossed on the table, saying these things. "I was at Second Bull Run," he said. "I've never forgiven them. I never will."

I got out of bed and started dressing. "It may interest you to know that Sam Bass is a Yankee," I said.

He cocked his eyebrow. "Oh? Where from?"

"Indiana."

"There are many Copperheads in Indiana." He swung his heavy legs out of the bed and reached for his underwear. "A Copperhead's a Northerner who believes in your holy Southern cause," he said. "In other words, a snake."

"Sam's too young to be a soldier or a Copperhead or anything else," I said.

"You called him by his first name." He was buttoning his collar in front of my mirror.

I felt myself blush. "I've heard a lot about him."

He said nothing else until he was dressed and had laid his

hand on the doorknob. Then he gave me the closest thing he had shown me to a smile. "Do you know what Southern women are?" he asked.

"What?"

"Whores."

The man frightened me, and when the *Herald* said William Pinkerton, the great detective himself, had come to Texas to capture Sam, I was sure he was my customer with the oily hair and the heavy legs, and I worried that I had told him something important. I told Norene I wouldn't entertain any more Pinkertons. She was a little angry, for they paid well.

I don't know why the Mesquite robbery upset Dallas so much more than the others. Sam got little out of it. Maybe it was all the gunplay and the wounding of the conductor. But Sam's name was everywhere in the saloons, in the stores and hotels, the livery stables and the streets. The banks hired extra guards, for everybody believed Sam planned to dash into the city and strip us of our last dollar. The newspapers wrote of little else, sometimes spreading the wildest rumors and alarms, sometimes crowing that all the law and guns congregating in the city would bring poor Sam to a quick and bloody end. I figured they might be right. The vision of Joel dead on the Kansas plain with a love poem in his pocket haunted me, and it wasn't hard to substitute Sam's image for Joel's in that scene.

Maybe Major Jones concluded that his Frontier Battalion regulars weren't sufficient to do the job. Or maybe they refused to stoop to pursuit of a train robber. The governor commissioned Junius Peak as a second lieutenant in the Rangers and authorized him to recruit thirty men for a month's service. Cowboys and buffalo hunters and even hotel clerks hurried to enlist, so they could brag forever that they had been Rangers.

I knew June Peak, though not professionally. He had just been elected city recorder, but his past was full of jobs not so meek. He had served in the war with both Morgan's Raiders and Forrest's cavalry and had been wounded twice at Chickamauga. He had been a deputy sheriff in Dallas, and later a city marshal. A few years back, he had been hired to wipe out a ring of cattle rustlers in New Mexico, and had done it. He had hunted the buffalo, too. His face wore a mild smile befitting a city recorder, but he was a dangerous man, and the bankers and merchants and newspapers were pleased with the governor's choice.

A U.S. marshal and a federal district attorney arrived from Tyler and issued a warrant for Sam and Jackson and Barnes and Underwood for the Mesquite robbery. Dad Egan volunteered to serve it. And a Pinkerton was working as a bartender in the Wheeler Saloon in Denton. That I got from Callie, who hadn't stopped entertaining Pinkertons. She liked them and called them "suave."

One night there was a commotion outside Callie's room, across the hall from mine. My customer covered his head with the sheet, and I opened my door a crack. June Peak himself was standing at Callie's door with a gun in his hand, and two men with him. Norene was with them, too. She saw me and motioned behind her skirt for me to close my door. I did, but put my ear to the wood and listened. "Come out!" June Peak said.

Apparently the door opened, for I heard Callie say, "What is it?"

June Peak said, "We don't want you, ma'am." Then he said, "Is your name Scott Mayes?"

Some reply was mumbled, and June Peak said, "You're under arrest for harboring Sam Bass. Get dressed and come."

I learned later that Scott Mayes was one of Sam's oldest friends. They had come to Denton together years ago. But he was no robber. June Peak was just rounding up everybody in Dallas who had ever known Sam. I was worried that it might happen to me, and I asked a lawyer friend if it was legal, and he said it was.

Every morning a bunch of June Peak's greenhorn Rangers left their tents at the Fairgrounds and rode off toward Denton. And the two-bit officers and bounty hunters sat in the saloons and dreamed of their future wealth until they were drunk enough to mount up and try to beat the Rangers to their prey. Denton County must have been full of them.

What the Pinkertons were doing, besides screwing everyone in our house except me and Norene, God only knows.

The news that Union Pacific gold was circulating in Dallas alarmed me. Each time Sam had come to me he had left four or five of the 1877 double-eagles behind. I knew where he had got them, of course, and I had been careful about disposing of them. A friend of Norene's named John McElroy ran a saloon not far from our house. Each time Sam left me, I sent Norene's nigger Willie to McElroy with the gold, and he gave me silver for it. I warned Willie never to tell anyone about the gold, where he got it or what he did with it. To ensure his silence I always let him keep the shiniest silver dollar of the change he brought back. "If you tell, no more money," I would say.

I never told McElroy the source of the gold, either. Not because I thought he might tell, for John McElroy was no friend of the law. I thought he would recognize the coins and cache them in a safe or strongbox. But the fool had banked them! And it suddenly occurred to me that if only John McElroy was depositing the double-eagles in the bank, and if he was getting them all from Willie, it wouldn't take the detectives long to trace them straight to the top of my bureau.

I folded the newspaper and laid it on the table beside my rocking chair. Norene was playing the piano, and two Pinkertons, both a little drunk, stood at her shoulder, trying to sing the song she was playing. They were waiting for their turn upstairs, and one glanced at me, then whispered something to Norene. "She's got the curse," Norene said aloud, and he said, "Oh."

I rocked and listened and worried. One of our new regular customers, a deputy sheriff from somewhere, stumbled down the stairs and tipped his hat to Norene and went out the door.

Beth came into the parlor and took one of the Pinkertons away. The other, who had the better voice, huddled with Norene, flipping through the songbook for a tune he liked. Willie appeared at the door and glanced at them, then at me. "Oh, there you is," he said. He crooked his finger, and I followed him to the kitchen. "You got visituhs, Miz Maude," he whispered, nodding toward the back door. "I knowed better'n to show *dem* in."

I laid my hand on the doorknob and took a deep breath to slow the pounding of my heart. I opened the door only wide enough to slip through into the alley. Sam was in the shadows, just out of reach of the light from the kitchen window. Another man stood deeper in the shadows. Down the alley, two horses stamped and snorted. I ran to him. He said, "What's the matter?"

"The house is full of law. You can't come in."

"Can't we sneak up the back?"

"No. Pinkertons are everywhere."

The other man drew a pistol from his belt. Sam said, "This here's Frank Jackson."

Jackson, still in the shadows, tipped his hat and bowed slightly. "Howdy do, ma'am," he said. His voice had a sad, musical quality. I stepped deeper into the shadows. Jackson took off his hat then and held it near his waist, over the hand with the gun. His hair was light and curly, his eyes so deep-set I couldn't see them.

"So you're Jackson." I winked at him.

"Yes, ma'am."

"How old are you?"

"Not as old as I hope to be, ma'am."

"You'd better take Sam away, then," I said.

"I didn't want him to come. That's why I came with him."

It took me an instant to catch his meaning. "How are things in Denton County?"

"Crowded, ma'am." He still held his gun under his hat. I knew he was watching the window.

Sam put his arm around my waist and walked me proudly, slowly, toward the horses. Jackson stayed in the shadows, his gun under his hat. Sam stopped and kissed me. "I guess I won't be seeing you for a while," he said.

"No, Sam. Stay away."

"I come to tell you about a proposition," he said. "I have a plan. When this is over, I'm going down to New Orleans and buy me a boat and go into the hide business."

"Yes, do that," I said.

"I want you to come with me," he said.

A shadow moved across the strip of light the kitchen lamp threw across the alley. Jackson moved his hat and cocked his pistol. The click was very loud. He glanced toward us.

"Will you?" Sam whispered.

"Yes! Now go!"

He kissed me quickly and motioned to Jackson. Frank sidled toward us, keeping his eyes and gun on the window. When he reached us, he uncocked the gun and returned it to his belt. He tipped his hat again. "Nice to meet you, ma'am," he said, then swung into the saddle. He smiled down at me while Sam mounted. Sam gave me a little wave, and they walked their horses down the alley toward the lighted street. They turned into the light, and I held my breath, half expecting to hear gunfire, but there was none. I stayed in the alley for several minutes, listening. There was nothing.

In the kitchen I stood against the door, blinking against the light. Willie was sitting at the table, behind the lamp, his black face glistening. "You got anuthuh visituh, Miz Maude," he said.

"Tell him I can't see him. Tell him I've got the curse."

"He say he jus' want talk. He look mean."

"All right, Willie."

The Pinkerton who hated Southerners was standing by the parlor fireplace, his elbow on the mantel. He smirked when he saw me and extended his closed hand. As I approached, he slowly opened his fingers. A shiny 1877 double-eagle lay in his palm.

I smiled. "For me?" I said. After all, I am a whore.

Frank Jackson

The haul we got at Mesquite certainly wasn't enough to convince me to stay with Sam and the bunch. It was clear that railroad robbery was going to take me no closer to the life I wanted than Ben's shop would have, and Ben's offer, or some other job in town, would at least have improved my odds for a long life. But no, I didn't go back to Denton. Sometimes we make decisions that can't be reversed. A man standing on the bank of a swift river can decide whether he will try to swim across or walk along the bank until he finds a bridge. He can turn one way and walk, and if he doesn't like the scenery he can turn around and go the other. But if he decides to swim, he has to do whatever the stream makes him do to get to the other side. Once into the current, he can't change his mind. He just fights like hell and takes his chances. With a little luck, he might make it. But only God knows what the bank will be like where he lands.

I took four buckshot out of Seab Barnes' thighs, and by the time I knew for sure that his wounds were healing properly my chance to return to Denton was gone. If it had ever been there. When Sam handed me some newspaper clippings that Maude had given him and I saw that my name was on a federal warrant, I knew I was smack in the middle of the river, and way downstream from Ben and my sister and Dr. Ross. No matter how far they stretched, I was beyond their reach. And when I read the clippings to Sam, he said, "Well, pard, we're all you got now," and he was right.

We were lying under the trees on the ridge above our cabin. Below us in the clearing, Seab and Arkansas were dressing a deer that Arkansas had shot that morning farther up the hollow. The trees were in full leaf now, and our hideout seemed even more remote from the rest of the world than it had in winter. Sam had a pair of field glasses and was leaning on his elbows, watching some riders out on the prairie while I was reading to him. The riders looked like ants to me. "They're Rangers, I think," Sam said. "About thirty of them."

We had spent most of our daylight hours for most of a week in this place, watching posses gallop around the fringes of our sanctuary. A couple of days before, Sam and Henry and I had watched two posses at the same time, one riding southward, the other northward. They spotted each other just north of the Clear Creek bottom, and each thinking the other was us, I guess, they opened fire. A member of the southbound posse grabbed his arm, and Henry said, "They winged the son of a bitch! The bastards are going to kill each other off!"

And we heard gunfire another time, apparently in the bottom, for we could see no riders. The shots echoed up the hollow, but they were so far away that we knew they weren't fired at us. "Posse work sure is dangerous," Sam said.

So we weren't worried. The riders that Sam thought were Rangers were so small and silent and seemed to move so slowly across the greening prairie that they were of another world, as distant as the moon from Sam and me on the ridge and Seab and Arkansas and the dead deer. Seab and Arkansas were cutting the skin away from the carcass, their knives working quickly, an inch or two at a time. Then Arkansas grabbed the big flap of skin that they had cut away and yanked downward. The skin peeled away with a ripping sound loud enough for me to hear. Henry was moving down the slope from the cabin. When he stepped into the clearing the sun was brilliant on his red underwear. He had surprised us and washed his clothes in the creek the day before. The Rangers on the prairie meant nothing to us.

The bullet hit the rock near my shoulder and zinged off into the sky. It hadn't come from the Rangers. I rolled onto my back, levering a cartridge into my rifle as I went. I fired blindly, before I even saw the riders on the ridge across the hollow. Sam fired, too, and we wriggled on our bellies down the slope to thicker cover. Sam fired again. The riders were dismounting, crouching, running, seeking cover. "It's old Dad," Sam said.

They were about two hundred yards away, and out of sight now. A buzzard, stirred from his roost by the gunfire, was circling. Our clearing was empty, except for the naked deer hanging in the shade. I could see no one. Sam fired again, blindly. "Hey, Dad! This is Honest Eph! Come fight me!" His high voice echoed through the hollow. A volley of rifle fire crashed over our heads, sending shreds of leaves down upon us.

"They see us," I said.

"No. They're shooting at the sound."

"Stop yelling, then."

Another volley cracked, and leaves and twigs fell to the right of me. Henry dropped with a grunt behind a tree not far away. "You all right?" I asked.

"Yeah. How many is there?"

"About a dozen, I think. Where are Seab and Arkansas?"

"Below us a ways."

"Hey, Dad! Why ain't you out grubbing brush?" Sam hollered.

The posse replied with another volley, closer this time. "Woo! They're laying down the lead!" Henry said.

"Sam, shut up!" I said.

"Hey, Dad!" Then bullets sliced all around us. I buried my face in the dry leaves and heard a slug thump into my tree. "Oh God, they hit me!" Sam groaned. I crawled to him, but found no blood. Beside him, his Winchester was a wreck. "A bullet hit the stock," I said.

"I can't feel nothing in my arm."

"You're all right. I wonder what those Rangers are doing."

"Rangers?" Henry asked.

"About thirty of them, north of here."

"Oh God!" Henry said.

We lay squinting across the hollow, watching for targets and finding none. I wished Sam hadn't left the field glasses on the ridge. Dad's men must have been wondering where we were, too, for there were no more shots. I guessed they were near the ridge, above the limestone bluff that rose above the trees across the chasm from us.

"It's a cinch they ain't going to ride down from there," Sam said. "And if they tried it on foot, we'd pick them off."

"Let's get out of here," Henry said.

"Hey, Dad! We're going home!" Sam hollered. "Go learn your brush-grubbers how to shoot!"

"Damn it, shut *up!*" I said.

No shots came. We lay there for some time, but none came,

and we saw nothing. "Reckon they're gone?" Henry said.

"Maybe," Sam said. "Wouldn't old Dad get a kick, thinking I spent the night up here on my belly?"

"I'm *staying* on my belly till I get to that cabin," Henry said.

We all did. We wriggled through the woods. Rocks and sticks poked us in the guts. We slid right onto the stone ledge where the cabin stood. Seab and Arkansas were sitting by the door with their rifles across their laps. Seab grinned. "Hey, Arkansas, did you ever see three snakes crawl out of the woods at the same time?"

"Never did. Reckon we ought to pop their heads?"

"Naw," Seab said. "These ain't poison."

Sam said, "If enough of them posses get together, they might come right up the creek and in the front door."

"A lot of them would die," Seab said.

"Yeah, but they might do it. Or they might just squat in the mouth of the hollow and starve us out."

"I wonder if those Rangers were regulars or Junius Peak's bunch," I said.

"What's the difference?" Arkansas asked.

"A lot of difference."

"I'll say!" Henry said.

"Let's get out," Sam said. "Tonight."

We toted our remaining supplies up the slope and buried them under rocks at the foot of the bluff. We packed little to take with us. Henry said, "Wait a minute. I ain't going to waste all that venison." He went down to the creek and returned a few minutes later with the backstrap of the deer. He wrapped the meat in a flour sack and rolled it up in his blankets.

We rode silently in the darkness, alert for sight or sound or smell of a posse's camp, but there was none. Jim Murphy's house was dark, but the black forms of several horses moved about the corral. We dismounted and left our horses with Arkansas and moved quietly to the fence and examined the beasts, to make sure they weren't a posse's mounts. We recognized them all as Jim's. "Remember them," Sam whispered. "We might need them."

Henry insisted on seeing his family before we went wherever we were going, so we headed over to Henderson Murphy's place, keeping to the roads. We felt sure the people in the few lighted houses along the way would assume we were a posse heading home from the hunt. When we reached Henderson's house Sam took some gold from his belt and gave it to Henry. The two of them dismounted and walked toward the house. A lamp shone through one of the two front windows.

"Who is it?" The voice came from the shadows in the yard. It coughed a hard, rattling cough.

"Sam Bass, Mr. Murphy. And Henry."

"Step into the light."

The old man came around a bush, bearing a shotgun under his arm. He stopped and coughed long and hard into a large handkerchief. "Hello, Sam," he said. "Hello, Henry."

"We're getting out, Mr. Murphy," Sam said.

"Don't blame you. Three posses passed today. Where you going?"

"Don't know."

"No, I guess you can't."

"Henry wanted to see his family."

The old man's face was dark and wrinkled, framed by a mop of white hair that glowed in the yellow light from the window. His stoop was worse than Sam's. His chest seemed caved in. "The kids is asleep," he said. "Sarah!"

The door opened immediately, and a tall, skinny woman came down the steps. Her face was as wrinkled as the old man's, but pale. Strings of hair hung down her forehead. Without a word she hugged Henry and kissed him. They spoke in low voices, and Sam and Mr. Murphy walked away from them, to us. "Evening, boys," the old man said. He looked us each in the eyes. "Ain't met this one," he said, indicating Arkansas.

"Arkansas Johnson, sir."

"Ah, yes." He laid his hand on my stirrup. "How are you, Frank?"

"Fine, Mr. Murphy."

He nodded at Barnes. "Seaborn Barnes, right?"

"Yes, sir, Mr. Murphy," Seab said.

Mr. Murphy nodded. "Be careful, hear?"

Henry kissed his wife again and laid the gold in her hand. "Thank you, Sam," she called.

"Henry earned it, ma'am," Sam said. He and Henry mounted, and we trotted away.

Instantly I knew it was a gun muzzle against my cheek. I reached for my pistol, but the cold metal pressed deeper into my skin, and the quiet voice said, "Don't." I moved my hand away from my gun, and the cold metal left my cheek, and I turned my head on my blanket. His face, hideous, was grinning. Hair almost white hung to his shoulders. His short beard across his broad chin was whiter. Only three teeth, all of them brown, all in the lower jaw, rose from red gums that glistened wetly in the early sun. One eye squinted, yellow as a cat's. The other was gone, its socket covered by a greasy black patch. A Confederate infantryman's overcoat, too warm for the season, sagged from his narrow shoulders. The heavy shoe near my head was split just above the sole, and I saw the pink toes. Where the other shoe would have been, a homemade wooden peg stood. The grimy hands held a double-barrel shotgun inches from my eyes. "Morning," he whispered. I moved my head carefully, looking for my companions. "They're asleep," he whispered.

"Who are you?"

"Wetsel. This is my place."

Now I saw the tiny log cabin fifty yards behind him, and a barn farther back, unnoticed when we unrolled our blankets, too tired and wary to build a fire or even eat. "Who are *you?*" he asked.

"Rangers. Looking for the train robbers."

"Ah." His yellow eye moved to our horses, still saddled, tied in the woods, and my companions, motionless under their blankets.

"Where are we?" I asked.

"Bottoms of Little Elm. Wake the others. We'll have breakfast."

I started to pick up my pistol and put it in my belt, but he said, "Leave it."

I moved from Sam to Seab to Arkansas to Henry, nudging them with my toe and saying quietly, "Don't go for the gun. I'm covered." They rolled out, confused. "This is Mr. Wetsel," I said. "He says he doesn't mind Rangers at his table."

Wetsel shook our hands, grinning. "Don't get many visitors. Come up to the house."

"You fixed breakfast yet?" Henry asked.

"No, but it won't take long."

"We got venison. You want it?"

The yellow eye widened. "Ah. Bring it along."

Henry picked up the backstrap and got his pistol, too, and stuck it in his waistband. Wetsel saw him but didn't object, so the rest of us got our guns. We walked slowly up the gentle slope, keeping pace with the old man. I noticed a plowed field behind the cabin and asked, "How do you follow a mule?"

"With a deal of difficulty and a lot of cussing," he said.

"The war, I guess."

"Yep. Vicksburg. Grant's grapeshot blowed it clean away."

"The eye, too?"

"Nope. A knife done that."

The cabin reeked of smoke and rancid grease. A yellow cat lay on a straw mattress in the corner. "The coffee's done already," Wetsel said. He served three tin cups, and poured for the rest of us into chipped china bowls. He laid the backstrap on the rough table, sliced thick chunks with a Bowie knife and slapped them into a skillet on the stove.

"Been here long?" Seab asked.

"Since right after the war. Drove an ox wagon all the way from Alabama. Ever been to Alabama?"

"No."

"Well, don't bother. Nothing but carpetbaggers and scalawags. Worse than here." He poked the hunks of meat with a long fork. "I hope you don't catch that Bass boy. He's just doing what the rest of us would do if we had the gumption, getting back at them Yankee railroads. Wouldn't mind doing it myself."

Sam smiled. "It's against the law."

"Yeah. I ain't blaming you. But it'd be funner than hell, hoorawing them Yankees. You caught sight of him yet?"

"Not yet."

"Well, I hope you don't. I hope he gets richer than Midas. *Somebody* ought to get rich down here, other than carpetbaggers and scalawags. I hate to see the Rangers on their side."

"Well, he's giving us a run," Sam said.

"I hope he runs clean away. I sure do."

Wetsel had only chair, so we ate outside on the ground. The venison was tougher than the old man's shoe, but he seemed to chew it without much difficulty. The cornbread and molasses were good, and the morning was cool and bright. We ate quickly, then Sam stood up. "We better move. The state pays our meals, Mr. Wetsel. How much we owe?"

"Nothing. But if you see that boy, just ride the other way."

Sam handed him a double-eagle. "That seems a fair price."

Wetsel stared at the coin, then squinted at Sam. "Ah. I figured."

"Don't say what you know, Mr. Wetsel."

Wetsel grinned, showing the three teeth and the wet gums and tongue. "You bet I won't. Don't forget your meat."

"You keep it."

"Well, much obliged, then. Stay clear of trouble, hear? Keep all your legs and eyes."

We watered the horses in the Little Elm. The old man watched from the slope below his cabin, his brass buttons gleaming.

The next weeks are only a blur in my mind. We were in the saddle constantly, riding through the swamps and jungles that are the bottoms of the Little Elm, the Elm Fork of the Trinity, the Clear and the Hickory. Sometimes days passed between our glimpses of real daylight, so closely did we stick to the dank and gloomy woods. The posses pursuing us were large and numerous. One, hot on our trail, would cross the trail of another whose tracks in the spongy ground obliterated our own. Sometimes one posse would follow another for a day or more, believing their fellow hunters to be us. They weren't working together on a plan to capture us, I guess. Each group seemed to be wandering alone, intent on winning the reward and the glory before their competitors could get them. All we had to do was stay out of their way. It wasn't long before we knew the bottoms as well as each other's faces, and sometimes we would sit quietly and watch a posse pass within yards of us, Sam leaning over Jenny's neck, peeking through the leaves and grinning like a fox.

One day Dad Egan himself passed within forty yards of us in the company of only one other man. "Why, it's my old pard, Army," Sam whispered.

Seab pulled his rifle from the saddle boot. "Let's take them."

"Go ahead," Sam replied. But as Seab raised the rifle to his shoulder, Sam laid his hand on the barrel and said, "No. There ain't no use."

"If it was the other way, he'd cut you down," Seab said.

"Well, it *ain't* the other way."

So we watched them ride slowly on, Dad sitting his horse erect as a soldier, and Army, a poorer horseman, waggling his feet in his stirrups as if they didn't fit him right. They looked clean and fresh, and probably hadn't been on the trail long. I envied them that. I hadn't been out of my clothes for weeks. They stuck to my body. My beard itched on my cheeks and neck, and I constantly scratched it. If old one-eyed Wetsel hadn't been fooled into thinking we were Rangers on that morning that was now dim past to me, it was a cinch that no one would think us anything but desperados now.

But those times when hunger forced us to risk a stop at some country store, we learned that if we had no friends we also had no enemies in that region except the posses. The storekeepers, careful to show no signs of recognition, would mention casually the passage of other horsemen on recent days, tell us how many they were and where they seemed to be going, and would offer bits of news they had gathered from them when they stopped. "Billy Collins was arrested the other day," they would say. "Looks like they're picking up everybody who's ever *knowed* Bass. Glad I ain't seen him." Some even hinted that their hearts were with us. And in that way that country people have of repeating each other's best phrases, those we had robbed had acquired a name. They were the "high-and-mighties," fat, rich men who were thought responsible for the poverty of the farmers and the storekeepers. As with old Wetsel, they were considered Yankees and scalawags who were plundering the broken South, and the veterans of the Lost Cause and their children weren't at all unhappy that the "high-and-mighties" had become the victims for a change. They accepted Sam's gold without question or complaint.

Soon Sam began to see himself as they saw him. He spread his money around more and more lavishly, as if our robberies hadn't been for our own gain but part of a campaign to seize wealth from the enemies of the people and return it to its rightful owners. He hadn't thought it through that far, of course. He just liked to be called "generous," and had forgotten that our attacks on the trains hadn't made us rich and that his Union Pacific gold wouldn't last forever.

When it appeared that horsemen were multiplying like flies in the Little Elm country, we moved back northwestward, toward the Hickory bottoms. We stopped at a store near Bolivar, owned by a man we knew, and bought enough provisions to last several days, and some cooking utensils. We picked a campsite in a ravine on Hickory. Seab and Arkansas and Henry were so famished that they decided to gather wood and get the cookfire going before they tended their horses. Sam and I unsaddled and laid our saddles and saddlebags under a tree and led my bay and Jenny to the creek, then tied them on the bank. We were about to return to the fire to help with supper, but Sam said, "What the hell. Let them do it." We lay down on the grass to enjoy the last rays of the day's sun. Henry stooped to put the pot on the fire. Seab was cutting something. Arkansas was coming out of the woods carrying firewood. They had unrolled their blankets, but their horses stood saddled just beyond the fire. Henry looked at us and said something about loafing. Seab laughed.

Then came a voice from the woods: "Throw up your hands! This is the law!"

Henry dropped to one knee, drew his pistol and fired twice toward the voice. Arkansas threw down his firewood and sprang for his rifle, which was on his blanket. Seab was lying belly down by the fire, looking. "Jesus! There's dozens!" he shouted.

The bullets raised puffs of dust around Seab and Henry. One hit the fire and toppled the pot. Arkansas bolted for his horse and mounted. Seab ran for his horse, too. They rode to Sam and me and stretched their arms to us, lifting their feet from their stirrups to let us mount behind them. Henry fired two more shots, then mounted and rode past Seab and me. My bay and Jenny were whinnying in panic.

A mile or so into the brush, we stopped and listened but heard nothing. "We'll wait a while, then go back and have a look," Sam said.

"I think we better keep going," Henry said.

"No. I want Jenny back."

We waited for two hours by my watch, then rode back, listening. A hundred yards from our camp we dismounted and took off our spurs and crept forward, our pistols drawn. Our fire had been scattered, but the coals still glowed. We heard not a sound, and crept to the very edge of the brush, then into the open. Our horses were gone. So were Sam's saddle and mine, our blankets and provisions. Everything was gone except the pot that had been on the fire. It lay on its side among the scattered coals. Then I realized I had lost my medical saddlebags, and I walked away from the others into the woods and almost wept. I must have stayed for some time, for Seab came looking for me. "Sam feels bad, too," he said. "He lost Jenny. We all feel bad." He steered me back to the campsite. Henry and Arkansas were talking to Sam, but he wasn't listening. "Come on, let's go," Henry was saying.

"Yeah, that posse's out there somewhere," Arkansas said.

Sam looked at me and said, "Our luck's turning, pard."

Seab said, "Well, it'll turn even more if we don't get out of here."

We had to travel slowly, despite the posse at our heels. We didn't talk much, and I kept thinking of what Dr. Ross had written: *I've given you all you need to be a physician in this wild land. All except a cool, comforting hand (which you may have already) and a beard. And, O yes, a black coat, which I urge you to purchase . . . .*

It was all gone. Even the coat. Even my hands were cracked and calloused from weeks of clutching the reins and pushing thorns and branches away from my face. All I had was a stubble of beard, which itched. But I tried hard to put those things out of my mind. and may even have slept. I remember my head on Seab's shoulder and my hands pressed against his hard belly, and his warmth.

When the first thin line of dawn was on the horizon we arrived at Henderson Murphy's. The house was dark and, still skittish from our night's trouble, we left the horses with Arkansas and approached on foot, guns drawn. Seab and Henry hunkered behind the horse trough, and Sam and I climbed the steps. He knocked, but no one answered, so he knocked again. There was movement inside, and a woman's voice faintly called, "Who is it?"

Sam hesitated, then replied, "Sam Bass."

Mrs. Underwood opened the door. "Where's Henry?" I motioned for Henry and Barnes, and they joined us on the porch. "Thank you, Jesus!" She embraced her husband.

"Is Mr. Murphy here?" Sam asked.

"They taken him away, Sam. And Jim, too. They said it was for helping you."

Sam's small body seemed to shrink. "When?"

"Yesterday. They was taking them to Tyler, they said."

"Who taken them, Sarah?"

"Dad Egan. And that brother of his, Army."

Sam glanced at Seab, who stared back at him very steadily.

"Lord, Henry, what's it coming to?" Mrs. Underwood groaned. Henry patted her shoulder but said nothing.

"Is there any horses, Sarah?" Sam asked.

"No. They taken them, too." She wiped her eyes with her hands. "You boys come in. I'll fix you a bite to eat."

"We better not," Sam said, "but if you got a bit we could take with us, we'd be obliged."

Mrs. Underwood and Henry went into the house and closed the door. They returned in a few minutes, Henry carrying a lumpy cloth sack and a skillet. He kissed his wife without a word, and we returned to Arkansas and the horses. "More trouble?" he asked.

"More trouble," I said.

We rode on to Jim Murphy's place and cleaned him out, taking the seven horses in his corral, two saddles, a pack saddle, three good rifles, several boxes of ammunition, blankets and quite a bit of food. "Old Jim must have knowed we was coming," Henry said. We loaded a packhorse with all he could hold, and Seab and Arkansas switched their saddles from their worn-out mounts to fresh ones after Sam and I had taken our pick of the bunch. Riding up Cove Hollow well mounted and armed, I felt we had regained some control over our lives, although Jim's unknowing hospitality hadn't really made up our losses.

The tiny corral at the cabin wouldn't hold ten horses, so Sam decided to keep five saddled at all times and tied in the woods near the door. "Last night ain't going to happen again," he said.

But Sam was still afraid of a frontal assault on our stronghold. So after we rested a few days and did our laundry, we loaded our packhorse and went back down Clear Creek, leading our spare mounts. Five men and ten horses made a brave array in that jungle, and I felt ready for anything, especially a plan. But all we really needed then was a breathing spell away from the posses and the odor of gunpowder, and Sam thought we might get that farther west, where the mighty railroads and their concerns hadn't yet spread.

We watched the countryside change from the rolling prairie and wooded watercourses that we knew so well to hills and cedar brakes, and we traveled for days without seeing another rider. On Big Caddo Creek in Stephens County, about a hundred miles from Denton, we found a cabin on a hillside that some poor fool had tried to make into a farm. He had either died or become wise, for it had been deserted so long that weeds were growing in the dirt floor. We moved in and spent several days pulling the weeds and repairing the corral fence. Arkansas found a worn-out shovel in the barn and even cleaned the stalls, and Henry and Seab rode into Breckenridge, fifteen miles away, with some of Sam's gold and bought a wagonload of oats and groceries and several jugs of liquor and hired a man to haul it. The teamster looked over the place and said, "You boys going to work it?"

"We're thinking on it," Seab said.

"Well, good thing you got plenty of help. You'll need it."

For almost a month we *did* feel that we were settling there. In the evenings we would sit behind the cabin with a jug, looking up at the ruined fields on the hillside, and argue what would grow there and how long it would take to make the place pay. None of us were farmers, and there was no knowledge in our talk, but it was a pleasant way to spend the twilight. Maybe you've noticed it. Men talk differently at twilight than at other times of day. Their voices are softer, to match the light, and with whiskey warming their blood and crickets and night birds beginning their songs and horses moving in their quiet way about the corral, well, it all becomes a kind of music, full of peace.

"I sure wish my woman was here," Henry would say every night. And Arkansas would grumble, "Mine, too."

We even met some of the neighbors. They would ride by on horseback or be driving wagons home from Breckenridge, and some would stop and share our jug with us. Some would just wave as they passed. I don't remember all the names we made up for ourselves. Sam was "Sam Bushon," and I called myself "Frank Allen," after our first train robbery. The people seemed to accept us at face value. If any were suspicious of the gold we were spending at King Taylor's store or McClasen's, they didn't let on.

We had done nothing but run since the Mesquite robbery of two months before, and our bodies and minds soaked up the quiet. We even stopped talking much about our next job, the big haul that would give us all new lives. We fattened, and so did our horses. Lazy. That's what we were. And if we had been left alone, maybe we would be there yet, with crops growing in those rocky fields. It's not likely, I guess. But we had no thoughts of moving.

Then one day four farm boys passed our place on their plow

mules. They kicked the beasts hard and constantly, urging them along the road, and each carried what must have been his household's whole supply of arms and cutlery. "What's happened?" Sam called to them.

"Posse forming at King Taylor's!" one of them shouted. "Sam Bass is in the neighborhood!"

Sam decided we stood a better chance of avoiding posses if we split into smaller groups for a while and traveled separately toward more familiar ground. So Seab and Arkansas and Henry took the packhorse and our spare mounts and went one way, and Sam and I, with enough provisions to last a week, headed eastward into the rough hills and cedar brakes of Palo Pinto County. If our brotherhood didn't reconvene somewhere along the way, we were to meet at Cove Hollow.

By evening Sam and I were about seven miles west of the town of Palo Pinto. We spotted a large log ranch house, and since the hills seemed empty, we thought it safe to stop and ask for shelter. We tucked our pistols and knives out of sight under our vests and knocked on the door. It was opened by a pleasant-looking gray-haired lady holding a lamp. Sam said, "Evening, ma'am. My name is Bushon, and this here's Mr. Allen. We've had a hard ride today, and wondered if we might find a little food and shelter here."

The woman held the lamp high and close to us, looking hard at our faces and clothing. I was glad we were reasonably clean. She smiled and said, "Our men are gone. I take it for granted you are gentlemen?"

"Oh, yes, ma'am," Sam said.

She nodded. "I'm Mrs. Roe. Put your horses up and come in. Supper's on the stove."

When we returned from the barn, two young women were in the kitchen with Mrs. Roe. One was a slip of a girl, redheaded and freckled. The other was blonde and heavy-boned, but also freckled. I noticed Mrs. Roe had freckles, too. "These are my daughters," she said. "Mrs. Maddox and Mrs. Maddox. They married brothers."

I asked, "Where have your men gone?" It was a bold question, but I wanted to know whether posses were out in the neighborhood.

"Tom and Jake went to help build the church in Slaughter Valley," the redhead said. "They should be home tonight. And Daddy's gone to heaven. Are you religious, Mr. Allen?"

"No, ma'am."

She gave me a sly little smile. "Well, we don't take spirits ourselves, but Mama keeps a jug for visitors. Would you care to sample it?"

"Thank you, ma'am."

She poured the whiskey and showed us into the parlor and lit the lamp on the little round table. It was a fancy lamp with a fancy shade covered with pictures of little red roses. The whole room was fancy, and large. It held a pretty red rug and a big horsehair sofa and a smaller settee covered with red roses like the lamp, two rocking chairs and even a piano with a large Bible on top. Lace things hung on the backs and arms of everything. A large painting of a solemn, bearded man, whom I guessed to be Mr. Roe, stared from an oval frame above the fireplace.

"Rest yourself, gentlemen," said the redheaded Mrs. Maddox. She went out and closed the door quietly behind her.

I raised my glass to the painting. "To you, sir," I said. "You didn't leave your widow empty-handed."

"Nice spread, ain't it?" Sam said. "Too bad the girls are married. Maybe we should ride to Slaughter Valley and make something fall on them Maddox boys."

Mrs. Roe's chicken and dumplings would have made a couple of murders worthwhile. I never ate anything better, even to this day, not even counting in the fluffy biscuits and the green beans and sweet, early corn from her garden. Sam and I ate until we were about to split, then Mrs. Roe said, "Save some room for the apple cobbler." The cobbler was swimming in cream, and I said, "Do you folks eat like this every night?"

Mrs. Roe smiled shyly and said, "I like men who eat."

Sam and I stayed at the table and drank another cup of coffee while the women washed the dishes. The shine of the lamplight on their hair and the quiet swish of their skirts as they moved about the small room and their soft voices made me sad. Well, not sad exactly. More a feeling of losing something important, or not getting something I was supposed to have. Mrs. Roe dried her hands and said, "Would you gentlemen join us for evening prayers?"

"We'd be happy to, ma'am," I said, and we followed her into the parlor. She took the Bible down from the piano and handed it to Sam. "Would you do us the honor, Mr. Bushon?"

Sam blushed. "Mr. Allen does it better, ma'am."

"Mr. Allen can read, then, and you can choose your passage."

"I like the one about Joseph's dream," he said.

She found the passage and handed the Bible to me. I read about the seven years of plenty and the seven years of drought in Egypt.

"It all come true," Sam said.

"Egypt must be a lot like Texas," the blonde daughter said. We laughed, and then we knelt, and Mrs. Roe said a long prayer thanking God for rain and grass and asking Him to withhold His judgment and forgive our sins and protect Mr. Bushon and Mr. Allen on their journey. Then we rose, and Mrs. Roe picked up the lamp.

"I'm sure you gentlemen must be tired," she said. "Let me show you to your room."

The rosewood four-poster left just enough space in the little room for a trunk and a small washstand with a mirror over it. It was the most beautiful bed I had ever seen, and I said so.

Mrs. Roe beamed. "It was my mother's. She died in it. We brought it all the way from Louisiana." She turned back the white coverlet. The sheets and pillows glowed in the yellow light. "I hope you'll be comfortable. Good night, gentlemen."

She set the lamp on the washstand and left, and Sam sat down on the bed and ran his hand over the pillow. "God, I wish I was a Maddox," he said.

"Which one would you court?"

"The blonde one. I like them strong."

"The redhead's got more fire."

We heard the women talking in the kitchen, then the back door slammed. I looked out the window. The blonde daughter was walking toward the woodpile, carrying a lamp. She pulled the ax out of the chopping block with a single yank, and returned to the kitchen. "Hey, Sam, she brought the ax into the house," I said. "I reckon they don't want any monkey business."

We laid our pistols and knives on the bed and were about to undress when there was a knock at the door. Sam glanced at the weapons, but said, "Come in."

All three women were standing there, the blonde holding the ax. Their eyes widened when they saw the guns. "I think you gentlemen should give us those weapons for the night," Mrs. Roe said, her voice trembling. "It looks like our men aren't going to get back tonight, and . . . Well, we're only women."

"We'd like to do that, ma'am, but we can't," Sam said politely. "Mr. Allen and me has enemies, and if they was to catch us without our guns, we'd die. Don't worry, ma'am. We won't do you no harm."

Mrs. Roe paled. "Well, I must get something out of that trunk, then." She moved tentatively into the room, and the blonde daughter took a step forward, ready with the ax. Sam and I didn't move while Mrs. Roe rummaged in the trunk, then slammed the lid. Her hands were full of shotgun shells. "Good night, gentlemen," she said.

"Sure do wish I was a Maddox," Sam said when they were gone.

Our bodies sank gratefully into the deep feather mattress. The rocking chairs in the parlor were creaking. The ax lay in the lap of one skirt, I guessed, and the shotgun in another.

Next morning, the ax and the shotgun were nowhere in sight, but the rings under their eyes told me the women hadn't slept. They were polite during breakfast, but didn't say much, and Sam and I ate in a hurry, then went to the barn and saddled up. As we led the horses back to the house, all three women stood at the door watching. "Much obliged for your hospitality, Mrs. Roe," Sam said. He laid two golden coins in her hand, tipped his hat and said, "Goodbye, ladies." The women didn't reply, but the redhead smiled. We mounted, and Sam pointed to a gap in the hills to the west. "Keep a skinned eye when we ride through there, Mr. Allen," he said.

We rode westward through the gap and out of sight, then rounded a hill and headed back eastward, well clear of the house. "When them church-builders get home we'll have some riders after us," Sam said.

We spotted them the next day, resting in a cedar brake on Ioni Creek, but they didn't see us. That afternoon, we found Seab and Arkansas and Henry at McIntosh's store on Dillingham's Prairie. We drank a beer, then headed toward Denton County.

"What now?" Seab asked.

"Let's change our luck," Sam said. "Let's go find Jenny."

Arkansas was the only one of us not known in Denton, and he wasn't named on any of the warrants. So Sam sent him into town. When he returned to our hideout on Hickory Creek he said, "It's full of law. The hotels is full, and there's tents. That Pinkerton's still at the Wheeler Saloon."

"Did you find Jenny?" Sam asked.

"She's at Work's Livery Stable. People go around and look at her. Frank's horse is there, too."

"I figured," Sam said. "I figured they'd put her on show."

Next morning we rode together to the edge of town, arriving not long before daylight, then drifted in one by one and reassembled in an alley near the stable, not far from the square. The town was very quiet, very dark except for the lantern shining in the door of the stable.

"Henry and Seab and Arkansas will guard the door," Sam said. "Frank and me will go get our property back."

Sam and I dismounted as if we were customers. Charlie McDonald, who used to play marbles with me when I was a kid, came to the door. He didn't recognize us in the darkness. I pulled my gun and said, "Morning, Charlie. How are you?"

His eyes widened. He raised his hands. "Morning, Frank. Morning, Sam."

"We come to get our horses, Charlie," Sam said. "Go saddle them."

"I can't, Sam," Charlie said. "Dad Egan says they're evidence."

I don't know why I did it. I was nervous, I guess, and tired. I slammed Charlie on the side of the head with my pistol. He groaned and fell.

"Don't do that," Sam said. "Now we'll have to saddle them ourselves."

The stalls were full, the stable heavy with the odors of horses and manure and hay and grain. Some animals still stood sleeping. Others moved quietly in the straw that covered the floor, snuffling at their empty troughs. I heard a different rustle in the hayloft above me. I swung my gun to the ladder and said, "Come down or you're dead." A shaggy head showed itself. "Hello, Mr. Work," I said. "You got a gun?"

He dropped a pistol to the floor beside me. "Come take care of Charlie," I said.

The Denton Mare and my bay were in adjacent stalls in the back of the building. Both our saddles were on the partition between the stalls, my saddlebags and coat still tied on mine, covered with hay dust.

"Old Dad's careless with his evidence, ain't he?" Sam said.

"He never expected to have need of it," I said. We saddled quickly and led the horses out. Charlie was standing now, holding the side of his bloody head.

"You ought to be ashamed of yourself, Frank," John Work said. "Dr. Ross never trained you for this."

"Tell Dad he can't steal nothing from us that we can't get back," Henry said.

We galloped out the Bolivar road. Mr. Work was shouting, "Sam Bass! Sam Bass!" behind us, and I knew the law would be after us soon, but we made the edge of town without trouble and rode by a group of white tents that I assumed housed Rangers. A man stood in the door of one of the tents, pissing, and I waved; at him. He waved back. I guess he thought we were a posse getting an early start. As we passed Dad Egan's house we saw a boy and a girl taller than he walking from the house toward the barn. To my surprise, Sam split away from us and rode toward them. We followed. The children stopped. The lad was Dad's son, John. "Hello, John," Sam said.

The boy smiled into the dawn. "Hello," he said.

"Remember me?"

"Yeah. You're Sam."

"That's right. I used to carry you on my back."

"Yeah."

"I used to call you 'Little Pard.' Remember that?"

"Sure do." His voice was high and sweet.

"Who's your friend?"

"Hired girl."

"*Hired girl!* You mean Dad filled my place with a *girl?*"

The boy laughed, and the girl, her brown hair done up in tight pigtails, grinned self-consciously. "I reckon so," John said.

"Well, you tell old Dad I don't like that a bit, hear?"

"All right."

"Where *is* Dad, anyways?"

"Asleep."

"*Asleep?* What's that old rascal doing asleep? Why, the sun's already up!"

"He was up late. Mama told me not to wake him."

"And what was the old rascal doing up so late?"

"He was looking for you."

"Looking for *me?* I been all over Denton this morning, looking for *him.*"

"He's up at the house. Maybe Mama will wake him for you."

"Naw. Let him sleep. You just tell him Sam Bass come by looking for him, hear?"

"All right."

"But if anybody *else* comes by here looking for me, don't tell them you saw me. I want Dad to be the one to find me. All right?"

"All right."

"Remember now, Little Pard. I just want to see old Dad. Nobody else."

"Yeah, I'll remember."

Sam leaned from his saddle. "I got a present for you, Little Pard."

"You do?"

"Come here, and I'll give it to you."

The boy walked shyly toward the mare, and Sam bent down and handed him a double-eagle. The hired girl smiled stupidly, maybe hoping he had a present for her, too, holding her milk bucket with both hands. "Put that in a safe place and hold onto it," Sam said. "And don't tell old Dad I give it to you. He might not let you keep it."

"All right."

"But remember who give it to you, hear?"

"Yeah."

"And who give it to you?"

The boy smiled. "Sam did."

"Your old pard, right?"

"Yeah."

"Remember that, John. Remember I used to be your pard."

"I will."

"We got to go now." Sam waved and turned the mare, and John and the hired girl waved back.

It was as easy as that. The newspapers called it one of our most daring adventures and made us out to be as bold as Jeb Stuart's cavalry, but it isn't hard to ride into a sleeping town and steal a couple of horses, no matter how many Rangers are snoring in their beds. The timing's everything. An hour later and all those Rangers and deputies would be up and dressed and full of coffee, and it might have been a different story. I still regret hitting Charlie McDonald that morning. There was no reason for it, and it marred an otherwise peaceful visit to my hometown. We had been friends, too.

Dad Egan and Junius Peak considered our raid a personal insult.

By the middle of the morning it was raining hard, but the rain couldn't dampen our spirits. Sam and I were complete again, he astride The Denton Mare, and I with my books and instruments and vials and black coat tied behind me. We welcomed the rain. The water would wipe out our trail. We traveled fast, to cross as many creeks as we could before the water rose, and we saw no law that day.

Next morning, we weren't so lucky. We headed toward Cove Hollow and soon encountered Dad and two other riders. They gave chase, although they were outnumbered, and we ducked into the bottoms of the Elm Fork of the Trinity and lost them and switched back to Pilot Knob, where we bought some canned meat at a store. That was a mistake, I guess, for within an hour we spotted two posses on our trail. We gave them a run. Their mounts tired faster than ours, but the rain that had befriended us had gone, and our tracks were plain as painted signs on the soft earth behind us.

Denton Creek was swollen with brown, rolling water, but Sam and Jenny didn't hesitate. Sam pulled his rifle from the saddle boot and raised it high above his head, and the mare plunged into the stream, the rest of us behind them. The posses dismounted on the bank, dropped to their knees and fired, but none carried rifles, or were too excited to think of them, and we made the far bank and dashed into the woods.

Wet to the skin and caked with mud, we pushed on to Hardy Troope's store, not far from Davenport's Mill. The others stood guard while Sam and I went in. The storekeeper was showing two women a bolt of cloth. Sam called to him, and he replied, "In a moment, sir."

Sam shouted, "I'm Sam Bass, and in a hurry! You wait on me, by God!"

"Certainly, sir," the man said. "Excuse me, ladies."

We bought some more canned meat and coffee and a coffeepot and headed southwestward toward Tarrant County, hoping to find a secluded place to rest our horses. But another small posse saw us and blazed away. We had a long start on them and shook loose, but I felt like a dog tormented by a million fleas. When full dark came we doubled back and headed for Denton County and Hickory Creek. Our horses lifted their legs as if they were lead, and we were damp and miserable and hungry. Yet I hoped for more rain, for our trail was plain behind us, and I knew Dad Egan wouldn't give up this time. It was near midnight when we reached the familiar bottoms of Hickory Creek. Afraid to make a fire, we had no coffee and ate our canned meat cold and crawled into our damp and stinking blankets.

"Why do you think they're trying so hard, when they didn't seem to care much before?" Henry asked.

"Four reasons," I said. "Money, money, money and Dad Egan. They think the railroads are going to win, and they don't want to be on the losing side anymore."

It didn't rain.

A posse was trying to charge our camp, but was held back by the undergrowth. We grabbed our guns and fired a volley into the woods and received a sharp reply. Arkansas grabbed at his neck, but ran for his horse. Henry's horse was tied on the other side of our campsite, and he started toward it, blood blossoming on his left sleeve. Seab, already mounted, yelled, "Grab on!" and Henry grasped his hand and swung up behind him. We broke onto the prairie and headed at a run toward a farmhouse a quarter of a mile away. A horse stood tied to the fence in front. The rest of us kept riding, but Seab reined in, and Henry jumped down and untied it. "I'm borrowing your pony for a while!" he shouted at two terrified boys on the steps. We cut northeastward, passed behind the farm, and then were safe in the timbers and swamps of the Elm Fork.

The whole week was like that, a crazy, blind game in which we, our pursuers and Mother Nature all had our moves. We dashed about the points of the compass, with Denton as the center, holding nothing in our minds but safety. Rain would fall and wash away our tracks. We would lose the posse behind us only to pick up another when the rain would stop and leave our hoofprints branded in the prairie grass and the mud of the creek banks. We had no idea how many men were after us or what their strategy was, if they had one. We rode three days and nights without a wink of sleep, nourished only by what little food we could grab at country stores and eat in the saddle. We talked little, and when we did we whined.

Arkansas had only been grazed in the neck, but Henry's wound was more serious. The bullet had passed through the flesh of his upper arm, but had missed the bone. He was in pain and couldn't use the arm well, but there was little I could do but keep the wound clean and bandaged. Playing fox in the woods had lost its charm for all of us.

The people in the countryside, who had been friendly to us for so many months and had accepted Sam's gold so willingly suddenly were hostile and frightened. Once after a heavy rain that we thought should protect us for a while, we stopped at the store in Bolivar, where we had traded many times, and Sam and I went inside. But the man stood motionless behind his counter. "Ain't you going to wait on me?" Sam asked.

"I don't want to go to Tyler with the rest of your friends," he said.

Sam stared at him a moment, then began walking around the store picking up things and setting them on the counter in front of him. I stood in the middle of the store with my hand on my pistol butt, to make sure no hands disappeared under the counter. The man reached for nothing, not even a pencil to tally our bill. Sam laid a thousand rounds of ammunition in front of him, then a sack of flour, then several sacks of coffee and a stack of new, dry shirts and pantaloons. "How much?" he asked.

The man didn't move. "I ain't selling you nothing," he said.

Sam pulled a pistol and cocked it and held it under the merchant's nose. "Then I'm going to blow your head clean away," he said.

"Forty dollars."

Sam laid the money on the counter, and we picked up the supplies. "If any of them posses comes through, tell them to leave us alone," he said. "I'm tired."

We rode into the woods and found enough dry wood to build a small fire and had our first coffee in days, and cold canned fruit with it. We changed into our new clothes and left our wet, mud-stained, blood-stained rags in a stinking pile on the creek bank and laid a rock on top as a kind of monument.

"Why don't we ride to Cove Hollow and get some sleep?" I asked.

"Because that's where they *think* we're going," Sam replied.

I really had ceased to care. The thought of death as a long sleep had begun to hold a certain appeal. But we rode northward, out of the frying pan and into the fire.

June 13, 1878. It's a painful day to look back on. We were lounging in the brush on the bank of Salt Creek, trying to rest. I was lying on my back, my hat over my face. I was just beginning to doze when the shots and shouting came. I sprang up and fired my pistol before I even saw the huge party of men on the opposite bank. There must have been seventy or eighty of them. They were watering their horses when they noticed us, I guess, for all were dismounted, and several were lunging toward their saddles to get their rifles.

Arkansas, who had lain beside me on the grass, jumped erect, then started to fall. Something wet hit my cheek, and I glanced down. A piece of bone lay at my feet, bits of skin and hair still clinging to it. Half of Arkansas's face was gone. I was mesmerized by the awful sight, but Seab grabbed my arm. "Henry's got the horses!" he said. "Let's go!"

I ran into the trees, then turned and fired again. The men across the creek were mounting and plunging their horses into the swollen stream. I ran again. Sam and Seab were ahead of me, and in the dark shadows I saw the horses. I stumbled and fell. I had tripped over the dead foreleg of the pony Henry took from the boys. Sam and Seab were grabbing at their reins, which were looped over the low branches of a tree. I grabbed my own and jumped for the stirrup. "Where's Henry?" I cried.

"I don't know!" Sam replied.

Sam urged Jenny through the thickest part of the undergrowth. Twigs and thorns tore at my arms and legs and face, and I plunged ahead in panic, my horse as desperate as I. No gunfire sounded behind me, but I knew the posse was swimming the stream and would be on me soon. My back expected their bullets. Something did hit me, and I thought, Oh, my God, I'm dying, before I realized it was hailing. Hailstones the size of marbles pelted me and leaves and twigs fell around me. I prayed, actually prayed, that our hunters would drown.

But there was shouting behind me now. Some of the riders had made it across the water. Sam must have heard them, too, for he cut toward the creek, and the mare plunged into it, and Seab and I followed. I thought we were doubling back across the creek, but Sam held Jenny near the bank and let her swim downstream, and we followed. I looked behind me and saw we were downstream from the posse, and a bend in the creek and the trees on the bank had put us out of sight of our hunters' watering place. It was strange, lying on my horse's neck, hearing nothing but the rush of the water, feeling nothing but its wet and the movement of the animal's shoulders, as if trotting slowly, dreamily, with nothing for his hooves to touch.

At a place where the bank was high and the stream had cut a cavelike depression into the earth, Sam headed for shore, and we followed. The cave was scarcely large enough to hold the three of us and our horses, but we huddled there, holding our hats over our beasts' muzzles to muffle any signal they might nicker to the horses behind us. The earth above, held in place by dead and gnarled roots that hung around us like grotesque moss, gave us some shelter from the storm. But I knew that if any of our pursuers had remained on the other bank and decided to ride downstream, we would be visible to them and naked to their fire.

We stood for what seemed hours, listening for sounds of men or animals amidst the thunder and the rushing water and the crash of hailstones into the woods above us. Before our itching eyes the grass on the opposite bank turned white, as if it had snowed, then green again as the hail stopped and the pelting rain melted the stones. I kept wanting to look at my watch, to guess how long we had been there, but I was afraid to risk its music. At dusk a man walked on foot down to the edge of the creek, about a hundred yards upstream. I dropped my hat and raised my rifle. "Shall I kill him?" I whispered.

"Not unless he turns this way," Sam replied.

The man was tall and cradled a rifle in the crook of his elbow. I guessed from his bearing that he was a Ranger. He stood gazing at the opposite bank, then glanced upstream, then turned and disappeared. Sam sighed, and I lowered the rifle.

We stood in that muddy depression until full dark, and then stood some more. But sometime during the endless night Sam whispered, "Let's go," and climbed onto Jenny and slipped quietly back into the water.

Jim Murphy

It was a hot afternoon, but cool in the shade. I was sitting in my rocking chair on the porch of my Cove Hollow place, and I seen them coming while they was still some ways off. When I first seen them they was so far away I couldn't tell they was only three. Then they dipped below a little rise, and I didn't see them at all for a while. When they topped the rise I seen they was only three, and I wondered why. They was coming real lazy, at a walk, and the tails of their horses was switching. It was only the fifteenth of June, but the flies was already bad. I knowed who they was. I mean, I knowed who *one* of them was, as soon as they topped that rise. I'd recognize the gait of that mare even if she was on the moon. When I seen they was only three, I stood up and squinted at them coming, trying to see who wasn't there. I felt fluttery in my belly, and the closer they come, the worser the flutter got. I seen that Arkansas and Henry wasn't there. Jackson and Barnes, they was there. And Sam, of course, on that mare.

They was a mess. Their clothes was tore and covered with dry mud. Their horses was covered with mud, too, and all their rigging. Their faces was all scratched up, like they'd been in a fight with a wildcat or a woman. They pulled up by the fence and just set there, slumping in their saddles, looking at me. They looked older than I remembered them, and I never seen nobody tireder. They was a bunch of hard cases, all right.

"Well, look what the cat drug in," Sam said. His voice was thin and weak, like somebody that had been sick a long time.

"*You're* the ones the cat drug in," I said. "I ain't never seen a sorrier looking bunch."

They got down and tied their horses to the fence. They come up on the porch and flopped down against the wall. "Well, old fellow, how do you like the Tyler jail?" Sam asked.

"Not at all."

"How'd you get out?"

"Jumped bail."

"And your daddy?"

"Him, too. We just hopped a train to Dallas and then hired us a buckboard and come home."

"Well, they'll be after you," Sam said.

"Not for a while. It's you they want."

Jackson and Barnes wasn't saying nothing. They'd took off their hats and laid their heads against the wall. Their eyes was closed. I thought they was asleep.

"Is Sarah Underwood still at your daddy's place?" Sam asked.

"I don't know. I left him in Denton."

He peered off into the sun and didn't say nothing else, so I said, "How about a drink of whiskey?"

"Fine," he said, still looking off in the distance. So I went in the house and got the jug and four glasses and brung them out. Barnes opened his eyes and said, "We don't need no glasses."

"Well, it's Sunday," I said. "We might as well do it polite." While I was pouring the whiskey I asked, kind of casual, "Where's old Henry, anyways?"

"Don't know," Sam said. "He left us."

"I ain't seen him," I said.

Jackson opened his eyes and picked up the glass I'd set beside him and took a pull. We all was drinking for a while, not saying nothing, then I said, "Where's Arkansas?"

"Dead," Sam said. "Salt Creek, two days ago. The day Henry left."

"Who done it?"

"Rangers."

"Bastards," I said.

"That's the truth," Barnes said.

Sam said, "So we need a good man, Jim. Why don't you come with us now? We have lots of fun and plenty of money in our camp."

I could tell how much fun they'd been having, but I said, "I been thinking on that. But I been thinking on going back to Tyler and facing the music, too. They ain't got nothing on me."

Sam laughed a bitter little laugh. "The hell they ain't! You're a friend of mine, and that's all they care about. The best thing for you is to come with us and make some money."

"You the ones that cleaned me out?" I asked.

"Yeah, I owe you," Sam said. "We lost all your horses but that one Seab's riding. Can you wait?"

So I could tell how much money they'd been making, too. "No hurry," I said.

"How long you been back?" Jackson asked.

"About two weeks. I camped down on Hickory for a long time, figuring I'd run into you."

"Surprised you didn't," Jackson said. "We been in and out of there."

"You been other places, too. I read in the paper you was way over in Stephens County."

"Yeah, we been everywhere."

"The papers has been raising hell with June Peak," I said. "They say it's time for you and him to fight."

They got a laugh out of that, and we passed the jug around again. "It may have been Peak that jumped us at Salt Creek," Sam said.

"Bad?" I asked.

"They just got lucky," Sam said. "You coming with us, Jim?"

I rocked for some time and stayed quiet like I was thinking. Then I said, "I promised Daddy I'd help him thrash his wheat. If you can wait till I'm through, maybe I'll go."

Sam stood up. "All right, we'll wait. We need you in our business. Our horses could use a rest, anyways."

He went down the steps, and Jackson and Barnes dragged theirselves up and followed him. "We'll be up the hollow," Sam said.

"I'll be there," I said. The fluttery feeling was worser.

Daddy's cell was a ways down from mine, but I could hear him coughing. He coughed all day and all night, but it was worser at night. I thought he'd never stop, and prisoners would yell, "Shut up!" and "Cut that out!" Of course there wasn't no way he could quit. I worried when he coughed, and I worried when he didn't, afraid he was dead. "My daddy's got the consumption," I would tell the jailer. "He needs the sunshine."

"Well, Jim, this here's a jail, not a sanitorium," the jailer would say.

"But he's innocent," I would say. "There ain't no reason for him to be here."

"And are you innocent, too?" the jailer would say.

"Yes," I would say.

The jailer would put his hand on his hip and look at me kind of disgusted and shake his head. "You know, Jim, this is the damndest jail," he would say. "Every man in it's innocent. How you reckon them Rangers keep on making so many mistakes?"

It went like that for almost two weeks. Then one day June Peak come with the key in his hand. "Major Jones wants you," he said, and he unlocked the door and taken me to a little office. Major Jones was setting behind the desk, but he got up and waved to a chair and said, "Set down, Jim." I taken one chair, and June Peak taken another, and Major Jones set down again. I'd never laid eyes on him before. He was big, big as me. Heavy, you know. With a big brown mustache and little black eyes. "The jailer says you been raising hell about your daddy," he said.

"Daddy ain't done nothing wrong," I said. "He didn't know

what Sam Bass was doing. He's a good man. Everybody in Denton will tell you that."

Major Jones smiled. "Don't know nothing about nothing, eh?"

"No."

"Do you?"

"No."

Major Jones looked at June Peak, and they laughed. "He hid on your place," Major Jones said. "He come and went at your house whenever he wanted to. You even got his supplies for him."

"We been friends for years," I said. "I didn't know he was wanted."

"You didn't, eh?"

"No. Dad Egan never come after him. He never asked me nothing about Sam."

The two Rangers laughed again, then Major Jones said, "Well, Jim, you'll get a fair trial. Your daddy, too. If you're innocent you got nothing to worry about."

"Daddy's a sick man, Major. If jail don't kill him a trial will."

Major Jones shrugged. "What can I do? The law's the law." He swiveled his chair till his back was to me and looked out the window, rubbing his chin. "Of course, if we was to catch Sam Bass, everything would be different. I reckon half the men in this jail would go free then. I guess the charges against your daddy would be dropped then. Maybe yours, too, although we got a good case against you."

I didn't say nothing, and he swiveled his chair back around and faced me. "I'll lay it right on the line," he said. "You help me catch Sam Bass, and I'll see that you and your daddy *both* go free."

The fluttery feeling started in my belly right then. "What can I do?"

"Join his bunch," Major Jones said. "Help us lay a snare for him."

"Sam's my friend, Major."

"Better than your daddy?"

"No."

"Well, then."

"And after you get the snare laid, what am I supposed to do then? Kiss him on the cheek?

Major Jones smiled. "That won't be necessary, Jim. We want all the disciples, too."

I didn't say nothing.

"There's another thing," Major Jones said. "There's all that reward money."

"I don't care nothing about that."

"Well, it'd be quite a sum if we was to get all five of them."

I didn't say nothing.

"You want some time to think about it?"

"All right."

"When you decide, tell the jailer you'd like to talk to Lieutenant Peak."

Major Jones swiveled back to the window, and June Peak stood up and taken my arm and walked me back to my cell.

Daddy coughed all night, and the next morning I told the jailer I wanted to see June Peak.

Peak told me he'd arrange for the charges against my daddy to be dropped and would see that my bail got paid. I lied to Sam when I told him Daddy and me left Tyler together. Daddy got on the train for Dallas that same day, and my brother Bob met him. But Peak told me to hang around Tyler a few days like I was waiting for my trial. I did. I spent a lot of time around the federal courthouse, and the lawyers and officers and bondsmen got to know me pretty good. Then one day Peak showed me a document that the United States attorney had drawed up and signed. It said all charges against me would be dropped if I helped capture Sam or any of his bunch. "It's time you went," Peak said. "Just get on a train and get out. But be careful. The word'll spread fast, and the bondsmen'll try to have you arrested in Dallas. And stop somewhere and get that mustache shaved off. It's like a goddamn flag."

He got up and walked me to the door, then picked up one of the hats that was on the rack there. "Here, try this on," he said, and I did. "Fit?"

"Yeah, pretty good."

"Wear it, then."

"Whose is it?"

"Some lawyer that's trying a case today. Go ahead and take it."

I got on the train and slumped down in my seat and put the hat over my face like I was sleeping. At Mineola I got off and went to a barbershop and told the barber to give me a shave, mustache and all.

"You sure? It's a pretty one."

"Take it off," I said.

I caught the next train to Dallas and got through the depot without no trouble. I bought me a horse and rode to Denton to see my brother Bob. He told me Daddy had made it home all right. It was dark when I started out to Daddy's place to see him. I was riding past an alley, and this voice come to me real low, saying, "Jim. Come here."

I rode over, and Dad Egan was standing there, leaning against the wall. "I hear you done some business with Major Jones," he said.

"Goddamn!" I said. "Nobody's supposed to know about that but Jones and Peak and me!"

"He had to tell me," Dad said. "He was afraid I'd arrest you again."

I didn't say nothing, and Dad just stayed there in the shadows, not moving. "You know how to get in touch with me," he said. "I want to be in on it."

I turned my horse and headed on up the road toward Daddy's house, worrying about how many *more* sheriffs and deputies and Rangers and Pinkertons knowed about our business. The fluttery feeling was something awful, because I knowed if word about me was to get out, Sam would hear it, and old Jim would be a gone gosling.

Daddy was glad to see me and told Sarah Underwood to give me a cup of coffee. When she left the room Daddy closed the door. He was coughing as bad as in the Tyler jail. "Why'd they let us go?" he asked.

"They didn't have nothing on us, so they dropped the charges," I said.

"Is that right?"

"You seen Sam or any of the bunch?" I asked.

"No. Why?"

"Thought they might've come by."

"Not since I been home."

"Well, if he comes by, tell him I'm looking for him," I said.

Late that afternoon I saddled me a good horse. "You be careful," Daddy said. And I rode down to the Hickory bottoms, thinking I might run into Sam down there. I camped there for better than a week, and I seen a couple of posses, but I never found Sam or any of his boys. And the longer I stayed there the nervouser I got, so I just packed up one day and rode up to my Cove Hollow place.

If Sam knowed about the deal I made with Major Jones, he hadn't let on when he showed up at my place. But Jackson and Barnes hadn't been a bit friendly. They was tired at the time, and maybe a little scared theirselves. But maybe they knowed, and I tried to figure how I'd feel if I was in their place and one of my friends done what I done. I had to admit that if I was in their place, I'd blow my head off. But what's a man to do when his daddy's dying? Blood runs thicker than water, don't it? And when your daddy's coughing his guts out in a goddamn cell, well that's worse than hell. No son worth his salt can just let that happen. I wished it would take forever to thrash Daddy's wheat, but of course it didn't.

Halfway up to the cabin, I heard the gunfire. At first I thought it was meant for me, then I knowed it was too far away. Then I thought maybe a posse had finally got the nerve to come up Cove Hollow, but it didn't sound like no fight. Just a shot or two, then a long quiet, then two or three more shots. Rifle shots, echoing down the hollow.

When I got to the clearing below the cabin I seen what they was doing. Some tin cans was set on the creek bank, and they was shooting at them from the ledge. I seen the boys bellied down with their rifles and hollered, "Hold your fire!"

Sam hollered, "Come on up!" and Barnes and Jackson set up and started reloading. I worked my horse up the slope. "Wheat put up?" Sam asked.

"Yep."

"Good crop?"

"Pretty good. What the hell you doing?"

"Just practice. Take down your rifle and come."

I put up my horse and joined them. "How good are you on the shoot?" Sam asked.

"Not very good. Hello, Frank? Seab?"

They nodded but didn't say nothing. They sure had changed in the weeks I was in Tyler. Frank had, anyways. I'd never knowed Seab too well, and he was a quiet one anyways.

"Well, you better practice," Sam said. "The posses is getting serious, and the boys and me decided to get serious, too. See that can on the end? Play like that's old Dad sneaking up on us. What you going to do to him, Jim?"

I took careful aim and fired, and the can jumped. It was a lucky shot. Barnes laughed. " 'Bye, Dad," he said.

We practiced for half an hour, and I hit about one out of five, the worst of the bunch. But Sam said, "You'll do."

"Seen any posses lately?" Barnes asked.

"Not a one," I said.

"Now ain't that strange?"

"Maybe they're wore out," I said. "Or maybe they had to go get their crops in. Or maybe they think you left the country."

"That's what we're going to do," Sam said. "The boys and me decided its getting too hot here. We're going to strike out and find us a bank."

"Where?"

"Don't know yet. We're just going looking."

"Maybe Henry would like to go with us," Jackson said. "You seen him, Jim?"

"I ain't," I said, "but Daddy has. He showed up the night before I went to help with the thrashing and collected his wife and kids and taken off. He's running."

"That son of a bitch," Barnes said.

"Maybe he ain't so dumb," Jackson said.

"You know where we could get a good horse?" Sam asked. "That old crowbait of yours that Seab's riding is about give out."

I thought a minute. "Yeah. Bill Mounts. He bought a nice saddlehorse just the other day."

"Mounts? Down by Denton? Well, tonight we'll lift that horse." Sam stood up and raised his arms like a medicine show man trying to raise a crowd. "The old rascal will walk out in the morning and find that horse gone, and he'll go back to the house with his lips hung down and his face long as hell. 'Well, old lady, my fine horse is gone,' he'll say. 'Sam Bass got him! What shall I do! My horse is gone! I bet Jim Murphy told him about him! Oh! That Murphy!' " This was said with a lot of clowning and hand-wringing, and we all laughed. Sam laughed, too, and set down. "Oh, they'll give you hell for joining us, Jim. But you won't mind, will you? You've turned loose now."

"I've turned loose," I said. "We'll just rob them where we find them."

"Damn right," Sam said. "We'd just as well rob one as another now, because they're all after us."

So that night we rode down to Denton and stole Bill Mounts's horse, and then on east toward the Elm bottoms. As we rode along next morning Sam talked a blue streak about the Rangers, saying he'd made a mistake by running from them, and bragging about all the killing he was going to do if he run into them again. "Yeah, boys, we're going to quit this running," he said. "We're shut of old Henry, and I hope we stay shut of him. That old man just couldn't stand the racket, and I don't want no man with me that can't stand the racket. If I'd never ran from nobody, they never would've been so hot after me as they've been, and I ain't going to let that happen no more."

Jackson and Barnes didn't answer a word, and neither did I. Sam didn't seem to be talking to us, anyways. I think he would've did the same thing if he'd been by hisself. And it was hotter than blazes. The sun was bright and the air still and the prairie steaming. We sweated through our shirts, and sweat was rolling down my face and dripping onto my saddle. It wasn't weather for talking, or riding, neither. Late in the afternoon it clouded over and got cooler, and I knowed the weather was going to break. "We better be looking for a place to stop," I said, but Sam said, "No, let's push on." When darkness fell it started raining like the clouds had just been waiting for the sun to go down. It was dark as the inside of a hat, and we was in the middle of a big pasture and couldn't see nothing, and soon we was lost. We just wandered around with the rain hitting us in the face, and we could've been going in circles for all I knowed. But after a while we seen a farm house with a light in the window, and Sam dropped back beside me.

"Jim, ride up and tell them we're looking for a pair of stolen mules and a big, fine horse. Tell them we're June Peak's Rangers, and you live in Wise County, and your name is Paine. Tell them you met up with Peak and got three of his boys to come with you to help arrest the thieves."

I didn't see no need for such a complicated tale, but I rode up and knocked on the door, and when the old man answered it, I told the story the best I could. The old man invited us in, and his woman fixed us a good supper. After we ate, while we was still setting around the table, the farmer started talking about Sam Bass. "I heared the railroads beat him out of a big pile of money, and that's why he robs them trains," the farmer said.

"I don't know nothing about the man," Sam said. "Old June Peak had me out on a couple of raids after him, but I don't know nothing about him. There must be *something* good about him, though. He's got a lot of friends."

The old farmer filled his pipe and lit it and said, "Well, I think a heap of him myself, even though I've never seen him. He never done no harm to decent folks, and far as I'm concerned, he can rob them railroads all he wants to. More power to him."

That tickled Sam, and the next morning when we was riding away, he said, "Well, it wouldn't take much to make that old man solid with me. There's still some good people left."

Later than morning the horse we'd stole from Bill Mounts throwed a shoe, and we stopped at the village of Frankfort to have him shod. We left the horses at the smith's and stepped across the road to the store, and Sam bought some candy. We was setting in the store eating it, and this towheaded farm boy come in with a sack of peaches. He was about ten years old. He went up to the clerk and tried to trade him his peaches for some candy. The clerk wouldn't trade, and the kid got mad. "I worked hard all year and made nothing!" he hollered. "I got a notion to go find Sam Bass and rob some trains! I ain't making nothing farming!"

We all laughed at that, and the clerk did, too. The kid looked our way and seen we was eating candy, so he come over and said to Sam, "Stranger, if you'll give me some candy, I'll give you some peaches."

"How many peaches you got?" Sam asked.

"A dozen." The boy reached into the sack and pulled one out. It was a big, golden, juicy one.

"Well, that looks like a fine peach," Sam said. "Will you trade us the whole sack for the candy we got left?"

"You bet!" the boy said. So they made the trade, and the boy left happy.

We asked the store clerk and the smith if they'd seen anybody driving a pair of fine mules and a fine horse, but of course they ain't. We rode off and stopped about two miles out of town to fix our dinner. "What do you reckon that boy would've did if I'd told him I was Sam Bass and showed him a couple of double-eagles?" Sam said. "I bet I could've broke his eyes off with a board. I bet he never seen twenty dollars in his whole life. That's the way it is around here. We're coming into good country now. They know what Sam Bass is about."

We rode on about three or four miles, and nobody said nothing the whole time. Then Sam said, "You boys go on ahead. I got some business. I'll meet you again a couple of miles farther on." He spurred his mare and taken off toward some trees. The rest of us looked at each other like we wondered what was up, but we didn't say nothing. Sure enough, a couple of miles down the way Sam caught up with us, and three other men was with him. Just as they was riding up, one of the strangers said, "Blast that Murphy! Sam, you ought to kill him right now!"

I thought my belly was coming right up through my mouth. Oh God, the jig's up, I thought. I turned to Jackson and said, "Frank, did you hear that?"

"Yeah, Jim," he said. "Just set easy. I won't let them hurt you." Barnes was looking at me real peculiar. The men rode up to us, and fell in with us. Sam didn't make no introductions. While we was riding along one of the strangers said, "People around here say they expect June Peak to show up any time now."

"Yes, we're going to have hell," Sam said, real angry.

A little farther one, the stranger said, "Well, we'll be leaving you now. Keep your eyes open and watch each other." Then him and his friends turned and rode away.

"Who was that?" Jackson asked.

"Henry Collins," Sam said. "Joel's brother."

We continued some ways, still not saying nothing, but there was something in the air. Barnes had dropped back behind the rest of us. Every time we would slow down, he would, too, always keeping just a few yards behind us. Then we come to a place where the road went through a grove of big live oaks, and when we got into their shade Barnes stopped and pulled his gun and pointed it at me. "Sam!" he said.

Sam hadn't been watching Barnes like I had, and he looked surprised. Jackson did, too, and put his hand on his own gun, but didn't pull it.

"Sam, did Joel's brother ever tell you a lie?" Barnes asked.

"Not that I know of."

"Well, I think we ought to kill this son of a bitch right now." Barnes waved his gun at me.

"Take it easy, Seab," Jackson said.

"The hell I will! That bastard's in cahoots with the Rangers! I've thought it all along, and now Collins comes and tells us flat out!"

"Well, if that's the case, we *will* kill him right now," Sam said. He slouched on his mare, staring at me in that Indian way he had. For the life of me, I couldn't tell if he meant it or not. But Barnes meant it. He cocked the pistol and raised his arm.

"Now wait a minute!" Jackson said. "We ain't going to kill him just like that!" He drawed his own pistol and cocked it.

"Frank, ain't it strange that Dad Egan ain't been around looking for him?" Barnes was screaming. "This son of a bitch didn't jump bail at all! Ain't it strange that we ain't seen a single posse since he tied in with us?"

I considered going for my gun, but Barnes had such a drop on me I knowed I wouldn't stand a chance. I stayed still. Jackson glanced at me like he wasn't sure Barnes wasn't making sense.

"Can I have a say before you bust my hide?" I asked.

Jackson looked relieved. "Yeah. We owe you that."

I taken a deep breath and said, "Well, boys, I know it looks bad, but it ain't what you're thinking. Seab's partly right. I *did* make a deal with Major Jones, but it was just to get me and Daddy out of jail. I never had the slightest notion of really doing it. You boys got me in this trouble, you know. But you wasn't doing nothing to get me out of it. And I fallen on this plan to give Major Jones the grand slip. I'm free now, and I'm a hundred per cent with you boys. And I reckon if you'll think on it a while you won't kill me."

They didn't say nothing for the longest time. Sam just slumped there holding his reins. Jackson and Barnes, still holding their guns, didn't move a muscle. It was so still I could hear a mockingbird in one of the oaks. Finally Jackson said, "Jim, I would've done the same thing myself."

"No!" Barnes screamed. "It's too goddamned thin! How does it sound to you, Eph?"

Sam pushed his hat back and scratched his head. "I don't know how to fix that up under my hair. What do you say, Frank?"

"You and me have knowed Jim a long time," he said. "Sometimes he's been the only friend we had. I just don't think he'd give us away."

"I think he would!" Barnes said. "And we'd best kill him while we've got the chance!"

Sam looked me straight in the eye and said, "All right, he goes."

Jackson aimed his gun at Barnes's chest. "Well, he *don't* go. You ain't killing Jim without killing me, too. We talked him into leaving his home and coming with us, and I'll be damned if I'll let you kill him. He's been like a brother to me, and we mustn't hurt him."

"Well, I don't trust my brother no more," Barnes said.

"He's been a brother to all of us," Jackson said.

"Hell! Hell! Blast the brother!" Sam was in a rage like I'd never seen. "I *got* no brothers! I don't *need* no brothers! They're just brothers for my money!"

Jackson said quietly, "*I'm* your brother, Eph."

There was a spot of spit at the corner of Sam's mouth. He wiped it away. "Yeah, Frank, you're my brother," he said. He looked down and didn't say nothing for a long time, like he was studying his saddle horn. Then he looked at Jackson. "If you say Jim's all right, then he's all right with me, too." He turned and started down the road.

Barnes cussed and uncocked his gun and rode to catch him. Jackson stayed beside me like he was protecting me. In a few minutes we rode into a dark bottom, and I become alarmed. I thought Sam and Barnes might turn around and shoot me. Jackson must've noticed my fear, for he said, "Don't worry. I won't let them hurt you." Then he said, "But it *was* nearly hell, wasn't it?" He leaned to me and whispered, "If you ever *do* lay a plan to catch anybody, you'll have some place for me to get out, I know."

I didn't know whether he meant it or was trying to trick me. I said, "I don't want to catch any of you."

"Of course not," he said.

We traveled into the dismalest swamp I ever seen and was too busy looking out for snakes and bogs and fighting off the mosquitos to worry much about the fate of Sam Bass, or Jim Murphy, either. I don't know why Sam led us into such a place. The thickets and vines was thicker than in the bottoms around Denton, and the ground was so wet and soft our horses tired quick, fighting their way over it. Sometimes we was in black water up to our stirrups, and cattails and long, sharp-bladed grass growed all around. We couldn't see nothing ahead but more of the same, and I was afraid a water moccasin was going to take a nip at one of the horses, then we *would* be in a fix. It was the evilest place I ever seen. We was still in it when darkness fell, and we stayed in it so long I figured Sam must be lost.

Sometime after midnight we rose up on high ground again and stopped. I was bone tired and didn't get a wink of sleep. I laid there slapping at the mosquitos and thinking back on the day. It's a terrible thing not to be trusted. It was the first time I could remember *not* being trusted, and the showdown on the road filled my mind with fear. I thought of Daddy in his bed in Denton County and could hear him coughing, and I dearly wished I was with him. I cussed the day I met Sam Bass and swore to Almighty God that if I lived to get out of the mess I was in I'd live an upright and decent life and choose my friends with more care. I wished I could fulfill my bargain with Major Jones and begin that new life right now. But till Sam give me some idea where we was going and what we was going to do, I had no message for June Peak or Dad Egan and no way to send one. I was stuck. Maybe

Sam had a plan that everybody knowed but me, but I doubted it. We seemed to be wandering without no aim at all, and I couldn't believe there was a point or purpose to the hours we'd spent in that swamp. I knowed we was somewheres east of Dallas, and that was all I knowed. We was leaving Sam's old stomping grounds and headed God knows where, while the Rangers and Dad Egan's men was camped miles and miles away. At times that night I wished I was dead, but the memory of Seab Barnes's pistol aimed at me always drove that thought away.

The others must've had an easier night than me, for they was in fine fettle when we got up. Barnes was quiet and still sullen from our set-to the day before, but Sam and Jackson laughed and joked as we saddled up. "Well, boys, it's time to go down the country a ways and cash in these old pistols of ours and get us a good roll of greenbacks," Sam said. "Seab, how much you reckon your old pistol will draw?"

"I don't know," Barnes muttered. "About ten thousand, I guess."

"Hell! I want at least twenty thousand for mine," Sam said.

And Jackson said, "Well, if you scrubs can get that much, I figure Jim and me can draw at least fifty thousand apiece, because we're the best looking. The old banker won't be afraid to trust us."

Sam laughed. "What do you reckon that old banker will say when we tell him we want to cash in these old pistols?"

"Don't know," Jackson said. "What will he say?"

"Well, when I drop mine up to his ear, he'll throw his old top to one side and wall his eyes like a dying calf, and he'll say, 'Well, here's the boys! They want a little money! The damn old express company can't furnish enough for them, and I guess I'll have to give them some.' "

That convinced me all over again that Sam *did* have some plan in mind, so as I rode alongside Jackson all day I tried in roundabout ways to find out what it was. But either there wasn't no plan or Jackson was cagey enough to figure what I was up to, for he told me nothing. It was a spooky day. Sam always rode just ahead of us by hisself, and Barnes rode always behind Jackson and me. I glanced over my shoulder at him from time to time, and he was always looking straight at me. I knowed he was watching every move I made and listening to every word I said. I knowed he was looking for an excuse to kill me, and if he found one maybe he'd shoot first this time and consult with Sam and Jackson later.

We pushed on toward Rockwall, and when we sighted the town Sam sent Barnes ahead to buy some canned fruit and eggs and canned salmon and a bottle of whiskey. "We're cutting south from here," he told him, "so just ride south when you get the goods, and you'll find us. We'll camp early, so it won't take long."

I was glad to hear him mention early camp, for it was beginning to drizzle, and I knowed it would be a dark night. If we wasn't in camp by sunset we'd probably spend another night lost and wandering. We pulled off the road a couple of miles south of town and settled on the bank of a little creek. Jackson and me rushed around trying to grab enough firewood before it got too wet, and Sam was trying to get the fire going. I'd just dropped my load of wood by the fire, and Jackson was walking toward Sam and me with his own when he stopped stock still and stared and said, "Look!" He dropped his wood and pointed, and Sam and me looked. Rising out of the bushes, hard to see in the mist, was two tall beams with another beam fixed across them.

"What is it?" Sam said. We went over by Jackson and stood staring at the thing. Then Jackson walked toward it, and we followed after him. We pushed our way about forty yards through the wet bushes, and then we seen what it was. It was a gallows. I knowed that as soon as I seen the platform and the trap door hanging open like a tongue lolling out of a mouth. It was an old one. Its heavy timbers was dark, almost black in streaks where the water was running down them. But hanging from the beam that was fixed across the uprights was a brand new rope. About two foot of rope was hanging there, and the end looked like it'd been cut. Drops of water dripped from it through the open trap door. That gallows had been used, and not long ago.

We gawked at it for the longest time, not saying nothing. Sam stared at it real solemn, his mouth hanging open like the trap door. It was raining harder, and water was dripping off his hatbrim and soaking the back of his shirt. Just then, Barnes hollered, and Jackson yelled, "Over here!"

Barnes was saying something while he was coming through the bushes, but none of us was paying attention. And when he seen what we was looking at, he gawked, too. I knowed every man of us wasn't thinking on nothing but the man that had swung there, maybe only a day before, and how he felt while he swung, and what his last thought might've been. And what happened after that thought. "Don't unpack, Seab. We're getting out of here," Sam said. We pushed our way back through the bushes and packed what we'd unpacked and killed our fire. Without another word we climbed on our horses and headed south toward Terrell without another glance at that gallows. But the horrible sight stayed in my mind, and I guess it did with the others, too, for none of us said nothing at all. The rain was blowing, and lightning was cracking around us, and we didn't stop for nothing till we was three or four miles on down the way.

It was useless to try to find dry wood, and none of us seemed in a mood to eat. Barnes fetched the jug, and we set in a little circle under two blackjack trees with our blankets draped over our heads like tents, and passed the jug around. After three or four pulls on the jug I was sleepy, so I wrapped my blanket close around me and laid down where I was and put my hat over my face to keep out the rain. I heared Jackson say, "We'll be lucky if we don't all get the croup," and then I dropped right off.

I don't know how long I slept or what woke me. Maybe it was the rain when it stopped, or the voices. I heared the voices for some time, I think, before I realized what they was saying. And Barnes was saying, "It was a sign, Sam, I tell you, Murphy's a Jonah."

"It was a sign, all right," Sam answered. "I knowed soon as I seen it. But that don't mean old Jim had nothing to do with it."

"It was a warning, Sam, and if we don't do nothing about it, we'll die. It's plain as that. We *got* to kill him now."

"Yeah, you're right." I heared a click then, and knowed somebody had cocked a pistol. They say in moments like that your whole life passes in front of your eyes, but all I remember is the stink of my wet hat over my face, and I closed my eyes real tight, waiting for the bullet.

"If you kill him, you've got to kill me, too." That was Jackson. No bullet come, and nobody said nothing else. I *would* save Jackson, I thought, if I could find a way.

After breakfast Sam and Jackson rode to Terrell to look at the bank and see if it was worth our trouble. I wasn't tickled to see them go. I thought Barnes might murder me while they were gone, then make up an excuse to tell them when they returned. Also, if we was to rob the Terrell bank, I would be in trouble with Major Jones, for I hadn't had no chance to telegraph him, and he'd think I welched on our deal and joined Sam's gang in truth.

I tried to strike up talk with Barnes, thinking if I showed him I was friendly he might decide I wasn't such a bad egg after all. Of course I didn't let on that I'd heared his talk the night before. I played like everything was fine and that I was pleased to be on the scout with him. But he didn't bite. He answered with grunts, and then stopped answering at all and walked off to the horses. He curried his, the one we'd stole from Bill Mounts, and then set down on the ground and tinkered with his rigging, making some little repair or other. I knowed he was just keeping as far from me as he could, so I set down by the fire and drunk coffee and whittled on a cedar stick.

Sam and Jackson was gone a couple of hours, and come back with crackers and canned peaches and clean shirts for everybody. Jackson was wearing a new low-crown black hat. He called it a "doctor hat," and it looked good on him, wearing it the way he did, cocked over one eye. He was a handsome boy in spite of his dirty clothes and the stubble of whiskers he had, but he didn't look like no doctor. A gambler, maybe, or a whorehouse piano player. "They got a bank?" Barnes asked.

"Yeah, but it ain't much," Sam said. "We'll look for better."

Barnes asked a couple of questions about it, but Sam answered in a vague way. I figured he was still spooked by that gallows and wanted to get as far away from it as he could before practicing his trade again, and that was fine with me. So after we ate we rode off to Kaufman.

We went into camp in the early afternoon, and Sam sent Barnes and me into the town to look for a bank. I was tired of being in Barnes's company by myself because of the bad feeling he had, and as we was riding along I said, "Seab, I sure wish you wasn't so down on me. I'd like to be your friend." But he just looked the other way and said nothing.

We looked around the town, but didn't find no bank. So we put our horses up in the livery stable and went to the barbershop and got shaved, then found the biggest store in town and bought new pantaloons and coats to go with the shirts Sam and Jackson had brung us. I wrote my name on a slip of paper with a pencil I had and put the paper in the pocket of my old pantaloons and left my old clothes in a pile in the little room where I put on the new ones, hoping it would serve as a clue if the Rangers come through looking for our trail.

The man that sold us the clothes was old and shriveled and bald and white all over, except the green eyeshade and red sleeve garters he wore. He was so rickety you could knock him down with a feather. When he taken our money and went into a little room behind the counter, he left the door open, and we seen him taking our change out of a safe in there. It was a big safe, and I figured maybe that was where the town kept its money, but I didn't say nothing to Barnes. But he figured like I did, and when we got back to camp, the first thing he did was tell Sam about the safe.

"Well, I reckon we better go back and look into that," Sam said. So next morning him and Jackson and me went back to Kaufman, leaving Barnes alone at the camp. Jackson and Sam went and got a shave, then I showed them the store. The same old man was behind the counter, and he sold Sam and Jackson some new clothes, too. When he taken their money he said to me, "Wasn't you in here yesterday, young man?"

"Yessir," I said.

"Well, you left your old clothes here. Do you want them?"

"Nossir."

"I'll throw them out, then."

I knowed if the old man found the paper with my name on it,

it wouldn't mean nothing to him. So there went my clue.

The old man taken the money from Sam and Jackson and stepped into the little room. This time he opened the safe door wider, and we got a good look inside. When we left the store, Sam said, "Well, boys, there wasn't much in that safe but dust. That old man barely had enough to give us our change. Blast this country! It ain't worth a fig!"

So we set out for Ennis and camped that night between Chambers Creek and East Fork, then headed for Trinidad Crossing, where there was a ferry across the Fork. But the water was as high as it was upriver a few days earlier, and the ferryman told us his cable across the river was broke and the boat wasn't running.

"We'll just swim it, then," Sam said, and he headed his mare into the water. We swam about a third of the way across, and then the horses turned downstream. We turned them back against the current again, but they turned downstream again. The ferryman stood on the bank, laughing at us thrashing around out there and getting nowhere. "We got wet for nothing, boys," Sam said. "If Jenny says it's too strong, then it's too strong."

So we returned to shore and went looking for a grassy spot where we could lay back in the sun and dry off. We passed a farmhouse close to the road, and there was a pile of watermelons under a tree in the yard and a lot of people setting in the shade eating them. "Some party!" Jackson hollered at them.

"You bet!" said a big man I taken to be the owner of the place. "Come join us!"

"What's the celebration?" Jackson asked.

"Why, man, it's the Fourth of July!"

So we got down, and Sam introduced us around as cattlemen from Wise County.

"Wise?" the farmer said. "Ain't that up in Sam Bass country?"

"That's right."

"They caught that boy yet?"

"Not that I heared," Sam said.

The man handed us hunks of watermelon and said, "Well, he'll make another strike soon. I don't give a damn how many trains he robs, just so he lets the citizens alone."

"From what I've heared," Sam said, "I don't reckon he bothers nobody but them Yankee railroads."

We set under the trees with the farmer and several other men that I taken to be brothers and sons and talked cattle and ate watermelon. There must've been two dozen kids around the place, running races and playing tag, and a bunch of women on the porch that giggled and talked in low voices except when they was hollering at the kids. It was a pleasant afternoon. Jackson beat four of the young men in a watermelon seed spitting contest, and him and Sam laid aside their weapons and coats and rassled some of the kids, taking on three or four of them at a time. I didn't see how they could do it, having ate as much as they did, but they laughed and hollered as much as the kids. Towards sundown some of the kin loaded their younguns and wives into their wagons and taken off, but some was going to spend the night. "I ain't got no room in the house," the farmer told us, "but you're welcome to spread your blankets under the trees. It's going to be a hot night, anyhow."

We accepted, and he brought out the whiskey jug and passed it around amongst the men that was left. Before he taken his first swig he raised the jug and said, "Well, here's to the Republic. I wish to God she was the Confederacy."

We all said, "Amen!" and then drunk a while and had supper and talked cattle and politics some more. Then the farmer and the other men invited us to stay for breakfast in the morning and went inside. While we was spreading our blankets, Sam said, "I hope them kids knows someday that they was rassling with Sam Bass hisself."

The river had dropped some, and Sam and Jackson offered to help the ferryman fix his cable. They set out in a skiff and pulled the cable across the river and tied it on the other bank. Then the ferryman carried us and our horses across. "You boys has been so nice I'll just charge you half the fare," he said.

"Why, you old robber!" Sam said. "You ought to let us ride free!"

The ferryman grinned and said, "Well, son, even robbers has to make a living."

And Sam said, "You're right, old man," and he paid him.

The sun was so hot and the air so steamy it was hard to breathe, and flies was everywhere. They drove me crazy, and the horses, too. It wasn't no day for traveling. But there was a nervousness in Sam's manner. He was looking to make a strike, and looking hard. I knowed I had to get a message to the Rangers soon, for my belly told me Sam wouldn't back down from killing somebody now if he was crossed, and maybe all of us would be killed, too.

We hadn't went far when this dude on a mule come up to us at a crossroads. He was wearing a fancy brocade vest, kind of gold in color, and a black string necktie. His coat and shirt was frayed, and the vest was dirty, and his pantaloons was patched in several spots. His mule was a poor, spavined thing. The man rode bareback, and his legs hung a considerable ways toward the ground. He give us a friendly smile. "Good morning, gentlemen," he said. "Headed for Ennis?"

"Yep," Jackson said.

"So am I. Mind if I accompany you?" And he fell in beside Jackson and stuck his hand out and said, "Claudius Parker, schoolteacher."

Jackson introduced hisself as Frank Allen and give some names for the rest of us. "Where you teaching at?" he asked.

"Well, I happen to be between appointments now," Parker said in a prissy voice. "But I'll have a school by fall. That's why I'm going to Ennis."

"Does teaching pay good?" Jackson asked.

"Oh, no," Parker said. "Barely enough to keep me and Achilles alive."

"Achilles?"

"My mule, Mr. Allen. Poor beast. He's weak in more than the heel, I'm afraid."

"So you taken his name from Homer," Jackson said.

Parker looked at him in surprise. "Do you know *The Iliad*, Mr. Allen?"

"Why, yes," Jackson said kind of proud. "Matter of fact, I happen to have *The Odyssey* on me." He unbuckled a saddlebag and pulled out a little book and handed it to the teacher. Parker looked at it and made gasping noises like a woman about to faint, and him and Jackson commenced the goddamndest conversation I ever heard. They went on and on about one-eyed monsters and women that turns men into hogs and all sorts of outlandish things. I thought the sun had taken hold of them, and Sam and Barnes looked at Jackson like he was a lunatic. But Jackson and Claudius Parker didn't pay no mind. They rattled on and on, passing the book back and forth between them. Parker even started talking in tongues, and Jackson acted like it was the most natural thing in the world.

Nothing wears on you like somebody talking about something you don't understand, and finally Sam couldn't take it no more. Next time we come to a crossroads he stopped and said, "Well, Mr. Parker, we got to go down this road and look at some cows, so I guess we part company here."

Parker looked disappointed. "Oh," he said. He closed the book and handed it to Jackson. "It's been a rare pleasure, Mr. Allen. A rare pleasure."

"Same here," Jackson said.

"Well, gentlemen." Parker tipped his hat and kicked the old mule so hard that dust rose out of his hide. The broke-down old thing hustled hisself into a trot that was painful to watch, and we turned down the other road.

"Christ, Frank!" Sam said.

"There ain't nothing wrong with book-learning, Sam. And old Claudius has got plenty up under his hat."

"Yeah, plenty of slop," Sam said. Then he laughed. "I wonder what old Claudius would say if he knowed he was riding with Sam Bass."

We camped about a mile above Ennis, and Sam and me went to town to look around. We got us a fancy dinner at the hotel, then taken our ease, walking up and down the streets, looking at the stores and offices. We stopped into one of the stores and was looking at a fancy cartridge belt. "What do you think of it?" Sam asked.

"It's a fine belt," I said.

"All right, I'll buy it for you. To make up for the hard time we give you back there."

I said, "Aw, that's all right. You was just nervous."

"Well, we was wrong about you, and I feel bad about it, so take the belt. A present between friends."

So I agreed. He also bought hisself a nice pair of little saddle-pockets made out of cashmere goatskin. "Ain't they pretty?" he said. "Just right to carry money in."

We found the bank and went in, and Sam stepped up to the teller's cage and cashed a five-dollar bill. When we was back on the sidewalk he said, "There ain't no use trying that one. The bannisters is too high. We'd be killed before we could get behind them."

"Well, where now?"

"Waco," he said.

Jackson and me rode into Waco and got shaved, then went to a hotel to eat. We done these things nearly every time we come to a town now, for we was a long way from Denton County, and the boys ain't seen a posse in almost a month. They enjoyed walking around in the open and not worrying about somebody recognizing them and taking shots at them. They was having a good time being just ordinary people.

While we was eating, Jackson smiled at me and said, "Jim, are you going to betray us, or not?"

His question, coming right out of the blue, scared the hell out of me. I knowed if Jackson didn't trust me no more, I was dead. I said, "Frank, it pains me that you ask that. I thought you knowed me better. No, I ain't going to betray you. I joined up with you boys in truth."

Jackson kept on smiling. He said, "Well, I believe you, but I think you joined up with the losing side. If I was in your boots I'd go back to Tyler and throw myself on the mercy of the court. You got a family and you got land and you got money, and you ain't done no robberies yet. Even if you was to spend some time in jail you'd be better off than us. We're going to get killed. I know that."

"How do you know?"

"I've knowed it since Salt Creek," he said. "When I seen how many Rangers was against us and I seen Arkansas fall, I knowed that's what's going to happen to all of us. It's that or the rope anyhow, and my preference is Arkansas's way. I wish I was you. I'd be riding for Tyler now."

"Well, I'll think on it," I said.

"You're running out of thinking time. We're going to do

something soon. We got to, because we're just about broke. We might do it right here in Waco, and if we do, then the law's going to be on us again. And once them Rangers comes after us, you're sunk with the rest of us."

I said, "Why don't you get out, too?"

His smile turned kind of sad. "I got no place to go that's better than where I am. I've went too far to turn back now, and Eph and me . . . Well, we've been through too much to split now. I wouldn't know what to do without the little son of a bitch, and he wouldn't be nothing without me." He looked at the white china dishes on the table and the crystal lamp hanging from the ceiling and said, "This is putting on a heap of style for highwaymen, ain't it?"

"It's getting up a little," I replied, and I knowed we was through talking about anything that mattered. I felt lower than a snake's belly. Being trusted by Jackson made me feel worse than *not* being trusted by Sam and Barnes, and it was hard to look him in the eye during the rest of the meal. I was glad when he pulled out that tinkling watch of his and said, "Well, it's time we done our duty."

We strolled around Waco real casual. It was the biggest town we'd been in during our travels, and it was pure pleasure seeing the pretty, well-dressed women and several fine horses and carriages mingled in amongst the farmers and the mule wagons. We found out there was three banks, and Jackson decided he'd check them all before we returned to camp. He'd go in and change a bill and look the place over while I waited on the sidewalk. I kept trying to think of a way to get away from him and send a telegram to Major Jones, but I couldn't think of no way without Jackson asking questions and getting suspicious. I didn't have nothing to tell the major nohow, except where we was. We still didn't have no plan.

When Jackson come out of the third bank, the Savings Bank, he was excited. "If we mean business, this is the place to commence," he said. "They got piles of greenbacks and gold just laying on a big table in there, and the bannister's low. We can get it easy as pie."

"I don't know," I said. "All these banks is in the middle of town, and we'd have a lot of town to ride through to make our getaway. We'd have plenty of chances to get ourselves killed."

"I don't think there'll be no trouble," he said. "We'll map us a getaway ahead of time."

His enthusiasm scared me. If Sam decided to tap a bank in Waco, the deed would be did before I could get a message off, and certainly before the Rangers could get to us. And I knowed if Jackson was in favor of the idea, Sam probably would be, too. On the way back to camp I tried to persuade Jackson that Waco was too dangerous. He listened polite, but just said, "We'll let Eph decide."

He give Sam a real excited report, and Sam's eyes lit up when he heared about the piles of money in the Savings Bank. But I tried again. "Frank's too excited over what he seen there," I said. "We'd have a devil of a time getting out of that town. Maybe you better go up and have a look yourself."

Next morning Sam and Jackson went to town, and I was stuck in camp with Barnes looking daggers at me. Sam come back as excited as Jackson. "Boys, we've struck gold if we work it right," he said.

He sent Jackson and me back to buy coffee and bread. While he was busy with that, I sneaked to the post office and bought some paper and envelopes and stamps and stuck them in my pocket. Later, as we rode through the streets, I pointed out all the danger spots I could find, places where our run could be cut off, places where we would be exposed to fire.

Jackson didn't buy none of it. "Hell, Jim," he said, "we'll take that bank easy as a drink of water. If you're sticking with us, you got to know there's a mite of danger in our business. But we'll scare this town so bad they won't know what's up till we've took the money and gone." I didn't say nothing, and Jackson said, "If you're going to strike for Tyler, now's the time. It might be your last chance."

I wondered what would happen if I was to turn and start. Would he just watch me go? Would he shoot me in the back like Barnes would? I wasn't about to try, and I made no answer.

When I started to tell Sam about the dangers in the town, he interrupted me. "Hell, Jim! We can take that bank easy. Hell! Don't get scared. I'll get you some easy money in a few days, as soon as little Jenny rests up for the run."

There wasn't no use talking anymore, so I shut up and got very serious, staring into the fire. "Jim, hold your head up," Sam told me. "Keep in good spirits. Old Eph's going to get you some money."

Sam and Jackson and Barnes was in good spirits, all right, and we had a deal to drink. They was still laughing and carrying on when we rolled into our blankets.

So you could've knocked me over with a feather the next morning at breakfast. Sam turned to me and said, "Well, Jim, if you think there's too much danger in Waco, we won't hit it. We'll go wherever you say."

Jackson and Barnes went on eating, so I knowed they already knowed, and I become suspicious. Why had they changed their minds? But I said, "Well, I'm glad, boys. I was afraid you all would be hard-headed and run us into danger and get us killed. So we'll go down to Round Rock and pull the Williamson County Bank."

They agreed to that, and we rode out to get on the road south to Round Rock. The day was hotter than hell, and as we was riding through Waco Sam said, "Let's get us a cold beer while we got the chance." So we stopped at the Ranch Saloon and had several. When we was ready to leave, Sam taken out a double-eagle and dropped it on the table. The bartender heared it and come and taken it, and Sam watched him walk away. "Well, boys, there goes the last piece of '77 gold I had," he said. "It ain't done me the least bit of good. But let it gush. It all goes in a lifetime."

"You going to fool around and miss that boat?" Jackson said.

"Don't you worry," Sam said. "I'll have me some more gold in a few days."

"What boat?" I asked. I was jumpy, I guess. I feared maybe the Round Rock plan was just a trick and we was heading on down to Galveston.

"Sam's taking to the water," Jackson said. "He's even got hisself a captain's lady waiting."

Sam raised his glass. "Maude," he said. "It ain't going to be long now."

The bartender come back with his change, and he started to get up. "Wait," I said. "Tell me about the boat."

"It ain't nothing," he said. "Just a little joke that Frank and me has."

We camped that night on a high hill near Belton. Next morning Sam chose me to go into town with him to check for banks, in case we might be interested. "I got to shit first," I said, and I walked off among some bushes some ways from camp and dropped my pantaloons and hunkered down like I was taking a shit. I pulled out my pencil and the paper I'd bought in Waco and wrote two letters, both the same, to Dad Egan in Denton and Major Jones in Austin.

SB on way to Round Rock to rob bank. For God sake come quick.

I signed them "J. W. Murphy," then wondered if they would know who "SB" was. Then I thought, hell, who else would they think I'd write about? I knowed Major Jones would have the best chance to get to Round Rock, since the town is only about twenty miles from Austin, and Dad Egan probably wouldn't have no chance at all. But if Sam wasn't caught and the law decided to haul me to court, I wanted Dad to testify that I'd did my best. I stuck the stamps on the letters and folded them and put them in my pocket. Sam was mounted and ready when I come out of the bushes.

Belton wasn't much of a town, and I knowed it wouldn't take long to find out whether there was a bank or not, and I had to figure a way to get to the post office, so I said, "Sam, if this burg has a bank it's probably in the back of some store. Why don't you take one side of the street, and I'll take the other?"

He agreed, and I went into the first store I come to and asked where the post office was. The man told me it was way down at the other end of the street, on my side. I walked as fast as I could without seeming to hurry, for I seen Sam some distance ahead of me on his side. My heart was going thumpity-thump the whole way, for I knowed if Sam seen me sticking them letters in the slot, I was gone. I found the store where the post office was, way back in the back of the building. When I come in the door, I almost run to the back. An old man was standing in the post office window with a newspaper spread out in front of him. The mail slot was right under the window. I'd just dropped my letters into the slot when Sam come in. "What the hell you doing?" he asked.

"I was trying to buy this man's newspaper," I said.

The old man must've thought I was talking to him, for he said, "Eh? I won't sell it, but I'll let you borrow part of it."

"You want to hear some of the news?" I asked Sam.

"No. Let's get moving."

My belly was going flippity-flop, but I done my best to be calm, and when we was on the sidewalk I asked, "Did you find a bank?"

"Yeah, but it's a pitiful little thing. We'll wait for Round Rock."

So we moved south to Georgetown and rested a day, then moved on to Round Rock. We come in by the San Saba road and made camp in a cedar brake not far from town. We could see the whole town from there, and Sam said, "I been through here with Joel, but it sure has growed since then. A whole new town's coming up there in the east."

"It's the railroad," I said. "The railroad missed the town, so they're building over there now."

Sam laughed. "God bless the railroads. They're good to everybody, ain't they?"

Sam and Jackson went off to find the bank, and Barnes and me went to Mays and Black's store in the old part of town and bought some horse feed. Sam and Jackson got back before we did, and they was sitting on their blankets drinking a jug of whiskey when we come with the feed. Sam rushed up and shook my hand. "Damn it, Jim, you was right about coming to this place," he said. "We can take that bank too easy to talk about."

"Didn't I tell you?" I said.

"You did, you old son of a bitch. You got the makings of a real highwayman."

We drunk the rest of the jug that night, and everybody was in good spirits. Next morning Barnes said he wanted to look at that bank, too, so I offered to go with him, just to show I wasn't worried about him. We rode in and got a shave, then walked over to the Williamson County Bank. It was a busy one, and they had more greenbacks in sight than a tree has leaves. Barnes cashed a bill at the window, and when we was walking to get our horses he said, "I wish we had fresh horses. We could take that bank this evening."

"I do, too," I said. "But if we go to stealing horses now, the law will get on us before we get mounted. The best thing to do is stay here four or five days and let our horses rest and play like we're wanting to buy cattle."

"Yeah, that's the right idea," he said.

Sam and Jackson had their plan already set. As soon as we dismounted, Sam stood up and said, "Well, she goes about half-past three o'clock Saturday evening. And here's the way we'll do it. Seab and me will walk in first. Seab will throw down a five-dollar bill and tell the banker he wants silver for it. While he's getting his change, I'll come in and throw my pistol on the banker and tell him to get his hands up. Seab will jump over the counter, and Jim and Frank will show up at the door and get the drop on whoever comes in after us. Anybody got questions?"

"No," Barnes said, "but I got something I want to say in front of everybody." He come over to my side of the fire. "Boys, I want you to know I think Jim's all right. I'm glad Frank kept us from killing him. He's the man we need. But blast him, I just couldn't fix him all right before. I'm proud to say now that he's my friend." He shook my hand.

"I'm *your* friend, too," I said.

Mary Matson

I sees him way up aside the hill. I can't tell nothing about him, he's so far off. Just this man and this hoss coming down the hill out of the cedars, that's all I knows. But he gets down off the hill and comes into the road, and I sees the hoss is a sorrel, the way the sun shines off him, and the man, I think he's old, he slump in the saddle so. I's walking in the road, toting a batch of laundry on my shoulder, going home, and the man, he's riding at me on that sorrel. When he gets close I sees he ain't old, he just slump that way. He's got dust all over his clothes, like he travels far. He rides on past me and smiles at me, and I smiles back. Then he turns that hoss and comes back and stops him in front of me so I got to stop, too.

"What's your name?" he says.

"Mary. Mary Matson."

"You sure is pretty, Mary," he says. "Where you live?"

I points to my house on the edge of the colored town, and he says, "The one with the oaks back behind?"

"Yessuh," I says. "That's the one."

"Who lives with you?" he says.

"Nobody."

"Ain't got no daddy or mama?"

"Nawsuh. They's dead."

"Ain't got no man?"

"Nawsuh. None that lives with me."

"What you carrying?"

"Laundry. That's what I does."

All this time he leans on his saddle horn, smiling down at me, and I's smiling back at him. Pretty smile and pretty man, I's thinking. Dark. Got some Injun or colored blood in him. Easy to talk to. I don't mind.

"How old is you?" he says.

"Sixteen. Seventeen. Don't know for sure."

"How come you live by yourself?"

"Daddy, he die."

The hoss, he sneezes and shakes his head, but the man don't pay no mind. "I's wanting to stay here a few days," he says. "I's looking for a place to live."

I points my thumb over my shoulder, down the road. "White folks lives down there. They got a hotel down there."

"Don't want to live down there," he says. "I wants to live here."

"Ain't no place here," I says. "Just colored houses."

"You got a house. Why don't I stay there? Pay you fifty cents a day and give you more when I leaves."

"I just got one bed," I says.

He smiles real big then. "That's fine with me."

I giggles and don't say nothing.

"Come on," he says. "It's all right, ain't it?"

"I don't mind."

Then he says, "Oh, I got three men with me."

"Lord, I can't put up no *four* men!" I says.

"You can cook for four men, can't you? Biscuits and greens and things?"

"Sure, but I can't take them in the house."

"They can sleep in the trees back behind. That's all right, ain't it?"

"I don't mind."

"We'll come around dark, then."

He turns the hoss, but I says, "Hey, mistuh, you got a name?"

"Yeah," he says. "It's Samuel."

Samuel gives me a wave and lopes that red hoss back up the road. Pretty hoss, pretty man, I's thinking.

After dark I hears them riding past the house and into the trees. In a while I hears them walking back, talking low, their spurs jangling. They knocks on the door, and I opens, and Samuel's standing there, still smiling. "Supper ready, Mary?" he asks.

"Yeah," I says, and they comes in. One of them, a big, redheaded man, he sniffs and says, "Nigger house, all right." The other two don't say nothing. One of them's small and dark like

Samuel, but heavier. I figures he's maybe Samuel's brother. The other one's tall and skinny. He's got yellow curls all over his head, and he smiles like Samuel, but I knows he ain't nobody's brother.

They sits at the table, and I dishes up the food for them. They don't talk much while they eats. Mostly about the food, and they likes it. But I can tell Samuel's the boss, and they shows respect for the curly-headed kid, too. The other dark one just looks at his plate and don't say much at all. The big redhead moves his eyes around the room all the time and looks at the others' faces a lot. There's something about them eyes. They looks scared. Maybe they don't like looking at a nigger house.

After they eats, all of them rolls cigarettes, and they smokes and puts the ashes in their plates. They don't say nothing while they's smoking, but when they finishes, Samuel says, "Let's go outside," and they goes.

I cleans up the dishes and puts my irons on the stove and gets to work. I been ironing for a long time when I hears the spurs and the door opens and Samuel comes in. He walks right over behind me and puts his arms around my waist and kisses me aside my neck. I don't move, and he says, "Kiss me, Mary." So I puts down my iron and turns around and puts my arms around his neck and kisses him. Then he pulls me close and kisses me again, real hard. "Come to bed, Mary," he says, and I don't mind. My innards is saying I wants him.

He turns back the sheet and sits down aside the bed and pulls off his boots while I's putting my laundry in the basket. He strips down naked and lays back on the bed and sighs. I's looking at him out the corner of my eye while I's working, and I sees he's whiter than I thought, and that scares me. I starts slowing down my work, but he says, "Come on, Mary," so I takes off my head rag and lays it on the ironing board and goes to blow out the lamp. "Don't," he says. "Not yet." So I leaves the lamp alone and starts undressing. He watches me, and when I's naked I starts for the lamp again, but he says, "Not yet. Just stand there a minute." So I stands there in the middle of the floor, and he looks and looks at me. "Turn around, Mary," he says, so I turns around, and when I's turned all the way around, he smiles. "Blow it out," he says.

I crawls into bed, and he puts his arms around me and holds me tight. His hands touches me all over, and I likes it, and I pushes myself as close against him as I can. He kisses me on the mouth and aside the neck and on the titty, and it feels good. I ain't never felt so. Then he climbs on me and has his way, and pretty soon he's got me moaning.

When we's finished, he rolls over and says, "You like that, Mary?"

"Oh, yeah, I likes that."

"You ever did it with a white man before?"

"No. But my mama did, back in slave days. She tell me white men is mean."

"You think that, why you doing it with me?"

"I figure you for part colored. Or Injun. You ain't all white."

He laughs at that. "Injun, maybe, but no colored," he says. "I's a Yankee. They don't do it with coloreds up there."

"Where a Yankee?"

"Indiana."

"Mistuh Lincoln's state?"

"No. Next door to it."

"You in his army?"

"No, but my brother was. He got killed."

"I was borned in the war, while all the white men was away. My daddy told me. He was slave. Mama, too."

"You want to do it again?"

"Yes," I says. And we does it again, and another time after that. By the time Samuel goes to sleep, my bed's smelling of our juices and sweat, but I don't mind. I likes the smell.

I don't go to sleep when Samuel does. I's laying on my back, looking at that ceiling, pleasuring in the sweet, lazy, wore-out feeling that Samuel give me and listening to his breathing. After while, though, he starts talking. I thinks he's talking to me, but I can't hear what he's saying, so I says, "What, Samuel?" He maybe can hear me, because he talks again, like he's talking to me, but I can tell now he's still asleep. The only word I understands is "hoss." So I just turns over and goes to sleep myself.

At daylight the birds wakes me up, and I gets out of bed and makes coffee and brings him a cup. He's awake, and he smiles while he watches me bring it to him. I sits aside the bed and drinks my coffee with him, and when he finishes he takes my cup out of my hand, too, and sets them on the floor. He grabs my arm and pulls me down on the bed with him.

"Your friends will be wanting breakfast," I says.

"Let them wait," he says.

"You sure is a needful man," I says.

For the next three days a couple of them would saddle up their hosses and ride down toward the new town from time to time. Sometimes it would be Samuel and the goldheaded kid, sometimes the scared-looking redhead and the other dark man. They'd stay maybe an hour and then show up again and unsaddle the hosses and tie them in the grass down by Brushy Creek. That's all they does. Rest of the time, they just lays around under the trees back there till I comes and tells them their vittles is ready. They comes to the house to eat, but don't say hardly nothing at the table. And sometime after dark, Samuel comes in and makes me stop my ironing and takes me to bed.

One day, a Thursday it is, I's walking down to the trees at noon to tell them dinner's fixed. I hears them talking, but I don't think nothing of it. Then I hears Samuel say, "I tell you, they was Rangers! They was dressed like cowboys, but I *knowed* they was Rangers!"

"Sam, you's just jumpy," the big redhead says. "You's seeing things that ain't there."

I guess they hears me coming then, because they don't say nothing else.

That night while we's in bed I says to Samuel, "What business you in?"

"Mules," he says. "Government mules."

"What you do with mules?" I says.

"I buys and sells them," he says. "I goes around the country looking for good mules, and when I finds one, I buys him and sells him to the Army. The Army needs lots of mules."

"And what does them other men do?" I says.

"Why, they helps me with the mules," he says. "Ain't no man can handle all them mules by hisself. Mules is hard."

"How long you going to stay here?" I says.

"Saturday," he says. "We's leaving Saturday."

I's grieved to hear that. I likes Samuel, and I's getting used to having him in my bed. But I don't say nothing. Then Samuel, he gets fidgety. Real jumpy, just like the redhead said. And I says, "Samuel, why you acting this way?" And he says, "I don't know, Mary."

Well, next morning that pretty goldhead and the redhead saddles up right after breakfast and heads down to the new town.

The other little dark one stays down in the trees with the hosses, and Samuel hangs around the house all morning, watching me iron and looking out the window at the graveyard, up towards the hill. The goldhead and the redhead gets back about time for dinner, and Samuel goes to the door. He's standing in the door, and the redhead comes up to him and says, "We didn't see no Rangers down there," and Samuel says, "Hush."

After dinner Samuel goes down to the trees with the others, and I don't see nothing of him for three or four hours. Then I sees all four of them leading their hosses past the window. The door's open, it's so hot, and in front Samuel hands the reins of his red hoss over to the goldheaded kid and comes in.

"Mary, I wants you to have this," he says, and he gives me a ten-dollar bill.

"You leaving?" I says.

"No, we's just going down to the town for a few supplies," he says. "I'll be back."

"Why you giving me this money, then?" I says.

"Well, I just wants you to have it," he says. And he kisses me aside the neck and goes out and climbs on that red hoss.

Frank Jackson

Everyone in the niggertown had taken to the shade. It was so quiet I could hear dogs scratching themselves under the shanty porches and flies buzzing in the dusty bushes beside the road. Heat climbing from the road made the way ahead of us wavy and bright, painful to the eyes. Slow nigger voices drifted through the open doors of the houses. The voices and the creak of our saddles and the soft thud of our horses' hooves in the dust all seemed separate and distinct and loud. I was sweating under my coat and wished I could take it off without revealing my pistol.

The new town was as dead as the old. Sun reflected white off the stone of the new buildings and the street. A team of mules stood hipshot in their traces, heads bowed, while a boy unloaded fodder at the livery stable. The boy stood up in the wagon bed and watched us for a moment, then bent to his work again. A man in black stepped into the barbershop down the street. A few horses stood at the hitching rails in front of the stores and offices, all hipshot, all dozing. A wagon loaded with lumber and a cookstove and a spool of fence wire was in front of the hardware store, and a boy, about ten, I guess, overalled and barefooted, stood beside it holding the lines, a piece of candy sticking out of his mouth like a cigar.

"Sam," Jim said. "Why don't I go back to the old town and check for Rangers there? I'll meet you after you buy the supplies."

"All right," Sam said, and Jim turned his horse and trotted back the way we had come.

We turned left a block and tied our horses in an alley on the north side of the business district. We walked through the narrow space between two buildings, blinking in the shade, then stepped into the main street, blinded again by the sun. We walked abreast down the street for a block, then turned to cross to Henry Koppel's store on the opposite corner. Sam's hand brushed his coat back, revealing the butts of his pistols. He pulled the coat closed and buttoned one button. The boy in front of the hardware store wrapped his lines around the brake lever and went inside.

Koppel's clerk was alone, sitting on a box behind the counter, fanning himself with a newspaper. He got up when we came through the door. "Hot enough for you?" he asked.

"Hot enough," Sam said.

"What can I do for you?"

"Well, we need some things," Sam said, placing his hands on the counter. "Let's start with the tobacco."

"Smoking or chewing?"

"Smoking. About eight sacks, I guess."

As the clerk turned to get the tobacco down from a shelf, two more men came in. One leaned against the wall beside the door and stuck his hands in his pockets. He started whistling. The other walked to the counter where we were, smiling. He nodded at Sam and put his hands on the counter, too. Then his right hand moved and touched Sam's coat. "Don't you have a pistol on you?" he asked.

"*Yes!*" Sam cried, and he went for his gun. Seab and I did, too, and suddenly we were firing.

"Don't, boys! Hold up, boys!" the man screamed. He stumbled backward, clawing at his coat, trying to get to a gun, I guess. Then he fell, his coat open, his white shirt bloody.

Now the man by the door had a gun in his hand, and we fired. We fired and fired. All sound was lost to me in the roar. My nose itched with the stink of gunpowder. The room was so full of the smoke of our firing that I couldn't see the man by the door. I ran through the fog toward the daylight and bumped into Sam. He was running, too. The man who had stood by the door was on the floor now. He fired at us again, and I fired at him.

Sam and I reached the sidewalk, gasping. Sam's right hand was dangling at his side, dripping blood. Several fingers seemed to be missing. Then Seab dashed through the door, too, and the man who had been on the floor by the door stood up and fired a shot after him.

The street was full of men, all firing. Three knelt on the sidewalk behind us as we ran, firing and firing. The man in black ran out of the barbershop and fired. A one-armed man stood in front of Koppel's store now, firing as we ran down the block toward the hardware store. A big man, a badge glinting on his chest, stepped around the corner in front of us and fired. I fired back at him, and he ducked around the corner again. The boy was holding the lines at the lumber-loaded wagon again. The horses were rearing and pulling in their traces, and the boy was scared, but he held onto the lines. A man ran out of the store and grabbed the lines and climbed to the wagon and stood there pulling on the lines, shouting something, and the boy ran into the store.

We bent low and ran into the street, trying to cross to our horses. Bullets raised puffs of dust all around us, and we fired back at nothing in particular. We made it to the shady passage between the buildings and ran on to the alley, and turned toward our horses. Someone fired a single shot at us from the back of one of the stores, and someone at the livery stable fired several rifle shots, then stopped. I saw his face above the stable fence, looking at his rifle. It was jammed or empty, I guess. Seab fired at him, and he ran away.

We had almost reached the horses when Sam screamed, "*God!*" and I knew he was hit again. I turned and saw a tall man silhouetted against the bright street at the end of the alley. I fired at him, and he ducked behind the building. Sam was falling. I grabbed him under the arms and pulled him toward the horses. Seab was untying his horse when he fell, his face gone, like Arkansas's. He sprawled in the dust, his arms and legs spread like a star.

I held Sam up with one arm and untied his mare. The man at the end of the alley, the one who killed Seab, I guess, was on his knee, aiming. He fired but missed us. I ignored him and lifted Sam to Jenny's back and wrapped the fingers of his good hand around the reins. His coat and shirt were bloody. I untied and mounted my own horse, then grabbed Sam's arm and held it to keep him from falling. "Can you ride?" I shouted, and I thought he nodded. I swatted Jenny on the haunch and held onto Sam's arm while we rode toward the end of the alley. The man at the other end was firing. A bullet sang off the stone of the building beside us, but we made it to the street, and I turned us right, toward Brushy Creek. I let go of Sam's arm, but he started weaving, so I grabbed him again.

I urged the horses across the creek, then turned them into a lane toward the niggertown. I looked behind me, but saw nobody after us yet. A couple of houses down the lane, a little girl was hanging head down from a low branch of a tree in her front yard, swinging by her knees. "Get in the house!" I shouted. "Get in the house, little girl!" She swung up, then dropped to the ground and stared wide-eyed. "You'll be killed!" I shouted, and she turned and ran.

Soon we were in the old town, among the nigger shanties. I looked behind me, but no one was coming. As we passed the Mays and Black store I noticed several men lounging on feed sacks on the porch. I thought one was Jim, but when I looked again he was gone. I was punching cartridges into the cylinder of my pistol, and Sam was trying to do the same, but he couldn't with his crippled hand, and he kept dropping the cartridges on the ground. I took his pistol and loaded it and handed it back and noticed he was very pale. I grabbed his arm again. Our horses were moving at a trot now, and it was hard to hold him, and the jarring gait wrinkled his face with pain. I spurred my horse into a slow, gentle gallop, and Jenny adjusted her gait to his.

I took the road toward the graveyard, and when we got to the house of the woman Mary, I started to turn in, but Sam said, "No, don't stop here."

"Our rifles are here," I said.

"Don't stop here," he said, so I didn't. The woman Mary came to her door with a basket of laundry on her shoulder. She stopped and stared, her eyes likes small moons, and started to speak.

"Get inside!" I shouted, and she ducked back, and I moved us on until we reached the Georgetown road, and turned northward. A nigger was coming toward us on a wagon. He saw the blood on Sam and stood up and pulled on his lines and drew his mules to a stop. We passed near him, and Sam told him, "We gave them hell in the new town, but they got us some." The nigger said nothing and stared as we passed.

We galloped along the Georgetown road for a way, the sun hot in my eyes, then I turned us into a narrow lane, heading for the broken hills to the west and the cover of the cedar brakes on them. I looked behind me, but no one was coming. The countryside seemed empty and still. I turned off the lane into an unfenced pasture and struck for the hill on the other side. We reached the cedars, and I knew we weren't visible now from any of the roads. Sam was pale as death and whimpering at every movement of his mare. "We'll stop," I said. "I think we're safe for a while."

I helped him down from Jenny's back and half-carried him to a huge live oak that stood alone among the lower cedars. I laid him in its shade and propped him against its gnarled trunk and tied our horses to one of its branches. I returned to Sam and lifted his shoulders and tried to take off his coat. He looked at me, pain and pleading in his eyes, but said nothing, and I twisted him and tugged until I freed him from the coat. It was soaked with blood, but I folded it and put it behind his back and took one pistol from his belt and laid it beside him. He lost the other one when his hand was hit, I guess.

The hand was shattered, the middle and ring fingers missing. It was still bleeding. Sam looked at it and said, "Just like old Wetzel's leg. Blowed clean away." His voice was thin and weak. I unbuttoned his shirt and worked until I had it off. "Move up a bit," I said. "I've got to take a look at this." I helped him move away from the tree, and he groaned. I thought he was going to faint. "Easy," I said.

I turned sick when I saw what had been done to him. His lower back was covered with blood, some dry and dark, some fresh, just oozed from the hole. The bullet had entered him an inch or two to the left of the spine. The hole was perfectly round, like a bleeding eye. The hole in front, about three inches to the left of his navel, was larger and jagged and bloodier. I guessed the bullet had hit a kidney, or hadn't missed it by far. There was nothing I could really do. "Bad, ain't it?" Sam said.

"Pretty bad. But I'll fix you up. You'll be all right when we get away from here. How do you feel?"

"Like death," he said.

"Well, I won't have to take the bullet out of you. It went clean through."

"I'm luckier than Seab was at Mesquite," he said. Then he looked quickly around him. "Where *is* Seab?"

"Still in the alley."

I got up and untied my saddlebags and opened them, rummaging for my bandages. I wished I had some water to cleanse the wounds. "Sit up straight as you can," I said, and I wrapped two thick bandages around his middle, tying them as tightly as I could, then tore his shirt into wide strips and tied them around him, too.

While I bandaged his ruined hand, Sam watched me curiously, as if it were happening to somebody else. His eyes were tired and glassy. "Where's Arkansas?" he asked.

"Dead. At Salt Creek. You remember."

"He was a gooder man than we thought, wasn't he, pard?"

"Yeah, he was real good."

I got the bottle of laudanum from the saddlebag and uncorked it and handed it to him. "Take a few pulls on this," I said. "It'll help the pain."

He drank a swig and made a face. "God," he said. "Why can't that be whiskey?"

"Take another one," I said. I helped him lie back on his bloody coat. He handed me the bottle, and I corked it and laid it beside his pistol. "If the hurting gets worse, have some more of that," I said.

I got up and walked down into the cedars. Tears were coming into my eyes, and I didn't want Sam to see them. I walked to the outer edge of the brake and sat down and hugged my knees and bent my head to my knees and cried. I cried until I couldn't squeeze out another tear, then dried my eyes on my coat sleeve and sat there sucking at the hot, still air.

"Frank!"

I walked back through the cedars. Sam moved his eyes to me. "Where'd you go?"

"To look for the law. It looks like we made it."

"You done right, crossing the creek and sticking to the roads a while. They'll have a devil of a time finding our trail." He tried to smile. "What time is it?"

I pulled out my watch and looked. "Five-thirty. What does it matter?"

"I wanted to hear the music," he said. So I opened the watch again and let the tune play through, then closed it. "You want to hear it again?" I said.

"No. Where's Jim?"

"He wasn't with us. He went back to the old town."

"Reckon Seab was right about him?"

"I hope not."

"Yeah, I'd hate to think it, after all these years. I was right about the Rangers, wasn't I, pard?"

"Yeah, Sam. Rest now."

"Them Rangers will be all over us in the morning."

"We'll move out when it gets dark. We'll give them the grand slip."

"We always give them the grand slip, don't we, Frank?"

"You bet."

He closed his eyes. I stayed as still as I could, hoping he would sleep, and I thought he did. I took off my coat and folded it for a pillow and lay down beside him, watching the hot sky through the crooked branches and the leaves of the old oak. I didn't feel like sleeping, and didn't want to. I was just waiting. I lay there a long time, watching the sky change color, moving toward evening.

"Hey, Frank."

I sat up and leaned on my elbow. Sam hadn't moved. His eyes were still closed. "What, Sam?"

"Give me old Margaret and William, will you?"

When all was wrapt in dark midnight
And all were fast asleep,
In glided Margaret's grimly ghost
And stood at William's feet.

Her face was like an April morn
Clad in a wintry cloud,
And clay-cold was her lily hand
That held her sable shroud.

Tears were clouding my eyes again, so I stopped. Sam listened, and when he knew I wasn't going on, he said, "I want it all, pard." So I began again, haltingly, and made it to the last verse.

And thrice he call'd on Marg'ret's name,
And thrice he wept full sore;
Then laid his cheek to the cold earth,
And word spake nevermore.

Neither of us said anything for several minutes, then Sam said, "Did you know Joel wrote poems?"

"No."

"He wrote love poems and read them to Maude. Not as pretty as that, though."

"Hush now, Sam. Save your strength. It's almost dark."

He got quiet then, and I buckled my saddlebags and tied them on my horse. I sat down against the trunk of the tree and watched it get dark, and when it was full dark I shook Sam's shoulder. "Wake up," I said.

"I ain't asleep," he said.

"It's time to go."

He opened his eyes. "I ain't going. I can't ride no more."

"Then I'll stay, too."

His eyes moved to me. "No, you ain't. Them Rangers will be here tomorrow."

"I'll fight them," I said.

He made a noise that may have been a laugh. "I'm gone, Dr. Jackson. You know that. You take Jenny. She'll take you farther than that nag of yours. And bring you luck, too."

"No. You'll want her when you're feeling better."

"Take her. I promised you could ride her someday."

"No, goddamn it!" I was angry. My heart was breaking, and I was crying again, and I hated it.

"All right. But go, Frank. Right now."

I was about to stand up, but he said, "Frank?"

"What?"

"Kiss me."

I knelt and kissed him on the lips. He patted my shoulder with his good hand. "Go, brother," he said.

I untied my horse and climbed into the saddle. I didn't look at him again. I walked my bay through the cedars, then spurred him to a gallop and turned him west.

Dad Egan

By the time my train got to Waco the coaches were buzzing. Some said all had been killed. Some said only one. Some said two officers were killed and the whole gang escaped. It was impossible to find out the truth. But something big had happened. and I had missed it, and from Waco to Round Rock was the longest ride of my life.

The depot was full of Rangers, many just arrived. I introduced myself to one standing on the platform. Yes, Sam Bass had been in Round Rock, he said. He or someone in his gang had killed A. W. Grimes, a Williamson County deputy sheriff, and badly wounded Maurice Moore, a Travis County deputy who had come up from Austin with Major Jones. One of the bandits had been killed, but he didn't know which. The trail of the others had been lost on Brushy Creek, but Major Jones would resume the search at daylight. "Where is Major Jones?" I asked.

"At the jail," he said. "The Judas has been taken there."

"The Judas?"

"Jim Murphy."

He gave me directions to the jail, and I lifted my saddlebags to my shoulder and went into the depot. The floor was strewn with saddles and blankets, and about two dozen men, most of them Rangers, lounged on the benches and sat on the floor against the walls, cleaning rifles and pistols and talking quietly. I picked my way through the clutter and stepped into the warm night. The buildings were brightly lit, and the streets and sidewalks were crowded for such a small town so late in the night. There were few women, and nearly all the men were armed. It looked like Denton had a month or two before. Another Bass war was in the making. The crowd was thickest and noisiest around a small building down the street, and I knew it was the jail. Two Rangers stood in the door, guarding it, but they stepped aside when I gave my name. A lamp burned on the jailer's desk, and another in one of the cells, among several men. "How do you know this is Seaborn Barnes?" someone asked.

"Take off his pantaloons if you don't believe me," said another. "He's got three buckshot holes in his right leg and one in the left. He got them at Mesquite."

The voice was Jim Murphy's. "That won't be necessary," I said. "I'll confirm the identification."

The men in the cell looked at me. A small man wearing spectacles held the lamp. I took him to be a doctor. Jim looked pale and sick. He glanced at me, then quickly looked away. The others were Rangers, and I didn't know them.

"I'm Sheriff Egan of Denton County," I said. "I'm sure I'll know the man." But when I saw him in the shadowy light I wasn't sure. The bullet had struck in the middle of the face, almost in the nose, and had crushed the bone. His dark hair was matted with blood. "Well, maybe you'd better take off the pantaloons," I said.

One of the Rangers lifted the body while another worked with the belt and buttons until he bared the body's legs. The scars were there, scarlet against the pale skin. Another Ranger laid his hand on Jim's arm and said, "You're under arrest."

"Let him go. He's working for us." The voice came from behind me. I turned around. Major Jones was sitting alone in a dark corner of the office. "Hello, Dad," he said. He stood up and shook my hand. The Ranger removed his hand from Jim's arm and looked at him with more contempt than I've ever seen in human eyes. Jim slid out of the cell and joined Major Jones and me. "Come to the hotel with me, Dad," the major said. "We've got to talk." He moved toward the door, and Jim started to follow us, but Major Jones said, "Go hide yourself, Murphy. And pray that Frank Jackson doesn't find you. I'll see that you get the money." His voice was heavy with contempt. Jim looked at me with pleading in his eyes. I pitied him, but followed the major out the door.

Men are strange creatures. With the exception of myself, Major Jones wanted more than anybody to see justice done to Sam Bass. And Jim Murphy had been responsible for the end of

Seaborn Barnes's ignominious career and might yet help bring the bandit chieftain himself to bay. He had saved the Williamson County Bank, too. Yet there was no more friendless creature in Round Rock that night than Jim Murphy. Seaborn Barnes, burning in whatever pit Satan reserves for his kind, at least had the company of kindred souls. And he had the respect of those who had killed him. But there wasn't a man in Round Rock who would have lifted a hand to save Jim Murphy from Frank Jackson or anybody else. In the minds of some men there are causes higher than justice. I remembered the Ranger at the depot calling him "Judas," and I regretted it, for I had always considered Jim a decent man. But the name fit. To Pontius Pilate our Lord was an outlaw, of less consequence to him than Sam Bass was to Major Jones and me. But to Judas Iscariot he was a friend sold for silver, and I knew Jim Murphy would never have another friend, nor would his soul be at peace again.

I wondered why Major Jones had warned Jim against Frank Jackson and not Sam, but I withheld my questions until we had worked our way through the crowd and the major had poured himself a glass of whiskey in his hotel room. "Bass was wounded badly," he said. "He'll probably be dead when we find him. *If* we find him. If he died, Jackson may have hidden his body or even buried him by now. That young man was still very healthy when we last saw him."

The major was weary and not at all elated to be so near the end of his mission. He told me of Jim's letter, a duplicate of my own, and the mad dash to beat Sam to Round Rock. When he received the letter on Wednesday, he immediately telegraphed Lampasas, the station of the nearest Rangers to Round Rock. The major and Deputy Moore, who had been wounded in the battle, then came the twenty miles from Austin on the train. He was disappointed that only three Rangers had arrived before him. The rest of the Lampasas squad had been sent the previous day to San Saba, but were notified to ride for Round Rock at once. He had telegraphed Austin to send most of the men stationed in the capital, and had prayed the trap be sprung quickly, for his decision left the state treasury almost unguarded.

But the battle had occurred before the Austin and Lampasas men arrived, before anyone was ready. Grimes and Moore had been fools to confront the bandits alone, even if they didn't know who they were up against. The barn door had been opened prematurely, and only one of the escaping horses had been caught. "We've damn sure shut the door behind them, too," the major said. "Bass and Jackson aren't going to ride back to Round Rock. The worst thing is, I don't know whether there are enough decent horses in this town to mount my men. The Lampasas men practically killed theirs getting here. The bunch from San Saba rode a hundred and ten miles in twenty-three hours, and their mounts might as well be shot. We had nothing but livery stable nags this afternoon, and they gave out before we were three miles out of town."

He had men scouting the ranches and farms for horses, he said, and hoped they found some. "Goddamn it, Dad," he said, "I hate working with local officers. They're politicians first and officers second, and don't know beans from billiard balls."

I must have flushed, for he said, "I didn't mean you. Anyway, Grimes and Moore should've known better. They both used to be Rangers, and in my command, too."

I tried to think he meant no harm. Sam Bass had haunted the minds of both of us for months, and until today we had only Arkansas Johnson to show for all our trouble and expense. And even Salt Creek had happened by accident. "I'd like to turn in," I said. "I wonder if they have another room here."

"I reserved you one," he said. "I figured you'd show up."

I went downstairs and registered at the desk and took my saddlebags to my room. For once, I wished I was a drinking man like the major. I paced the tiny room, unable to sleep, unable even to sit down, listening to the shouts and laughter of the drunks in the saloon below, all claiming credit for the bullet that smashed Seaborn Barnes's face. Finally I pulled on my boots and walked down the stairs and headed for the livery stable at the end of the street. The door was open, and a lantern hung lit inside, but I found no one until I climbed to the loft. A boy was sleeping there. I touched him with my toe, and he sprang awake. "Are you the hostler?" I asked.

"Yessir. I'm in charge till Mr. Highsmith gets here in the morning," he said.

I showed my badge and said, "Come down. I want to show you the horse I want in the morning."

He did as I told him, and I walked along the stalls until I found the horse that Sam had stolen from Bill Mounts and Seaborn Barnes had failed to ride out of the alley. "That horse was stolen in my county," I said, "and I claim him to return to his proper owner. I'll get him at daybreak."

"I can't do that, sir," the boy said. "He's the one the dead outlaw rode. The Rangers want him."

"If I don't get him, I'll have you *and* Mr. Highsmith in jail for possession of stolen property," I said. "Sheriff William F. Egan will ride that horse, and he'll be saddled and waiting at daybreak, son."

Yes, it was a bluff. But I was determined that *one* officer would be well mounted the next day, and that officer would be me. Sam would be found, all right, but not by the Texas Rangers. He would be taken by a politician from Denton County who didn't know beans from billiard balls.

I went back to the hotel and slept well.

Major Jones's men rounded up a dozen good mounts during the night, so he wasn't angry at finding me sitting Barnes's horse in front of the hotel. My foresight wasn't wasted, though, for he assigned all the good mounts to his own Rangers and left the local officers to quarrel over the livery stable nags, which they were doing when the Rangers and I rode out to Brushy Creek just after daylight. I was surprised that Jim Murphy was among us. "If Sam's alive, he'll kill you on sight," I said.

Jim's face turned even redder than usual, and he glanced away without reply.

"I asked him to come, to identify Bass," Major Jones said.

"We don't need him," I said. "I know Bass as well as anybody."

The major gave Jim a little nod, and he turned back toward town.

Sam's trail had been lost at the creek, and we figured that he and Jackson had turned either upstream or downstream after they forded the water. Maybe they separated there, but I doubted that because of Sam's condition, and I remembered Jackson's devotion to him from the earliest days of their acquaintance. I suggested we split our party and scout the creek both ways until we found the trail. The major agreed and assigned two Rangers, a private and a corporal, to go with me. In a little-traveled lane not far upstream we discovered the tracks of two horses that obviously were traveling together. The Rangers were expert trackers, and we moved along the lane at a slow gallop, keeping the trail in sight without difficulty until we came to the edge of an unfenced pasture. There the tracks disappeared into the grass. Beyond the pasture was a low hill with a cedar brake near the top and a huge live oak rising from among the cedars. The Rangers were from Lampasas and had never trailed Sam before. They didn't know his love of timber as I did. So I said, "Scout the trail here. I'll rejoin you in a minute." Before they could reply, I spurred across the pasture, but slowed and drew my pistol as I neared the cedars. I reached the edge of the brake and stopped and listened but heard nothing. I peered into the somber green boughs but saw nothing. "Sam! Sam Bass!" I called. There was no reply. I moved the horse into the cedars, scanning the shadows, half expecting to see a gun barrel pointed at me, but there was nothing. Until I reached the live oak.

Sam wasn't there, but he had been. A bloody black coat was folded neatly, lying against the trunk. I dismounted and unfolded it and saw the bullet hole in its back. Almost on the spot where it had lain was a large dark blot. He bled a lot there. And there were several narrow pieces of cloth that looked as if they had been torn from a shirt and a brown bottle about a third full of some liquid. I pulled the cork and sniffed. Laudanum. I walked to the edge of the brake and cupped my hands to my mouth and shouted at the Rangers below. When they got to the live oak, I was holding the coat spread before me. "Damn!" the corporal said.

It didn't take long to find the trail out of the brake. Or rather, the trails. One man walked, leading a horse. The other rode, at a run, toward the west. "Jackson left Bass here and took off in a hurry," the corporal said. "Right after dark, probably. He'll be hard to catch. Since Bass was walking, I reckon he was too weak to climb on his horse. I doubt he's gone far."

We followed Sam along a northward course, but lost the trail again among the rocks on the side of the next hill. "I'll go see what's on the other side," the private said. He had barely reached the ridge when he called, "Farm house down there."

While we were riding down the other side, a woman came out of the house and stood in the yard, watching. As we neared the fence, she called, "Who are you?"

"Texas Rangers, ma'am," the corporal said.

"Are you looking for a wounded man?" she asked.

"Yes, ma'am."

She squinted at us, worried. "He was here last night."

"When last night, ma'am?"

"Late. I was in bed, and he knocked on the door and begged

for water. But I was alone and afraid to open."

"How do you know he was wounded, ma'am?"

"I watched him through the window as he went away. He was staggering, and didn't get on his horse. There was blood on my porch this morning." The woman looked embarrassed. "I wish I'd opened the door, but I didn't."

"You did right, ma'am. He's dangerous."

"Who was he?"

"Sam Bass."

"Oh, my God!"

Sam's trail wasn't hard to follow. If his wounds had been bandaged, as I assumed from the strips of cloth I found, the bandages had been soaked through, and he was bleeding again. I prayed he wouldn't bleed to death before we found him. Remembering the hundreds of hot and wet miles I had pursued him through the bottoms and prairies of North Texas, I wanted him to know who had captured him, when that hour came. Was it a vengeful thought? I don't think so. Sam Bass was my personal bandit. By helping him keep body and soul together when he was a lonely child in a strange land, and especially by loaning him the money to buy that accursed mare, I had been the sponsor of the trouble he had inflicted. I had cast my bread upon the waters as the Scriptures direct, but it was plague that floated back to me. And since it was I who had loosed the plague upon the land, I didn't want to leave its cure to others.

About a mile from the farm house we struck the new Georgetown spur of the International and Great Northern Railroad. The line was still under construction, and we lost Sam's trail among the litter of the project upon earth that had been much trodden by men and mules. But a construction gang was working only a few hundred yards away, and we rode to it. The nigger hands took our approach as an excuse to stand up and lean idly on their sledges and pickaxes, and their white overseer didn't object. "Morning," he said. He took off his hat and wiped his brow. "Going to be another hot one, ain't it?"

"So it seems," I said. "We're officers of the law, looking for a wounded man leading a sorrel mare. Have you seen him?"

"What if I have?" the man said.

"His name is Sam Bass. He's a fugitive."

"Sam Bass! Well, I'll be damned!"

"You've seen him, then."

"Yeah. This morning. When the boys and me was riding to the job."

"Where was he?"

"Laying under a tree aside the roadbed. I thought he was just resting. He hollered at us, and one of my boys went over and give him some water. He said he was sick."

"Where's the tree?"

He pointed down the track. "Just follow it," he said. "Big oak, maybe a mile down."

We struck down the track at a run. The tree stood alone between the railroad and a pasture. The mare was tied to one of its branches. Her red hide glistened in the sun. The Rangers and I drew our weapons, and I called, "Sam Bass!"

There was an answer, but I couldn't understand it. The voice was small and weak. We reined our horses to a slow walk, our pistols ready. "Sam! Are you armed?" I shouted. "If you resist, we'll kill you!"

"Don't worry, Dad. I can't even lift the damn thing."

The Rangers and I rode in, cautiously. Sam was lying on the other side of the tree from us, and when I saw him I knew we had nothing to fear. His face and shoulders and chest, all naked, were so drained of blood that they glowed in the shadow. The end of his right arm, wrapped in a blood-soaked rag, seemed little more than a stump. Heavier bandages around his waist were so soaked that not a white spot was to be seen on them. A pistol lay near his left hand, but he made no effort to pick it up. "Hello, Dad," he said. His eyes were shiny and so vacant that I was surprised he recognized me. "What took you so long?"

I didn't reply. I dismounted and hunkered before him. His dark eyes were looking back at me, I guess, but they didn't seem focused.

"Is this man Sam Bass, Sheriff Egan?" the corporal asked.

"Yes. Go find Major Jones. And go to Round Rock and get the doctor."

The Rangers departed. I picked up Sam's pistol and put it in my belt.

"Are you going to shoot me?" he asked.

"Of course not."

"What are you going to do with me?"

"Take you to town."

"Why don't you shoot me? Better that than be lynched."

"You won't be lynched," I said.

"We killed somebody, didn't we?"

"Yes. Deputy Grimes."

"Was he well liked?"

"I don't know. I didn't know him."

"I never meant to. He shouldn't have jumped us like that."

It amazed me that he could talk so. "Can you see me?" I asked.

"Yes. I'm pretty doped up, but I can see you. What are you doing here, Dad?"

"Major Jones telegraphed me," I lied.

"He knowed, then."

"Yes. He knew." Then I asked, "What brought *you* down here, Sam?"

He made a noise that was either a cough or a laugh. "You," he said. "You drove us down here. You and easy money. We thought we had us a soft thing, but it turned out pretty serious. Dad, you got any water?"

"I'll get it."

I hunkered again to lift the canteen to his lips and asked, "How many were you?"

He swallowed first. He had trouble taking the water into his mouth, and it dribbled down his chin. "Four," he said. "Three that meant business and one drag."

So he knew about Jim, or suspected.

"How's my old pard Army?" he asked. "And little John?"

"They're fine."

"I had a chance to kill you and Army once. Seab wanted to do it, but I didn't let him."

"I'm glad," I said.

He smiled a little at that, then said, "Let's don't talk, Dad."

He closed his eyes, and I feared he was dying. I went to the roadbed and stared down the tracks, hoping for the Rangers or the doctor. It was too soon for them to come, I knew, but I was nervous. I've never liked to look at death. I walked to Sam's mare and laid my hand on her soft muzzle. She snuffled.

"She's thirsty," Sam said.

"I'll give her some water," I said. I poured the water I had left into my hat and put it under her muzzle. She drank it with loud sucking noises.

An hour passed before I saw the Rangers. Major Jones's entire search force was riding down the roadbed, followed by a hack.

As the major dismounted he said, "Is he alive?"

"Yes, barely," I said.

The bespectacled doctor who had been at the jail climbed from the hack and carried his little bag to Sam. Sam opened his eyes. "I'm Dr. Cochran, son," the man said. "I've got to look at you." Sam said nothing, and Dr. Cochran knelt beside him. "Who bandaged you?" he asked.

"Frank Jackson."

"He did a good job, under the circumstances."

"Frank always done a good job," Sam said.

Major Jones stepped up to him then. "Where *is* Jackson?" he asked.

Sam's eyes narrowed, as if trying to recognize the face before him.

"Major John Jones, Texas Rangers," the major said.

"I don't know where Frank's at. Long gone, I hope."

"But where? Back to Denton?"

Sam gave him the same glassy, vacant stare he had given me. "Leave Frank be," he said. "He wanted to quit, anyways."

"I can't do anything for him here," Dr. Cochran said. "Let's put him in the hack."

"There's a farm house not far from here," I said.

"No, let's take him to town. I didn't bring much with me."

Four Rangers lifted Sam and carried him to the hack and laid him on some blankets there. "Is he going to die?" Major Jones asked the doctor.

"Oh, yes."

"When?"

"Soon, I think."

Sam whimpered as the hack rolled across the rough prairie, but quieted when we reached the road. I was surprised how quickly we reached the town. We must have found him no more than three or four miles from Round Rock, but the way had seemed much longer when we were tracking him. We entered the town near a graveyard and went into the colored section. The darkies must have heard we were coming, for woolly heads lined the road, staring in wonder at the still form in the hack. The doctor stopped in front of the first house we came to, and Major Jones went to the open door and knocked. A young negress, a girl, really, came to the door. Her hair was wrapped nigger-fashion in a red rag. Major Jones said something to her, and she looked at the hack and screamed and ducked inside. The major went inside, too, and in a few minutes returned. "It's all right," he said. "Unload him." Four Rangers lifted him as they had before and carried him through the gate. The other Rangers remained mounted, but the major and the doctor and I followed.

The shanty was shady, but hot. The cookstove was near the front door, and a fire roared in it. Several irons were heating on its top, and two piles of laundry, one damp and wrinkled, the other ironed and neatly folded, sat on two chairs near an ironing board. The negress was seated at the table now, her head buried in her arms. She was rocking back and forth and moaning rhythmically, as niggers do when scared or grieving. "Lay him on the bed, boys," Major Jones said. Then he went outside to give orders to his men, and the Rangers who had carried Sam trooped out after him. Dr. Cochran took a pair of scissors from his bag and snipped at the bandage across Sam's belly. He looked at the wound, then stood up and muttered, "I'll need some things," and went outside, too. Maybe the negress thought I had left, too. She raised her head and looked toward the bed. "Samuel," she said.

"Mary?" Sam replied. "Is that you?"

She rose and moved toward him.

"You know each other?" I asked.

The negress wheeled, fear and anger in her eyes.

"It's all right, Mary," Sam said. Then to me, "Yeah, I know her, Dad, but she don't know who I am."

The negress remained tense and poised, like a cat about to spring, until Sam repeated, "It's all right, Mary. That's Dad Egan. I've knowed him a long time." The black muscles relaxed then. She sat down on the side of the bed and looked at the bloody hole in Sam's belly.

"God, Samuel!" she moaned. She covered her face with her hands, as if about to cry, but she didn't. She sat like that, still and quiet, until Major Jones and the doctor returned. It was so quiet I heard the high, clear voices of nigger children playing somewhere and the murmur of the crowd outside the yard.

Major Jones wanted to question Sam immediately, but the doctor wouldn't let him. The major and I paced the room while Dr. Cochran and the negress cleansed the wounds and tied clean bandages on them. The doctor gave Sam a draught of something, and the negress removed his boots and fluffed his pillows and straightened the bedclothes around him. Finally the doctor stood up. "All right, Major," he said. "I'll come back later." He shut his bag and departed.

"Did you know Joel Collins?" the major asked.

In a thin voice Sam began answering questions about his career of crime in Dakota and Nebraska. He confessed his part in the Union Pacific robbery and several stagecoach robberies in those territories that had never been attributed to him. They spoke so softly I could still hear the children and the crowd outside. The negress still sat on the bed, fanning flies away with a paper fan with a picture of Jesus on it.

Twice that afternoon the murmur of the crowd increased, and I went to the door to see what was happening. A black hearse with glass windows stirred the first commotion. Two black horses moved it slowly up the road, and many citizens and Masons in full regalia trooped along behind it. Deputy Grimes was going to his rest. Not more than an hour later, the other funeral procession passed. It was only a nigger wagon pulled by a team of worn-out mules. Two niggers sat on the seat, and another, holding a shovel, sat on Seaborn Barnes's box, the new pine lumber glowing yellow in the sun. "Joel, Bill Heffridge, Tom Nixon, Jack Davis, Jim Berry and me. We done the U P robbery," Sam was saying. "Tom Nixon's in Canada. Ain't seen him since the robbery. Jack Davis was in New Orleans, I think. The others is all dead."

Major Jones was sitting in a cane-bottom chair, writing Sam's replies in a notebook with a pencil that he moistened in his mouth from time to time. He spoke gently, like a father to an ailing son. But when he moved on to the Texas robberies, Sam refused to give any information that the whole state hadn't read in the newspapers. "It ain't my profession to tell what I know," he said. "It would hurt too many good men."

Major Jones asked, "How many good men?"

"Too many."

"Men like Henry Underwood?"

"I don't know where Henry's at."

"What about Frank Jackson?"

"I don't know where he's at, either."

"Was he at Allen? Hutchins? Eagle Ford? Mesquite?"

"No, I don't think he was at any of those places."

"You don't remember?"

"That's right. I don't remember."

"Jackson rode with you a long time."

"He's a good friend of mine," Sam said.

"But he didn't commit any robberies?"

"It's against my profession to blow on my pals, Major. If a man knows something, he ought to die with it in him."

The major gave me a look of exasperation and licked his pencil. "How did you start on such a life, Sam?" he asked. "Sheriff Egan says you were a good man when you worked for him."

"I started sporting on horses. It just went on from there. Let's stop now, Major. I ain't feeling too good."

Major Jones stood up and closed the notebook. "Would you like me to get a preacher for you?"

"No. I'm going to hell. I got lots of friends there."

Major Jones shrugged. "Come on, Dad. Let's get some rest, too. We'll come back in the morning."

The crowd outside the yard had gone, but the major instructed two of the Rangers who were standing on the porch to sleep there. I turned for another look at Sam, perhaps the last I would see of him alive. I was shocked. The negress was bending over him and seemed to be kissing him.

The hotel was full of newspaper correspondents and other lovers of misery who had been arriving on every train since the fight at Koppel's store was telegraphed through the state. They circled in the lobby, very like buzzards, but noisier, shouting questions and passing rumors. They swarmed at us when we entered, but two of Major Jones's men pushed them aside, uttering threats. The Rangers stopped at the foot of the stairs and blocked them while the major and I climbed to his room. One of the Pinkertons from Dallas was there, sipping a glass of the major's whiskey. I had met him before, but I didn't remember his name. He didn't offer it, since Major Jones apparently knew him, too. "Make yourself at home," the major said sarcastically, pouring himself a drink. He waved the bottle toward me, not expecting me to accept, and I didn't.

The Pinkerton gave us a supercilious smile. "What did you get?" he asked.

The major pitched him the notebook. He read through it quickly and said, "Not much."

Major Jones breathed a weary sigh. "No, not much."

"Maybe I'd better question him," the Pinkerton said.

"It wouldn't do any good," I said. "He'll probably be dead by morning, anyway."

The Pinkerton reached for his hat. "Then I'll go now."

"*No!*" Major Jones's voice filled the room. The Pinkerton gave him a look of pure hatred, but removed his hand from the hat. "Let the poor devil go in peace," the major said.

The Pinkerton smirked again. "The man's a criminal, Major. It's my duty to recover at least some of that money."

"He hasn't got a dime," the major said.

"What happened to it?"

Major Jones waved his arm in a half-circle. "Scattered all over Texas, sir. If he had any left, he gave it to Jackson."

"Where's Jackson?"

"Read the notebook, damn it."

"Well, I'm going to ask." His hand moved toward the hat again.

"My men won't let you in," the major said. "They'll kill you if they have to."

The Pinkerton glared at me. "Sheriff, do you support Major Jones in this?"

"Absolutely," I said.

He grabbed his hat then, and jumped up. "Rebels!" he shouted. "Every stinking one of you!" He left and slammed the door.

Major Jones gave me a tired smile and raised his glass. "I wish you were a drinking man, Dad," he said.

Major Jones and Dr. Cochran and I rode out to the shanty in the doctor's hack. The morning was already blistering hot, but country folks were arriving in their wagons and buggies, wearing their Sunday best. They gathered in knots in the hotel lobby and on the sidewalks, exchanging news and gossip, pointing at Koppel's store and up the road toward the niggertown. "I guess he hasn't died," the doctor said. "Nobody came for me."

The crowd outside the fence was larger now, with more white faces. The two Rangers who had slept on the porch were lounging there, smoking, gazing without interest at the people beyond the fence. They stood up when they saw us. "I'll relieve you in a little while," Major Jones told them.

Sam was sitting up in bed. The negress was bending over him, feeding him broth. "What day is it, Dad?" he asked. His voice was as weak as before, but his face had a little color.

"Sunday," I said.

"Of the month, I mean."

"The twenty-first of July."

"Important day, Dad. Remember?"

"No."

"Mrs. Egan used to fix me all the pancakes I could eat."

"Your birthday!" I said, and he smiled. "How many?"

"Twenty-seven. Twenty-seven years old today."

I nearly wished him happy returns, but caught myself. He looked younger and smaller, so pale on that nigger bed, than he had so long ago when he rode into the Denton square, determined to be a cowboy. The doctor grasped his wrist and felt his pulse, counting it on his watch. Then he dropped the wrist and shook his head.

"How am I doing, Doc?" Sam asked.

"You're dying, son. Why don't you tell Major Jones all you can while you've got the chance?"

"I ain't dying," Sam said calmly. "Old Dad'll have a chance to hang me yet, if he can hold onto me."

The negress took the bowl away and went to work with her laundry. The irons clattered on the stove. She burned herself and muttered something and sucked her finger. Dr. Cochran checked the bandages but didn't change them. He gave Sam some liquid in a cup, and Sam made a face as he swallowed it. Dr. Cochran closed his bag and left. Major Jones sat down in the only rocking chair and started rocking. The rockers creaked on the loose floorboards. I sat down in one of the chairs at the little table. "Sam," the major said.

"I got nothing to say." Sam closed his eyes and went to sleep, I thought. No children were playing outside. The crowd had gone. Over the creak of the rocker I heard the irons moving on the cloth, making a kind of whispering noise, then there would be a clatter when the negress laid down a cold iron and picked up a hot one. She came to me once and asked, "Does you want something to eat?" I shook my head, and she went back to the ironing board, her bare feet scratching softly on the bare floor. We sat there a long time, I think, for I heard the church bells once and wondered whether they signaled the beginning of the service or the end. I took out my watch and saw that it was noon and wondered why I hadn't heard them earlier. Maybe the bells ring only at the end in Round Rock. Then Sam awoke with a kind of weeping noise. "Oh, God, I'm hurting!" he said.

Major Jones rose and went quickly to the bed. "Sam, you've done much wrong in this world," he said. "You now have an opportunity to do some good before you die by giving some information which will lead to the vindication of that justice which you've so often defied and the law which you've constantly violated."

The speech surprised me. I wondered if he had composed it as he rocked, or had he spoken it many times to dying outlaws?

"No. I won't tell."

"Why won't you?"

"I done told you. It's against my profession to blow on my pals. Get the doc. I'm hurting bad."

The major stood up and slapped his legs in disgust. He picked up his hat and stomped out the door, and I took his place on the bed. "Are you dying, Sam?" I asked.

"Yes, Dad. Let me go."

He closed his eyes, but I still heard his breathing. Then he opened his eyes and said, "Water."

I waved at the negress., She was standing motionless beside the ironing board, staring at us. She stooped and dipped a cup into the water bucket, and Sam said, "The world is bobbing around."

The negress brought the water, splashing a little on the floor in her haste. She sat down on the bed beside me and lifted his head and moved the cup to his lips. Sam drank, then closed his eyes. In a moment they opened again, wide, and he stared at the negress as if recognizing her for the first time. "There's a horse for you in the corral," he said.

And she said, "Thank you."

Afterword

It's the hope of the historian to dig into a legend and find facts. It's the hope of the novelist to take facts and mould them into some personal version of truth. For the facts, I've depended heavily on four writers—an anonymous author (presumably T. E. Hogg) who published *Life and Adventures of Sam Bass, the Notorious Union Pacific and Texas Train Robber* in 1878; Charles L. Martin, whose *A Sketch of Sam Bass, the Bandit* appeared in 1880; Walter Prescott Webb's classic *The Texas Rangers: A Century of Frontier Defense*, first published in 1935; and Wayne Gard's equally classic biography, *Sam Bass*, first published in 1936. Because of their efforts, more facts are known about Sam Bass than most of the notorious Western outlaws, and my debt to them is great.

Although I've taken care not to contradict historical testimony, I haven't hesitated to bend the facts and invent situations and personal histories and descriptions when the needs of my story required it. That's why this book is a novel.

Dallas
February 1983

Bryan Woolley

The text was set in 11-point Goudy Old Style by Typesetters Unlimited, San Antonio. Printed and manufactured by Edwards Brothers, Ann Arbor, Michigan. First printing - September 1983.